JENNIFER HARLOW

HIGH
MOON

A
F.R.E.A.K.S.
SQUAD
INVESTIGATION

DEVIL ON THE LEFT BOOKS

1

COPYRIGHT

ALSO BY JENNIFER HARLOW

THE GALILEE FALLS TRILOGY

Justice

Galilee Rising

THE F.R.E.A.K.S. SQUAD SERIES

Mind Over Monsters

To Catch a Vampire

Death Takes A Holiday

High Moon

THE MIDNIGHT MAGIC MYSTERY SERIES

What's A Witch To Do?

Werewolf Sings The Blues

Witch Upon A Star (03/15)

A HART/MCQUEEN STEAMPUNK ADVENTURE

Verity Hart Vs The Vampyres

For Sophie

4

"A gentleman is simply a patient wolf."

-Lana Turner

"Right on, sister."

-Beatrice Alexander

ONE

BEWITCHED, BOTHERED, AND BEWILDERED

Watching the man you love suck face with a gorgeous woman is not the best way to start a birthday. Welcome to my world.

He sits at a back booth, lips and every other body part pressed against that succubus, appearing to love every second and caress, the rat bastard. And how can he not be? The evil slut queen of doom has everything I don't. Long, straight hay-colored hair, big blue eyes, big breasts, long lean legs, tight body all encased in a skintight black dress clinging to her perfect curves that only a plastic surgeon could ever recreate on me. I've envied women like her all my life, and now that succubus has my future husband in her enticing clutches. Literally. An actual succubus is clutching his soft brown hair and kissing him as if her life depended on it. Which I guess it does—as she feeds off sexual energy to live—but still. Does *he* have to frigging enjoy the whole experience so much?

Howdy. The jealous, insecure, emotional wreck before you is Special Agent Beatrice Alexander of the covert branch of the FBI known to the underworld as the F.R.E.A.K.S. We fight the monsters under your bed: the vampires, the ghosts, and the soon to be decapitated succubi of the world. Those terrors in horror movies? Real. Trolls, zombies, even giant snakes. Killed them all so the citizens of America can go about their normal lives. Why am I so lucky? Because technically I'm one of them. I can move anything with my mind. It's called tele or psychokinesis. I can carry in groceries or stop hearts without lifting a finger. And let me say doing the latter is mighty tempting right about now.

The man having his tonsils examined by the succubus is my teammate Special Agent Will Price. He's technically a monster too, at least once a month. He's a werewolf, not that I hold that against him. After all us freaks can't help who or what we are. We're actually a lot like everyone else. Though Will did literally *eat* my last boyfriend. The psycho was trying to kill me at the time, so I gave Will a pass on that. But this...

Will shifts in his seat to get closer to her. They haven't broken apart in over forty-seven seconds. Forty-seven! He's kissed her longer than he's ever kissed me all three times combined. I don't care that she's more or less bewitched him. I don't care that it's all for a case. My hands ball into fists, fingers digging so deep in my own flesh it hurts. A cool hand touches mine. I look away from this nauseating PDA toward the hand's owner. My friend, the delectable Oliver Montrose gazes at me,

7

his gray eyes warning me not to put into action what I've been contemplating. Namely storming over there and cold cocking that female dog with the butt of my Glock. Though she *so* deserves it. In Virginia Beach alone she's been linked to two deaths. Two young seamen were found naked and dead in their own beds of apparent heart attacks after going home from a club with a hot blonde. Who knows how many others she's sucked dry over the years?

For those not in the monster killer business, a succubus is a woman who Hoovers up the life-force from her lovers, much like a vampire feeds off blood. Now, I don't begrudge a life form getting whatever they need to live. I watch *Animal Planet*. Sometimes it's kill or be killed. But a succubus doesn't need to kill any more than a vampire does. A little can go a long way. Some people are just evil. And right now evil has Will in a lip lock.

"Whatever course of action you are contemplating inside that beautiful head of yours, I suggest you forget it post haste," my vampire friend warns. His hand remains heavy on mine, a reminder about restraint. We don't want to blow our cover. While Will plays doctor, Oliver and I sit at the bar, just another couple enjoying the Virginia nightlife. A few stools down, Agents Rushmore and Wolfe, in their chic Ralph Lauren polo shirts and buzz cuts, nurse ginger ales, and keep their eyes locked on the same booth. Chandler is lucky enough to be out in the parking lot waiting for the signal to take her down. Darn you, innocent bystanders. Darn you.

Lord, I hate clubs. They're loud, crowded, expensive, and filled with hormone crazed men and women with no sense of shame or decorum. I've lost count of how many strange crotches have rubbed up against my backside while "dancing." I'd only been a handful of times before I joined the F.R.E.A.K.S., and now it seems as if I live in one. Why preternaturals feel so at home in these places is beyond me. I guess to them it's nothing but a smorgasbord. Easy pickings. Everyone's mind is so filled with sex and booze they forget basics like safety and common sense. And now Will has joined their ranks.

"I wasn't contemplating anything," I snap, downing my screwdriver. "I'm not bothered by them. Not a bit. It's work. We're *working*. Another drink, please! Now! *Now!"*

"That is not a wise idea, my dear."

"Wise is so overrated," I mutter.

I glance back at the couple. Still making out, still…*oh, no she isn't*! Her graceful hand slides up Will's thigh, resting on the bulge in his pants. At first she just traces the outline with her fingertip, and then rubs against him with her whole harlot hand. He doesn't push it away.

Rage boils over. Involuntarily I leap up, every inch of me tense and ready to rip her shining hair out at the roots. Before I'm totally upright, a hand on my shoulder presses me back into my seat. "No."

"But she—"

"No," Oliver says as if I'm an ill-behaved dog.

9

"But he—"

"No."

Torture. This is nothing more than torture. This is worse than the time I was actually physically tortured. At least that ends. Bones heal. *This* will be seared into my brain for years to come. I could kill her, just pop a vein in her brain or squeeze her heart until it stops. But I reign in the homicidal part of my nature, instead gazing at my ridiculously handsome friend in an effort to calm me the frak down.

I don't normally act like this. I'm a good, sane person. Or at least I was until I fell in love with a man who refuses to acknowledge he loves me back. He does. I mean, I'm eighty percent sure he does. The man all but said he did, and his kisses shouted it from the rooftops. He just won't give in. Won't let himself admit it because apparently I make him nuts. I cloud his judgment. Of course my worst offense is I give him hope. But to a control freak who watched his wife get eaten by a werewolf, these are apparently bad things. I'm in love with an idiot.

And absence did not make the heart grow fonder, at least in his case. Me, I was watching *Beauty and the Beast* with my goddaughter and burst into hysterical tears at the end when Belle saves the beast. Will has fared better in the past two months. I had to remain in San Diego longer than expected because of my elbow. I broke it while I ran from a crazed cop hopped up on troll blood. Long story. Ended with previously mentioned psycho ex-boyfriend being eaten by the current object of my affection. I needed surgery to repair the damage, then it healed wrong and I had a month and a half of physical therapy before I was cleared for duty. I got back two weeks ago. So I was stuck in San Diego with nothing to do but watch sappy movies and think about Will.

He returned only one of my ten phone calls, and then just asked after my health and family. I could tell he couldn't wait to get off the phone. And since I've been back, well this is the longest he's been in the same room with me. I walk in, he walks out. When we're working, I'm either assigned to a different team or barely acknowledged. If he didn't blush every time he looked at me, I'd be put off. But I'm no quitter. I love him, and per the songs, that can conquer all, including the neuroses of a bull-headed werewolf. I'm banking my heart on it.

"You must calm yourself," Oliver orders. "You are acting as wretchedly as he usually does. If you recall, this was your plan."

"Yeah, but *you* were supposed to be bait. Or one of the other guys. Not him."

"A succubus feeds off living energy, which I am lacking and werewolves possess in abundance."

"Yes, and thank you for pointing that out in the meeting. Why didn't you just wrap him in a bow for her while you were at it? Whose side are you on, anyway?"

"The victims'," he says. Fudge. Now I feel like a total jerk. "It is our job to keep predators off the street the quickest and safest way possible. And occasionally that requires sacrifice." He glances back at Will, and Grin Number Two, with the tips of his fangs, forms. "Though I doubt William minds playing the martyr at this moment."

I have to look again. Great, not only is she feeling him up, but he's returning the favor, kneading her breast with his strong hand. Can she feel those rough calluses? Does she even care how he got them? Years of rowing on the Potomac River, that's how. And yet she gets to second base with him before I do. "This is hell. I am in hell."

"I do not know why you are distressing yourself over *that man*. I really do not. He has not showed you the slightest regard since your return. Or prior to that while you convalesced. He made his position abundantly clear."

"You don't understand," I sigh. They pull apart for air, and she says something that makes him smile. He usually never smiles, except for me. She's even stolen that from me.

"Understand what, Trixie?"

Will caresses her face and dives in for more. "Some things are worth fighting for. They make no rhyme or reason to anyone but you, but you just *know*. It's outside logic, it's outside reason, it's just something you sense in your very core. And if you don't listen to it, if you allow it to slip through your fingers, then you spend the rest of your life regretting it. You spend the rest of your life an empty shell. If that's not worth a whole damn war, let alone a fight or two, I don't know what is."

Will moves his lips down the succubus' neck, and I turn back to Oliver, who studies me with a mix of sadness and anger that takes away only a fraction of his exquisiteness. I can safely say he is the most physically handsome man I've ever seen. Pale skin, lush red lips, cleft chin, wavy shoulder length brown hair with blonde highlights, and straight nose all in perfect proportion. The impossible balance of masculine and feminine. The only other man who holds a candle to him in the looks department is the Lord of San Diego, and even Connor doesn't come close to this level of perfection. Not outside and certainly not inside. No one does. "You are…" he touches my face with his ice cold fingertips, "such a fool."

"Guys?" Rushmore says inside my earpiece with his New Jersey accent. "I think they're leaving."

"About freaking time," I say.

Ever the gentleman, Will gives his hand to the succubus to help her out of the booth. She titters like a schoolgirl as she pulls down her skirt, which has ridden up enough to be whorish even in a club. He says something, no doubt chivalrous, to make her feel better, drawing a pretty smile from her plump lips. Double gag me as he wraps his arm around her tiny waist before leading her toward the exit.

"Chandler, headed your way," I say into the black brooch on my red sweater.

"Copy," Chandler says through my earpiece. "I have the car in sight."

Oliver tosses money onto the bar, and we stand as Agents Wolfe and Rushmore do the same. When I glance up again, Will and the succubus have disappeared amongst the

13

dancing horde. If he follows the plan, he'll take her to the car where we'll arrest her with less of a chance of collateral damage.

"Now, when we apprehend her, do you promise not to use excessive force?" Oliver asks as we maneuver toward the exit.

"Only if she gives me a reason," I say pointedly. Like say she blinks in my general direction.

"You sound exactly like him," Oliver says, meaning Will. "Remember what happened when he allowed his jealousy and rage to get the best of him?"

Yeah, he ended up eating my ex-boyfriend. "Shut up. I can remain objective."

Rushmore and Wolfe flank us as we stroll out of the club. The moment we're outside, the agents lift their shirts to pull out their badges from their pockets and hang them around their necks. I retrieve mine from my purse, along with my gun. Standard procedure, I promise. Oliver rarely carries. I suppose he doesn't need a gun with his super-strength, speed, mind control, and charm. That last one works better than all the others combined.

We run outside toward our SUV parked on the side. Chandler climbs out, eyes narrowed with confusion. My heart catches in my throat when I see his bewildered expression. Oh crap. "Where is he?" Chandler asks.

"What do you mean?" Wolfe asks.

"He never came out," Chandler says. "What—"

I don't hear the rest. I take off back toward the club.

"Trixie, wait!" Oliver shouts after me.

I charge past the bouncer through the door. The patrons milling around inside the front entrance take one look at the gun and back away from me, as they should. Wildly, I glance to the left then right down the hallways with more tables and chairs lined up along each. Crap. Crap! I don't see them. He vanished. My fellow agents sprint inside and before they stop moving, I bark, "Oliver, you take left. The rest of you, back in the main room."

They obey without question. Good boys. I hurry down the right hallway while couples on barstools at high tables assess me and the gun. Run away, people. Run away. I stop halfway down at the coat check where a wide-eyed Latina stares at me. "Did a man about 6"2' with brown hair wearing a gray suit jacket pass by with a hot blonde in a black dress?"

"I-I think so."

Thank God. I continue down the hall until I reach a curtain with a "Restricted" sign tacked on. I push it aside and enter the backstage area with boxes of booze lining the tiny hallway and waitresses milling around. The one closest to me can't take her eyes off the gun. "FBI," I say. "Did a tall man and blonde woman—"

"Down there," she says, pointing toward the back.

"Thank you."

There are only three doors, and two are open. The first is a break room were more startled waiters sit around. Directly opposite this room is a kitchen. I do a quick scan, but no joy.

15

That leaves door number three, the closed one at the end of the hall. A man moans. Yep. I yank on the handle, but it's locked. Another moan. *No.* Before I realize I'm doing it, invisible hands rip the door off at its hinges. It falls inside the room with a thunk.

Oh, God.

In the large storage room the succubus straddles Will, who lies on a pallet of boxes, his pants around his ankles. Her outline, her aura, actually glows as if gold dust surrounds her entire body, save for her eyes which are black and dead like a vampire when it's feeding. Will doesn't seem to notice, his head lolling side to side on the box as if he's just taken a hit of heroin and is chasing the dragon. The dragon he should be slaying snarls at me for interrupting her meal.

"Lunchtime's over bitch."

With one thought, she flies across the room as hard as my mind can toss her. The boxes she lands on crumble, the impact breaking the glass inside. Liquid seeps out and runs down her limp body, plastering her dress even tighter onto her body as she slumps onto the floor like a rag doll. Down but not out. Before she can get up, I walk over to her, kicking her once in the head for good measure. It whacks against the wall again, leaving a splatter of blood. The glow vanishes, along with any thoughts inside her pretty head. *Now* she's out.

"Trixie?"

I pivot toward the busted door where my partner stands with his gaze glued to the broken and bleeding succubus. "See? I told you I could remain objective."

Before he can retort, the other three agents join their teammate at the door, their expressions similar to his. As if I'm scarier than a murderous succubus. But their attention, and mine, diverts to the groaning werewolf beside me who is trying and failing the simple task of sitting up. That's not the first fact I realize. His black boxers barely contain his massive erection. Yeah, of course my eyes go there first. Thank God it's dark in here otherwise all the men could see me blushing.

"What happened?" Will asks, still in a haze.

I'm the closest, so I walk over to help him up. The men, save for Oliver, enter and approach the unconscious succubus. Oliver stands guard at the door just in case lookie-loos walk by. Rushmore feels for a pulse. "She's alive," he proclaims.

"Of course she is," I say indignantly.

"Where are my pants?" Will asks.

"Around your ankles," Oliver says as if he's a Rhodes Scholar talking to a dunce.

"Oh." Will leans down to get them but topples to the floor the moment he moves. I catch him and sit him back up, glaring at the smirking Oliver. "I don't feel very good."

"Will he be okay?" I ask.

"In an hour or so," Oliver says.

"She's out cold," Wolfe reports. "I think she has a concussion."

"What do we do now?" I ask Oliver.

"You are the director of this farce, my dear. You tell us."

Ugh. Which means I have to care about Slutty McWhoreface on the floor there. Will rests his head on my shoulder and closes his eyes. I'll care later. "We need to get Will back to mobile command. Dr. Neill should see him."

"It would be a waste of time," Oliver says. "There is nothing physically wrong with him. He simply needs to eat, drink, and rest to replenish his stolen energy. No pill can cure that. The doctor should examine our poor friend on the floor there, though."

"Okay. Fine. Then the three of you take her to mobile command while Wolfe and I help Will back to the hotel to rest."

"Or *I* can escort him," Oliver suggests, "and *you* can keep guard on our killer."

"No. She's still dangerous, and you're the only one immune to her. We'll be fine." I turn to the three agents. "Chandler, Rush, you bring the cars around to the side." I reach into Will's coat pocket and toss Chandler the keys. The men obey as always. "Wolfe, help me get him up."

Wolfe throws Will's arm around his shoulders, aiding him to his feet. The big man sways but remains upright this time. Now the mortifying bit. Having no choice, I bend down, my head an inch from where Not So Little Will salutes. I quickly pull up his pants. "Thank you," he mutters.

18

"Let's get them out of here," I say. "Oliver, you carry her."

As I sling Will's other arm over my shoulders, Oliver picks up the slumbering succubus and follows us out. There's nobody in the hallway as we come out. Will is practically dead weight but manages to put one foot in front of the other. "You look so pretty tonight," Will says to me, obviously still floating somewhere around Jupiter.

"Thank you."

He rests his cheek on the top of my head. "You're so pretty."

Oliver scoffs behind me.

We find the back door though the break room. The one waiter remaining drops his Powerbar when we come in. Yeah, yeah, we're weirdoes. It's still not polite to stare. Wolfe opens the door, and we shuffle out into the chilly February night with a salty breeze coming off the ocean. Our two SUVs round the corner, parking beside the dumpster. Rushmore climbs out of the first, running toward us to help with Will. We toss him in the backseat as Oliver puts his invalid in Chandler's car. I climb in beside Will with Wolfe replacing Rushmore behind the wheel. Before I can even put on my seatbelt, Will lays his head on my shoulder again, but this time he wraps his arms around my waist as if I were a teddy bear, and immediately falls asleep. He likes to cuddle. Good to know.

Oliver comes up to the window, sets eyes on us, and scowls. "How cozy."

19

"Shut up. Can you handle things there?"

"I shall arrange for her transport to Montana." There's a secret prison a quarter mile underground a field in Montana where the preternatural bad guys, or in this case girls, are housed. Never been and don't want to.

"Thank you. If you need me, call my cell," I say.

Will nestles further into my neck and sighs. Oliver's eyes narrow. "Behave yourself."

"Of course."

"I was not speaking to you."

Wolfe drives us away.

*

Wolfe and I all but carry the barely conscious werewolf back to the hotel room he shares with Agent Chandler. The parking lot, the foyer, two hallways, and an elevator. I may never walk upright again. The moment we fling Will on his bed, he falls back asleep. Good. Hard labor complete, I send Wolfe back to mobile command in case the men need further assistance. I can handle things on this end. As Will slumbers, I find the others to fill them in. Nancy watches some slasher movie in our room. She always waits up for us no matter how late we get in. Either because she worries or because she doesn't want to miss any of the action. Probably both. I tell her to pack as we'll be leaving in an hour or two. Like everyone else, she obeys me without question. Andrew is also asleep, but I relay the same message to the sleepy man. After tossing my few belongings into my suitcase, I return to Will's room to do the same for him. He doesn't stir as I enter or as I move onto the bathroom and throw his shaving paraphernalia into the toiletry bag. I should order him some food. He'll be—oh, my.

As I'm shifting the items in the black bag, I notice two small squares at the bottom. Trojan condoms, lubricated and ribbed for her pleasure. How long have those been in there? I've known Will about nine months, and I'm all but certain he hasn't had a girlfriend or even a lover in that time. I've never even seen him flirt. Not even with me. Heck, the man barely smiles. So why would he have those? Maybe he really was a Boy Scout and just wants to be prepared for any eventuality. Okay, what I'm really wanting to know is if this is an old or new habit. Have they been in there for say, nine months? Or...oh Lord. What if in the two months I was gone he found someone else and just never told the team? She...ugh. Ick. I'm doing it again. Overanalyzing everything. He's a guy, they carry condoms. End of story, Bea. I zip up the bag.

Will remains asleep when I leave the bathroom. As I zip up his suitcase, he suddenly stops breathing. Oh God. My own breath seizes too. No. No. I knew we should have...he sighs contentedly a second later. Okay, end of heart attack. He's fine. I think. I wonder if what she did to him is the same as a concussion. If I should wake him up every hour or something. At the very least I should probably stay here and watch him. Just in case. For...health reasons. Yeah. Who knows what that female dog did to him? I plop into the chair in the corner with a sigh myself.

He looks so peaceful, not a state I'm used to seeing him in. Pensive, yes. Angry, oh yeah. Never peaceful. It suits him. Softens his ruggedly handsome face. Even the crooked Roman nose doesn't take away from this current gentility. Shame his eyes are closed. They're a beautiful true green. His large frame, not fat just big, has none of the tension I'm used to seeing either. He's in his early fifties but appears fifteen years younger. It's a werewolf thing. He's nowhere near as good looking as Oliver, but I could gaze at him forever. He's the first man I've ever loved and our relationship has consisted of three kisses, five hugs, and countless arguments.

My best friend April thinks I'm nuts. Heck there are times *I* think I'm nuts. The man made my life hell for five months because he thought I was sleeping with Oliver. And he told me point blank I drive him crazy, and he can't see himself with me. That I'm "chaos incarnate," whatever that means. Of course the next time he saw me he stuck his tongue down my throat. Yeah mixed messages abound. I'm hoping actions speak louder than words in this case. No, it's not been easy, not by a long shot, but none of the great love stories are.

Will burrows deeper into the pillow and groans. A second later, his eyes finally open. He blinks a few times, but is unsure of his surroundings until his eyes lock on me. "Wha—"

"We brought you back to the hotel."

"Oh," he says, still sleepy.

22

I move to the edge of the bed sitting by his knees. "Can I get you anything? Water?"

"What happened?"

"We caught the succubus. She's at mobile command right now."

He rubs his temples. "I have a headache," he says weakly.

"I'll get you something." After rising, I unzip the suitcase to retrieve the toiletry bag, grabbing a handful of Advil. One of the bad side-effects of lycanthropy is medicine only works in large quantities. He'll be lucky if ten pills do the trick. When I return with the pills and water from the bathroom, Will's attempting to stand. "Oh, don't—"

He falls back onto the bed before I finish. "What the hell's the matter with me?" he asks.

"What's the last thing you remember?"

He glances up at me then takes the pills and water. "Just pieces. Walking down the hallway. Her kissing me. A dark room. Her…on top of me. Did she…I mean, did we…"

I fold my arms across my chest. "I got there in time."

"Thank God," he says before chugging the rest of his water. "It was so odd. It was as if she drugged me. I wanted to pull away but just…couldn't."

I snatch the glass from his hand. "Yeah, poor you."

"What do you mean by that?" he asks.

"Nothing. Just, well, it looked like you were having a lot of fun."

He glares up at me. "Well, I wasn't," he snaps. "I was doing my job."

"Okay. If you say so." I walk over to the mini-bar and place the empty glass on it.

"Wait. Are you mad at me?" he asks. "Why the hell are you mad at me? Bea, you can't be pissed at me for doing my job."

I spin around. "Why not? You get pissed at me for exactly the same thing all the time."

"So you *are* mad at me?"

"I…I just think you could have stopped the whole thing a lot sooner. That's all."

"It was your plan," he points out.

"I know! But you didn't have to enjoy it so damn much!"

"I did not—" He groans in frustration. "Why are we even having this conversation?"

"Because I just spent the whole freaking night watching you get felt up by Demon Barbie! How would you feel if you had to watch me make out with Oliver all night?"

"I don't have enough energy to fight with you, Bea."

"We're not fighting, we're talking. You know that thing we used to do before you started to leave the room the moment I walk in it?"

He manages to stand this time, spurred by his urge to flee from me no doubt. "I don't want to talk about that, okay?"

24

"That's nice. I do, though. You're weak now. I fully intend to take advantage of that fact."

"We have said everything we need to say. I—"

He takes a step but crumples to the floor in a heap.

"Will!" I say, rushing over to him. I help him sit up, his back to the bed, then lower myself next to him on the floor. "Are you okay?"

"I'm fine."

"Maybe Dr. Neill should examine you."

"I'll be better by tomorrow. Don't worry."

"How can I not worry? You almost fainted!"

He pats my hand, the first time he's willingly touched me in months. "I'm fine. Really. I just want to get the hell out of here."

"Our plane's on stand-by. They just have to arrange transport to Montana. She'll probably have to wake up first, though."

"What happened?"

"Her head had a not so accidental meeting with my foot after I threw her bony butt across the room. She'll live. Unfortunately."

He shakes his head. "Well, that's one way to start your birthday."

I raise an eyebrow. "You know it's my birthday?"

"February twenty-ninth. That's today. Born on a leap year. That makes you…?"

"A gentleman never asks," I chide.

"Sorry."

We sit, shoulders touching, in silence for a moment and not our usual awkward kind. "So, did you get me anything?"

"I never did show you how to pick a lock," he says. "With all the trouble you get into, seems like a good skill for you to have."

"You do realize that would mean being in the same room with me for ten, possibly twenty minutes, not seconds? Think you can handle that?" I ask with a smile.

"As long as you behave yourself," he says playfully.

"Doing a pretty good job right now, aren't I?" I ask, playing back. I start tracing the collar of his shirt. "I mean, here you are all frail and vulnerable, and I haven't made a move, let alone mentioned my dastardly, evil plan to get you naked in bed. Saint Beatrice, that's me." I slowly roll my tongue over my lips. "Unless you *want me* to misbehave."

His breathing grows ragged from the lust I can all but smell on him. I know I'm right because he scoots a foot away. "Yeah, I think I'll just get you a sweater."

Drat. "Can't blame a girl for trying."

"I wish you would stop. It's just a waste of your time and energy. You should be…chasing guys your own age. Normal guys."

"I don't want them. I want you," I state as plain fact.

With a sigh, Will rests his head back onto the bed. "You have it all figured out, huh? Let me ask you this: when you were a kid, is this how you imagined your life?"

26

"Not exactly. I thought I'd be married with a few children by now. Same amount of vampires in my life as I envisioned, though," I quip.

He doesn't take the bait. Instead, he scowls. Always so darn serious. "I'm fifty-two, Bea. When I was your age, I thought I had it all figured out too. The rest of my life was mapped out. By the age I am now, I'd be Captain of my own unit, living in a grand house I worked damn hard for, surrounded by my kids, my wife, my friends. But life doesn't turn out the way you want it to. It just doesn't."

"Um, Will? I'm happy to be the one to point this out to you, but in a way you sort of did get all of that."

"What?"

"Well, you live in a mansion you work hard for. You run your own unit, for the FBI no less. And you're surrounded every day by your friends. Despite *everything*, you got what you wanted. It might be a little different than you thought, but you did it. Werewolf or not."

Confusion and bewilderment fill his face, but the tension in his shoulders has left. Guess he never thought of it that way. "Huh."

"Except for the kids, I guess. But, you know, you do sort of need a woman, probably said wife, for that. A woman who wants kids. Who can put up with you. Who is as crazy about you as you are her. Can you think of anyone who fits the bill?"

27

He runs his hand through his hair, a sure sign he's nervous and uncomfortable. Good. "You do realize if we did have children, they'd be werewolves with telekinesis? Can you imagine?"

Only every day and twice on Sundays. I shift closer to him. "Yeah, their teenage years will be absolute hell, but I'm far more worried about if we have a girl."

"Why?"

"Um, I seem to remember a certain vampire whose larynx you crushed just for talking dirty to me. What happens when your precious, innocent baby girl brings a boy home? You'll toss him out the window just for looking at her," I chuckle.

"I would not!"

"If someone stole her lunch money, you'd storm the school and threaten the child with violent death!"

"I...okay, I probably would do that to them both, yes," he laughs. "But they'd both deserve it."

"We'll have to lock her in a turret just so you don't wind up in prison."

"A turret works for me," he says. "We'll build it right after the moat."

We both laugh, occasionally glancing at each other laughing, which makes the laughs come even harder. Oh, I adore his eyes the rare times he laughs. The corners crinkle and the green becomes true emerald when he's happy. Like now. Our laughs peter out, but our eyes never leave one another's.

Butterflies flutter not only in my stomach but every inch of me as if I'm being kissed everywhere, leaving nothing but lust and anticipation in their wake. His smile fades in time to mine. This is serious now, deathly serious, and we both know it. I can't make the next move. I want to, but it's in his hands now. My future, my heart, my soul, our fate all in his hands. I trust him. And it's not misplaced.

Hesitantly, eyes never leaving mine, he raises that important hand to my face, brushing a stray strand of hair from my cheek. His fingertips set the flesh on fire as they always do whenever he touches me. I need more. I nuzzle his hand, pressing it against my cheek with my own. Neither of us moves, blinks, breathes for a second. There is nothing but those eyes. His flesh. *Us.*

"Oh, fuck it," he says.

Will draws my face toward him, our lips finally meeting. Oh, Lord. We kiss hard and rough. Our tongues find each others' playing and teasing back and forth. Oh God, how I've wanted this. We wraps his arms around my waist, yanking me in closer, almost onto his lap. I run my fingers through his hair, soft like feathers. Still clutching me, still consuming me as passionately as I am him, he twists us onto the floor, pinning me against the carpet. His hands hold my wrists, stopping me from touching him as I *need* to, but I don't protest. I don't want him to stop kissing me for anything.

But I rarely get what I want.

29

The sound of a card-key in the door acts as a cold shower on his ardor. As the door opens, Will's body lifts off mine to sit up. I'm not as quick as him. Chandler walks in just as I rise too. It's obvious what we've been doing what with me still on the floor and Will's hair disheveled, but Chandler's stony expression doesn't change. The man still doesn't forgive me for playing the part of Helen of Troy in the war between Oliver and Will. They called a truce but it still weighs heavy on is all.

"I, um, fell," Will says.

I give a little wave. "Me too."

Chandler rolls his eyes. "I need to pack. Wolfe and Rush are accompanying mobile command and the prisoner to Montana. She's in the cell now."

It takes effort, but Will finds his shaking feet. "Oh."

I stand too. "Is she awake?" I ask as I pull down my bunched up sweater.

"Yes, but we sedated her for the trip."

"Is everyone else back?" Will asks.

"I brought Oliver with me and took the liberty of alerting the airfield. Wheels up in an hour."

"Very good. Thank you for, uh, taking charge while I was…incapacitated," Will says.

Will and I exchange a guilty glance which garners another eye roll from Chandler. "I'm gonna go check on Nancy, I guess," I say. Not looking at either one, I walk out. "See you, uh, both on the, uh, plane."

I shut the door and stand with my back against it for a moment, savoring the sensations still jangling through me. I touch my lips, still feeling his against them, still tasting him. The biggest smile I've ever had forms on my face. The smile of a victor. K.O., Bea.

Ya got him.

Two

Happy Birthday to Me

As usual, Nancy insists on sitting beside me on the plane, so I can't sit next to Will. Though I doubt I could have regardless, not with his new chaperone blocking me at every move. Chandler wouldn't leave his side. Not on the way out of the hotel, not in the car, and not on the plane. If I got too close, I'd be treated to a dirty look. The man gives rather frightening stink eye. Good on perps and psychokinetics alike. One would think I had spit in his face. Not that Will or anyone else noticed. Will refused to look my way and fell asleep on the plane before takeoff. I passed out a few minutes later.

The situation does not improve when we land. We exit the plane, he ignores me. We drive to the mansion, he pretends to sleep. We arrive home, he hangs back so he doesn't have to walk to his room near me. Thank goodness exhaustion prevents me from caring too much. I barely have enough energy to put on my pajamas before crawling into bed.

I awake from a dreamless sleep in my cloud of a bed around eleven, and the first thought that pops into my head is of me rolling around on the floor with Will. The second is, "Oh, crap. It's my birthday." But I push the negative away to focus on the memory of those kisses. His taste, his smell, his feverish body pressed against mine as he pinned me to the floor. Oh man can that man kiss. And if stupid Chandler hadn't shown up, I bet I'd be re-playing something more X-rated. I let my imagination stroll down Smut Street anyway. It is my birthday after all.

After a shower, various painful beauty necessities, a careful blow-dry, and make-up application, I carefully choose my clothes. Will falls more on the Madonna spectrum than whore, so I put on my black and pink swirled knee length dress with bell sleeves and black leggings. Adorable. He won't be able to resist me. I hope.

As I apply my lipstick, there's a knock on the door. My heart skips a beat. It's him! I check myself one last time in the mirror—for once happy with what I see—and hurry to the door. But my smile vanishes the moment I see Chandler waiting in the hall holding a brown package with envelopes on top.

"Oh, hello," I say.

He hands me the box. "This came for you when we were in Virginia."

It's from Nana. "Thank you."

I'm about to shut the door when Chandler asks, "May I come in?"

This can't be good. "I...can't think of a reason why not." I move to let him pass.

I'm pretty sure this is unprecedented, him being on this floor. The agents have their own apartments in town, so there's really no reason for them to leave the ground floor. And yet, here he is. The man dislikes me to the point of visible contempt, so why would he volunteer to bring up my mail? Chandler, a former recon Marine, stands with his back ramrod straight and hands clasped behind his back. I suppose he's a good looking man with hawk like features, olive skin, and expensive haircut. Even now he's in a crisp suit with gun clipped on his hip. Uptight is not a turn on.

"It's your birthday?" he asks as I set the package down on my desk.

"Yeah."

"Happy Birthday."

"Thanks." I fold my arms across my chest. "So, what can I do for you?"

"I wanted to speak to you about Will."

Here we go. "What about him?"

"Normally, I don't get involved in the personal lives of my co-workers."

"And I'm sure *they* appreciate that," I cut in.

His nose crinkles with displeasure. "Yes. And I preface what I'm about to say by acknowledging the fact your tactical, defensive, and offensive abilities are for the most part impressive. You are an asset in the field. Under other circumstances, I would be proud to serve with you."

"I feel a massive 'but' coming on."

He nods. "*But* I cannot ignore the fact that since your arrival, you have brought unneeded and unwelcome strife to our team. Whether it was intentional or not remains beside the point. The fact is due to your presence, the team fractured. We weren't as effective at our jobs as we should have been, and I just thank God the rift didn't cost any civilians their lives. And it should also be noted, during the time you were away recovering, things returned to the status quo."

"I'm not quitting if that's what you're not so subtly hinting at."

"It's not. I just see a potential problem, and I feel it's my duty to defuse it before it blows up in all our faces."

"Cut to the chase, please," I snap.

"Fine. I have worked with Will Price for five years. I even consider him a friend. Until your arrival, he was driven. Confident. A capable leader who saved my life a dozen times over. And in the last two months, that man returned to us."

"Since I was out of the picture," I say.

"He told me what transpired between the two of you. All of it. From your first meeting, your declaration at Christmas, even last night. And I am worried to say the least. We can't take another split, especially so soon after the first."

"And you want what from me?" I ask, no longer hiding my anger.

"I want you to think before you act. I want you to put the needs of your team, the lives of the people we save, ahead of yours."

I hold up my hands. "Now, wait a minute. If I remember correctly, I was not the one who started the war. It

35

was Will and Oliver with *you* adding fuel to the fire. I was just caught in the middle. And it was all because your friend got jealous and pig headed about some imaginary love affair I was supposedly having. And they've settled that."

"For now. But what do you think will happen if you and Will do become romantically involved? I'm the first to admit I don't like Oliver. I never have. He's arrogant, rebellious, and damn selfish. He hates Will as much as Will hates him. I don't know if it's a vampire/werewolf thing or what, but it is a fact. And Oliver has an attachment to you I never thought he was capable of. What do you think he'll do when he sees the two of you together?"

"He knows about my feelings for Will," I counter.

"Knowing about a crush and having to watch the two of you as a couple are two very different things. If you think Will's reaction was extreme, it will be like a match compared to the forest fire Oliver will reign down upon us."

"Look, I get where you're coming from. You want to protect the team and your friend. I respect that. I do. But you aren't giving any of us enough credit, especially Oliver. He would never do anything to hurt me or the team. He's not the bogeyman everyone makes him out to be."

"I knew this would be pointless," Chandler says, shaking his head. "I knew you'd just deflect and make excuses. I can only hope Will has more sense than you."

Without another word, he walks out, which is really good because I was about three seconds from tossing him

36

through the door without the benefit of opening it first. The nerve! And on my birthday. Oh fudge it. I am twenty-seven years young, I look fabulous, I have presents to open, and I made out with my dream man last night. I will not let Mr. Gloom and Doom ruin this day for me. And I know just how to wipe away his bad juju. Presents.

I open the birthday cards from Brian, April and the kids, and the gang at the salon. April already got me a present before I left. A dark green teddy with black lace trim from Victoria's Secret for what she calls my "grand seduction scene" with Will. I do look darn good in it. Sexy even. It covers all my trouble spots. Hope I'll have an opportunity to wear it soon.

Inside the package Chandler brought are two smaller boxes and two cards. One is simply wrapped with a familiar Snoopy design, but the other has rich, shiny paper and cloth bow. I open the card on the Snoopy one first. It's from Nana. Just "I love you, I miss you" written inside. My present is a black beret with matching gloves and scarf. All very useful in frigid Kansas. Then I open the second card. Of course. What a gentleman.

"*Dearest, Beatrice,*" it begins, written in flourished handwriting, "*I do hope this reaches you. I understand you have since departed San Diego. We are much poorer for it. Regardless, may I wish you many happy returns on this joyous day. I hope you will enjoy your gift. It was exceedingly hard to come by. Think of me whilst you read it. Yours, Lord Connor McInnis.*"

And what did he get me? A second edition of *Poems by Currer, Ellis, and Acton Bell*. Also known as Charlotte, Emily, and Anne Bronte. Charlotte is my favorite author. This book is over a hundred and fifty years old, incredibly rare and is probably worth thousands of dollars. He really shouldn't have.

I'm not surprised by the grand gift though. Connor could give Machiavelli lessons on how to maintain a powerbase. I met the generous vampire around Christmas when he tried to force me into becoming his consort, the vampire term for concubine. I said no and threats and guns became involved. All pretty standard when dealing with vampires. My salvation came when Will convinced him we were madly in love, and threatened a werewolf war. Connor backed off. Sort of. Really, he just changed tactics. Carrots instead of sticks. Hence the extravagant present. And the kiss we shared in his Ferrari. And the flowers he sent every week while I recovered in San Diego. I'm sure he'd send them here if he knew the address. I haven't seen him since the Christmas Eve kiss. I stayed true to Will despite the very enticing invitations he extended such as a trip to London and private New Year's celebration on his yacht. *That* is how much I love Will. I really would have liked to have seen London though. Maybe for our honeymoon.

After cleaning up, checking myself in the mirror, and fluffing my hair, I step out of my room. My first stop is the kitchen where Andrew and Carl sit at the small circular wooden table enjoying brunch. Carl is in his early thirties with short black hair, non-descript features, and only a few inches on me.

38

The first thing people notice about him, myself included, is the gloves. He never takes them off except maybe to shower. It's not a fashion thing. If he touches a person or object, he can sense things about them. Thoughts, feelings, even images. Very useful in investigations. I have a similar trait, though not as strong. If a person has an intense emotion, I sense it. Makes it hard to be in big crowds.

His dining companion Andrew has been with the F.R.E.A.K.S. the second longest after thirty-year-old veteran Oliver. He's in his early sixties with gray and black hair, dark brown skin, a kind face, and white eyes hidden behind square sunglasses. He's blind, has been ever since he was a boy, but for some reason he can see ghosts like we do normal people. He can hear and talk to them as well. Sometimes I walk into a room and find him chatting to thin air. There are a lot of ghosts in this house.

"Happy Birthday," Carl says as I stroll in.

"Thank you." I prepare my favorite breakfast, Count Chocula cereal with a Pop Tart on the side. S'mores flavor this morning. Diabetes ahoy. "You guys just get up too?"

"No," Andrew answers with his Louisiana drawl. "We had to buy your cake."

"Chocolate with vanilla frosting?"

"Of course," Carl says. "You told us five times."

"What can I say? I take my cake very seriously," I joke, joining them at the table.

"So, do you have any plans for the day?" Andrew asks.

39

"Oliver's taking me to Wichita tonight to see *Legally Blonde: the Musical*."

"That should be fun," Carl says.

"Yeah. And I usually make a bowl of popcorn, shut off the lights, slip under the covers, and watch *Gone with the Wind*." My mom and I started the tradition and I've kept it up all these years.

"I love that movie," Andrew says.

"Me too."

"Sounds like you have a full day," Andrew says.

"What about you two?" I ask.

"Nothing special," Carl says.

I take a bite of the Pop Tart. Oh, that's yummy. And thinking of yummy... "Oh, have either of you seen Will today?" I ask.

"I think I saw him going down to the basement," Carl says.

"Oh. Huh."

We make chit chat for a few minutes, talking about the op last night, and my awesome present from Connor. After I promise to read Andrew a few poems, I clean up and skip off. They of course know where I'm off to in such a hurry. Helen Keller could.

There's a hidden elevator to the two basements in the staircase. On the first level are Oliver's bedroom, the conference room, and laboratory. The floor beneath it houses the firing range, gym, and Will's moon cell. Curiosity brought me inside the cell once, and once was more than enough. It's nothing but a 20X30 concrete room with metal cage filling most of the space. For the lucky person guarding him on the full moon there's a couch, fridge, coffee pot, tranq gun, and magazines to kill time. The chemical smell with an undercurrent of urine adds nothing to the ambiance. And Will's stuck in there every month.

I find the future prisoner already pumping iron in the gym. About five hundred pounds worth. Sweat dribbles off his forehead onto the floor, and his arms shake a little as he pushes the barbell up. He lowers it again, and then with even shakier arms, presses it up once more.

"Do you need a spotter?" I ask, concerned.

The bar clanks on its holder as Will racks it. He grabs the towel from the floor and wipes his face. The happy, lustful man I played tonsil hockey with last night has vanished. In his stead is the grumpy, obstinate jerk I spent months fighting with. I can tell that bastard's back by the scowl and tense body. Great. Nothing can ever be easy, can it? "Looks like you're feeling better," I say.

"I am. Thank you," he says, back as straight as a razor. "Sleep helped."

"Good."

And right on cue the uncomfortable silence begins. I think we've spent more time in one of these traps than actually talking. He breaks it first. "Did…you sleep well?"

"Yeah."

"Good." He moves to the rowing machine and locks his feet in the apparatus. His back is to me now, which I'm fairly sure was intentional. This is what he always does. We get close, he freaks, I confront him, we fight, we forgive, and the cycle begins anew. There has to be a way to break the loop. It just makes me frustrated and dizzy.

I slowly saunter around him until I'm within his eye line. "How long have you been down here?"

He starts rowing, making it a point not to look at me. "Half an hour."

I sit down Indian style right in front of him. "Having fun?"

"Yes," he says gruffly.

"So, are you going to spend all day down here?"

"That's the plan."

"What about my birthday present?"

"What?"

"The lock picking lesson. Remember? You promised to teach me right before you kissed me."

His jaw sets. "I don't think it's a good idea."

"But it's my birthday present. I want to learn to pick a lock. No, I *need* to know. If I had known how to, maybe I would have gotten out of those handcuffs and that cabin a lot sooner. All that…stuff might not have happened." I pause for a moment as he rows harder. "Come on. It'll keep your mind off things. And you promised." He didn't really promise, but I'm hoping he forgot everything before the kissing. I fake pout. "I thought you were a man of your word."

Will stops rowing, looks up, and glares at me. I smile back brightly. I knew that'd work. He is a man of honor. "I don't want to talk about last night."

"Okay. Cross my heart."

"I have to get my tools." He climbs off the machine and stands.

"I'll go with you," I say, rising too.

"Why?"

"We can't practice down here. There are no locks," I point out. "We can use one of our doors. They both open with keys. And I have a pair of handcuffs in my room too. Come on." I walk out first, and he follows a few feet behind. On the elevator he practically hugs the wall, that scowl never wavering. "Will you please stop making that face? You'd think I was leading you to a firing squad."

His mouth loosens a tad. "Sorry."

The elevator doors open. "So, your room or mine?" I ask nonchalantly.

"Mine."

We start up the stairs, him behind me again. "Good. Mine's a mess. I didn't clean up the wrapping paper from Connor's gift yet."

Suddenly he grabs my arm hard, jerking me around. "He sent you something here?"

43

"No, he gave it to Nana who mailed it to the mail stop. Quit being so paranoid." For our safety the location of the mansion is top secret, like shooting you for knowing top secret. Not even my grandmother knows exactly where I live.

"Oh." Will releases my arm. "What did he send you?"

"A book of poetry by the Brontes. It was really sweet of him. I don't know how he found it. He is so thoughtful," I say with a quick smile.

Will prickles, the corners of his mouth twitching. The exact reaction I was hoping for. "Why is that vampire sending you expensive gifts?"

"It's my birthday, Will. Even vampires give presents to people they care about on special occasions." I spin back around and continue up the stairs.

For a moment he stays put, but then follows me up again. "Have you had contact with him since Christmas?" Will asks, all business now.

"He sent some flowers and asked me out a few times, nothing major. I turned him down."

"But he believes we're still a couple?"

"Hence why I turned him down. Though that trip to London was mighty tempting."

"He invited you to London?" he asks, shocked. "Maybe I should give him a call. Tell him to leave my girlfriend the hell alone."

"If you're going to do that over London, you also might want to threaten him. A lot. You know, for kissing me and all."

Once again he takes my arm and twirls me around. "You kissed him?"

"No, he kissed me. I only kissed him back for like a second."

"Why the hell would you do that?" he asks, more hurt than angry now.

"Because he's handsome. And he helped me. And it was nice to be wanted by an uncomplicated man. But I told him in no uncertain terms it would never happen again, and I haven't *seen* him since. Because of you." I pry his hand off my arm and start walking again. "Though if you keep acting this ornery, I might begin to think you're not worth missing a trip to London with a gorgeous millionaire for."

We continue the rest of the way to our rooms in silence. He opens his bedroom door, and we walk in. It hasn't changed since the last time I was in here. Still masculine with blues and greens. The bed is unmade with the covers bunched up at the end. Someone had a fitful sleep last night. I'm about to shut the door when he says, "Leave it open."

"Why? Don't trust yourself?" I ask with a smirk.

"The locks are on the outside."

"Right." Duh.

He picks out a gray shirt from his dresser. "I need to change. My kit's in the desk." He walks into the bathroom and shuts the door.

I open the desk drawer where a small brown pouch rests on top. When I pick it up, what lies beneath jars me. Without thinking, I pick it up. His wedding ring. It's nothing fancy, just a gold band, but a pang of sadness socks me in the stomach. Poor Mary Price. Would she like me? Is she looking down at me getting together a ghost posse to haunt me because she thinks me unworthy? I never met the woman but certainly feel a kinship to her. Not just because I want to bed her widower, but because from what I can glean, she was a good woman with a lot of love for Will. Something we have in common.

He never talks much about her. All I know is she was a nurse working in Washington, DC, and they were married ten blissful years. A picture of Mrs. Price stares at me from his dresser right now. She was tall, thin, and beautiful with olive skin, dark brown eyes and matching hair. Twins we are not. Then all that beauty was literally ripped apart. What would she—

Crud.

The bathroom door opens, and I quickly toss the ring back into the desk. I hold up the kit. "Got it!" I snap the drawer shut. That was too close.

Since I continue to find myself kidnapped and in locked rooms, I actually do want to learn this skill, so I'm on my best behavior as he instructs me how to use the tools, a paper clip, and a bobby pin to unlock a dead bolt, handcuffs, and even the desk lock. I'm a quick study. Forty-five minutes of alone time where after a demo, Will patiently stands by while I try. Where his voice never changes from that of authority. Where he refuses to touch me, even when I need him to when I hold the bar incorrectly. Where one time, the only time he got within two feet of me, he bent down and his hot breath on my neck made me goosepimply all over. The lesson winds down with us on his bed and me in handcuffs, though not in the way I'd always envisioned it. He sits on the edge across from me while I fiddle with a paperclip inside the lock. One minute of sheer frustration later, the left side pops open. Much faster than last time, but faster still...

In my boredom while I was recovering from surgery, I began experimenting with my power. One can only watch so many episodes of *Law and Order* after all. Before my experiments I used to have to see or visualize the object or person I was moving, or at least be in the same room with it. Now, if I know something is there I can bring it to me as long as I concentrate and know the path I want it to take. In this case, I know the machinations of the handcuffs and the lever used to keep the bar in place. I press down with my mind and the right cuff unlatches. "Ta da!"

"I think your way is quicker," Will says.

I hand him the cuffs. "Good to know both. My way only works in certain circumstances, yours works all the time."

He collects the tools and rises, walking over to the desk, and putting them back inside. "I suppose."

Guess the lesson's over. Time for our next class, Seduction 101. I lie on my stomach facing him, rest my hands on my fists, and raise my legs at the knees. "You're a good teacher, you know."

Will turns around, shocked for some reason, his mouth opening a little. "Um, thank you."

"No, thank you. It was fun." I bite my lower lip. I read in *Cosmo* this drives men wild. "So. What should we do now?" I ask with a mischievous smile.

The scowl resurfaces. "I'm sure you have plans."

I roll onto my back. "Not until tonight." With my head over the side, I stretch like a contented cat. "We have all day."

"Bea..." he scolds, annoyance growing with each letter.

"Yes, William?"

"Will you please get off my bed now?"

"I don't think so. I'm quite comfortable here."

His glower ticks up a notch. "You promised you wouldn't do this."

I flip back onto my stomach. "No. I promised not to bring up you mauling me last night. And I haven't. I said nothing about not flirting with you. I would *never* promise that."

He folds his arms across his chest. "You know, you sounded exactly like Oliver right then."

"Did I? Good for me. It is best to learn from a master."

"Guess he never got around to teaching you the definition of stupidity. It's up to me then. It's doing the same thing over and over again and expecting a different result."

Be it his snotty tone or the rebuff itself, righteous indignation courses through my veins, forcing me to my feet on the opposite side of the bed from him. "Huh. Silly me, but I seem to recall getting a different result last night. And in the hospital. Oh, and in mobile command at Christmas."

"You kissed me then," he says.

"But you kissed me back. And I pulled away first that time."

The scowl is replaced by a momentary twitch. "We've gone over this."

"Yeah, yeah. I'm chaos incarnate, and you're pushing me away for my own good, and blah dee blah. Just because you keep saying it doesn't make it true, Will. The truth is you're afraid, and you want to punish yourself, which is beyond ridiculous!" I throw my hands up. "*You* didn't kill your wife, Will. You becoming a werewolf is not some divine punishment for not being there when she needed you. It could have happened to anyone, you just drew the short straw."

"You know nothing about it, Bea, so shut your mouth."

"I know this: you're not honoring your wife by acting like a zombie. Because that's exactly what you're doing. Going through the motions. Not embracing life and love when it's offered to you. That's just…sick and wrong. And you look down on Oliver? He may be undead, but you're just a walking corpse who hasn't caught on he's dead yet."

"So why the hell do you want me?" he shouts. "If I'm a zombie, then," he stammers, "then-then why the hell can't you just leave me alone?"

"Because I love you! Haven't you figured that out yet, you asshat?" I shout back.

49

Okay, not the way I intended to impart that life changing information. Crap.

My hands cover my mouth, and my eyes bug out as much as his do. We let those words hang between us for a few seconds, me mortified and him shocked into silence. This is bad. This is *so* bad. I can't talk first. He has to say something, even if it breaks my heart. And he knows it. "You don't love me. You can't."

I remove my hands. "But I do. I have for months."

"But you *can't*," he insists through gritted teeth, almost disgusted by this notion. "I—don't do this to yourself."

"Too late. It's done," I say, shrugging my shoulders.

He can't look at me. He can't focus on anything. His eyes jut around the floor, the walls, in search of an answer. Every second of silence drops another boulder into my stomach. I was wrong. Everything I thought was wrong. He doesn't want me, at least not the way I want him. He might take my body, but my mind and soul mean nothing to him. If he did, he'd say something. Look at me at least. I want to curl into a ball and cry. If he kicked me it would hurt less then the agony he's inflicting now. I have to get out of here.

I'm about to run out of the mansion, out of the damn state, when he finally opens his mouth to ask, "Why?"

"Why?" I parrot back.

"Why do you love me?" he asks in disbelief.

All that strength. All that power. All that beauty. And he's as insecure as an anorexic girl in a beauty pageant. He breaks my heart, and not in his usual way. "Because you're strong. And smart. And handsome. Because your moral compass always points north even when it's to your detriment. Because you're passionate. Because you have integrity. Because you're brave. Because you're a *good man*."

"I'm not a man!" he roars. "How can you say that? I eat men! I prey on them. You saw that first damn hand."

"Yeah, Will, I did. I saw it. I saw you at your worst. You're most monstrous." I walk around the bed as fast as I can, stopping mere inches from him. "And I'm still here. Telling you I'm in love with you."

I'm on the verge of tears now. Two months I've waited for this moment. Two months of planning, scheming, psyching myself up. Because this is it. This is the precipice. The last battle. Me versus the monster. Winner take all. "I love you, Will. I do. I don't care that you're a werewolf any more than you care that I'm telekinetic. It is not what defines you, Will. Not to me. And it never, ever will." I put my hands on his chest, my right one over this heart. He doesn't pull away. "Why is that so hard for you to understand? After everything. Colorado. The war. The cave. Why can't you just…" I look into his exquisite eyes, so full of pain and longing, just like mine. "Trust me?"

Hesitantly, he places his hands over mine. "It's not you I don't trust, Bea." His hands fall from mine and ball into fists. "I just…I can't. I'm sorry."

He literally turns his back on me. He won't even give me the courtesy of saying this to his face. "Then you're nothing but a coward, Will Price. A massive, idiotic, cruel coward. You have no idea what your fear is making you give up here. A woman who-who-who loves you despite your damn temper. Your ridiculous possessiveness. Your prejudice. Who would…fight for you to her last breath. But I can't do it anymore. Do you hear me? Because God help me, I'm starting to think you *aren't* worth it." He doesn't turn around. "This is it, Will. Your last chance to prove to me you are. Because when I leave this room, it's done. You will have lost me. Is that what you want?"

He doesn't answer.

I bite my lower lip to stop the tears. "Then…I guess everyone was right," I say, voice breaking. "You *don't* deserve me." With as much dignity as I can muster, I stalk out of the room straight into mine, slamming both our doors behind me.

And that's it. I lost. The wolf won.

Happy Birthday to me.

I burst into tears.

*

"I hate men."

I lie in my bed hours after that heartbreaking debacle surrounded by tissues, ice cream cartons, and popcorn with Rhett and Scarlett sparing on the screen. Gone are my cute outfit and polished exterior, replaced instead with flannel Oreo pajamas and red, swollen face. It's as dark as it can get in here. Light pisses me off. "They should all be rounded up and shot," I say into the phone.

"A great idea on paper," April says.

"I mean, why can't they be like they are in the movies?" I ask with a sniffle. "Witty. Strong. Considerate. Rhett Butler wouldn't turn down Scarlett just because he's a big, stupid coward." And I crumble again, little cries escaping me. "He loves her so much!" I get another tissue and blow my raw nose.

"Okay, you have got to turn off that movie! It's making things a million times worse."

"No! I've already given that fleabag enough power over me. He's not going to ruin my birthday tradition too! Oh!" Strong, virile, roguish Rhett chases after wild Scarlet, picking up the protesting woman and carrying her up the stairs to screw her brains out. "No man will ever be that way for me."

"What?"

"So consumed with passion and love he has to have me right there and then. He just ignores my protests, scoops me up, and takes me to bed."

"I certainly hope not! That's rape!"

"You know what I mean." I sniffle again. "I'm gonna die alone."

"You're not going to die alone," April says, getting aggravated. Poor thing has had to listen to me whine and cry for almost two hours. I'm amazed she hasn't hung up.

"I am! I'm not skinny, I have crazy hair, and I'm a freak of nature! Who would want me?"

"Um, you want the list? Oliver? That Connor guy? Like all of Javi's friends? You're funny, you're hot, and you literally kick ass. Don't let this one douche bag make you forget that."

This makes me feel a little better. "Did I tell you what Connor sent me?"

"No. What?"

"Another Bronte book. It's a second edition."

"Wow."

"I know, right? Maybe I should just leave here. Become his consort and have wild, hot, monkey sex on his yacht. Be a kept woman with minions to do my bidding. Like stringing up a certain werewolf on the Coronado Bridge. Naked. And covered with bees. He'd so do that for me."

"Or you could join e-Harmony and meet a non-evil guy."

"Or there's Oliver. He's taking me out tonight. I could invite myself into his bedroom afterwards and rip off his clothes. He wouldn't turn me down." Except he did. I threw myself at him after a particularly scary night, and he had the good sense to put on the brakes. Shot down by a sex crazed dead man and now a half man. Is it any wonder I'm such a Cassandra when it comes to romance? Didn't think so.

"You just had your heart broken. A fling with your friend is not what you need."

"Then what am I supposed to do?"

"Exactly what you are doing. Eat too much, watch sappy movies, and bawl your eyes out. It's all you <u>can</u> do."

"I just don't understand how I could have been so wrong, April. I mean, I did everything right. I was patient. I made a good argument. And I wasn't even that wrong. He does want me. Just as much as I want him. He just…hates himself more than he cares for me."

"Bea, you can't save someone who doesn't want saving."

"I know. But I had to try."

"That's what makes you the best person I know."

Thudding footsteps in the hallway grip me with terror. It's him. Seconds after I fled his room, I heard him slam the door and leave. Where he went, I don't know. I was just so glad he wasn't around to hear me sob like a baby for hours. Guess he's back now. Whoop-a-dee-do. The fast footsteps grow closer. I mute the movie. "Hold on a sec, April," I whisper into the phone. The noise stops right outside my door. A shadow of two feet is visible under the frame. Crap, he's right outside. Though my heart thuds double time, I stop breathing. After a faint sigh, the shadows finally fade. His door shuts. I take a deep breath. "April, I gotta go."

"Feel better, okay?"

Before I can even set down the phone, I hear it. The sound of his door opening. The purposeful footfalls. I leap out of bed and rush over to my door, reaching it just as those two shadows reappear. I fling open the door just as he raises his hand to knock. Our eyes lock, and that's it. That's all he needs.

"I love you too."

Our smiling lips collide together like magnets. Greedy, rough kisses that make me want to swoon. My knees even buckle. He must sense this because his powerful arms surround me, pulling me into him so there's no space between us. Not good enough. I leap up, wrapping my legs around his waist and throwing my arms around his neck. Our mouths devour each other as he backs us onto my bed, falling on top of me, crushing me with his warm body while tissues and popcorn spill onto the bed and floor. I finally got him into my bed.

His mouth leaves mine to nibble then kiss down my neck as I moan and writhe against him. Oh Jesus that's lovely. He traces the edge of my skin this toe curling way until he yanks my top open, buttons popping and cloth ripping. I'm so shocked I jolt, but then his mouth finds my bare breast, flicking his tongue against my erect, sensitive nipple as his fingers expertly roll the other. My eyes cross, and I throw back my head in ecstasy. But it's not enough. Nowhere near enough. I sit up and tug at his shirt. He raises his arms to aid me and leans back down to find my mouth again. Our flesh meets, my sensitive soft breasts crushed by his hard chest. I toy with his lips and suck on his tongue all the time our pelvises grind against their mate. His bulge is barely contained and my nethers throb with each coupling. I'm so wet already my panties stick.

"I love you," he says between deep kisses. "God, I love you so much."

Our fingers entwine and he forces my arms down, pinning me to the mattress. He pulls his mouth away again, kissing down my neck, between my breasts, down over my not so flat stomach, and further south as those expert hands squeeze and tease my exposed, feverish flesh. His body forces my legs apart, and that's when I regain my senses. I have literally dreamed of this very scene and it ends very well for me but badly for him. Like howling in pain, rush to the hospital bad. In all my planning I forgot one very important fact. If we have sex, I can kill him. One little orgasm and his internal organs can pop like a balloon. He's about to take my pants off when I say, "Stop!" I sit up, meeting his confused eyes centimeters from my pelvis.

"What? Why?"

"You—you can't do that."

"Do what?"

"You know. Oral."

"Do you…not like it?"

"I-I don't know," I chuckle nervously. "I'm sure I would. A lot. But I can't, um, have an orgasm. I mean I can physically, but…not with another person in the room."

"I don't understand."

His confusion is making me feel more naked than the fact I am almost naked. "I'm afraid I'm going to hurt you," I whisper.

Then he does something totally unexpected. He chuckles, relief washing over his face. He sits next to me. "Really? I'm worried I'm going to hurt you too."

"You are?"

"Well, yeah. I've never had sex as a werewolf before. I'm scared to death I'll forget how strong I am and break something in you. Or I'll lose control and change when I'm about to...you know." He actually blushes. "I mean, I *think* I have control over the change. Jason really helped me out when I was visiting." Jason is the Eastern Pack leader. Will visited the pack this summer, I guess to learn how to be a better werewolf or something.

"Did you go there for me?" I blurt out.

"Yes," he says immediately.

"And did you treat me like crap all those months because you thought I was sleeping with Oliver? Because you were jealous?"

"Yes. It physically hurt me to look at you and not be able to touch you like he could."

"I never slept with him."

"I know. I was just using it as an excuse to push you away from me because, you were right. I was afraid." He closes his eyes. "And I am so sorry I hurt you. I would rather cut out my own heart than hurt you."

We sit in silence, letting those words heal any rifts left. I reach across and take his hand. He opens his eyes and watches

58

as I lean in and lightly kiss his lips. I rest my forehead on his and whisper, "I forgive you. Now, make it up to me."

Never taking my eyes from his, I stand. Will watches as I pull down my pants. My panties. I stand there completely and utterly naked in every sense of the word. He can see all of me. The scars. The cellulite. All my bumps and bruises, every imperfect inch. "It's time we stop being afraid and trust each other. And ourselves. Come here."

He slips off the bed, slowly walking toward me until our flesh almost touches. My body reacts as if it has, a shiver coursing down. His index finger finds the bottom of my jaw. He lifts up my chin, gently kissing me, but only for a second. Just the beginning. Those lips move down my neck, butterfly kisses barely connecting continuing down my collarbone to my arm, to the meeting of veins on my wrist on that thin skin. He's torturing me with tenderness. Finally his rough calloused hands touch me, cupping my breasts, thumbs then tongue toying with my nipples until he gets the desired effect. I toss my head back and moan. The moment I make the sound, his lips begin their assault down my stomach. He kisses the underside of my tummy, tracing the soft curve with those velvety lips. If he minds the extra mound of flesh, it doesn't show.

"Lay down," he orders in a husky voice.

He helps me to the floor, and just as my butt hits carpet, he buries his face in me. No preamble. No more tenderness. I gasp in surprise and pleasure as those lips and tongue begin their task of driving me over the edge. I writhe and nip my own wrist

59

to muffle the screams and moans I feel like shouting at the top of my lungs, especially as he kisses the outside of my pulsating opening. His tongue darts inside me, exploring as his thumb caresses my clitoris like a master. Round and round, fast then slow in time to the invader's strokes inside me. Then they change places, hard thumb thrusting inside me until it locates that sweet spot while his tongue flicks that sensitive bud. This time I don't stifle my moan. My back arches to draw him in closer. Deeper. I touch his bare back just to find an anchor in case I'm imagining this. But he's there. In me. Loving me.

Finally.

How long he continues, I don't know. Time doesn't exist right now, only the pleasure. And him. Every massage, every press, the tension grows inside me desperate for release. His thumb leaves for a maddening moment, only to be replaced by two other plunging digits massaging my G-spot, retreating, then forcefully impaling me again. And again. And again in time to his equally maddening tongue until I can't bear it anymore. With that last invasion, I cry out. My body vibrates and I dig my nails into him while the most intense, beautiful wave of heaven cascades through each pore of my being.

I can't move. Heck, I don't think I can remember my name right now. I am vaguely aware of something smashing onto the floor inches from our heads. Will lies down beside me on the floor. He wipes my stray tears off. Oh God, I'm crying. "Did I hurt you?"

"God, no," I say with a sniffle. This is so embarrassing.

60

"Why are you crying then?" he whispers, cupping my face in his rough hand.

"I just, I never…I don't know. This is just so much. I mean, you're here." I kiss the palm of his hand. "I've wanted this pretty much since the moment I met you."

"Me too."

"Really?"

"When you opened that door the first day…it took every ounce of willpower not to throw you against that wall and screw your brains out right then and there. And it's been pretty much the same every time I see you, or smell you, or hell just think about you."

"Ditto." I lean over and kiss him, tasting myself on his lips. "Guess we have a lot of time to make up for, huh?"

I unbutton his jeans, but he pulls my hand away. "Don't."

"Why not?"

"We can't. Not until after the full moon. I'm barely containing the wolf now."

"Days? We have to wait days?"

"Believe me," he says with a chuckle, "I like it less than you do. But I know I couldn't control the change if we made love."

I pout. "Well, I don't know if I can control myself around you that long. What are we going to do with ourselves?"

We both smile mischievously before he puts those lips to good use once again.

61

*

This is almost better than sex. Almost. We lie in my bed, me curled up against him, head resting on his chest with his arm around me. We're cuddling, and he doesn't seem to mind. I've found the rarest of men: a cuddler. Steven put up with it for about fifteen minutes before finding an excuse to pull away. But the man who killed him loves it. Go figure.

And he even let me pick what we're watching. I was shocked to find he's never seen one of my favorite movies, *The African Queen*, about a mismatched couple who fall in love battling Germans along a river. Will seems to be enjoying it, and I'm just enjoying having his body next to mine.

"What about when you found me in bed with Oliver that time in Dallas? Kiss me or kill me then?" I ask.

"Definitely kill. Both of you. *A lot*. And when I had your vampire admirer by the throat at Christmas? Kiss or kill?"

"Kiss. When you were standing across the billiard table during our peace accord?"

"Both." He pauses and strokes my hair. "What about in the cave with Steven? Kiss or kill?"

There goes the fun. "I don't know," I answer truthfully.

"I scared you."

I gaze at his saddened face. "He was trying to kill me. Would I have preferred you not to have ripped his heart out right in front of me? Yes. Does it make me love you less? No. He

62

tortured me and was going to shoot me. You saved my life. And I love you for it."

He actually smiles. "Say that again."

"What?"

"That you love me. Say it again."

"I love you, William Price."

"And I love you, Beatrice Alexander."

He grasps my tangled hair as we kiss again. My lips are sore as heck, but darned if I'll let that stop me. Close to ten months, countless fantasies of this very situation, a little bruising means nothing. I also know he's doing this to avoid the conversation, but it feels too good. Time for round four.

But the knock on my door kills that possibility.

"Trixie, dear?" Oliver asks in the hall.

Crud. I've lost track of time. In my bliss bubble I hadn't noticed the room getting darker as the sun set. "Shoot," I whisper. "Don't come in! I'm not dressed!"

"I do not see a problem, my darling."

Will tenses up against me, his signature scowl affixing itself. "I need about half an hour," I call. "I'll meet you downstairs."

"Very well, then." I hear his footsteps walk away.

"What was that about?" Will asks.

"Um…Oliver is taking me out," I say.

"Where are you going?" he asks as the scowl tightens.

"To see a play."

"That should be fun."

"You're okay with this?" I ask.

"Well, I would much rather be the one showing you off, but I know he's your friend. He's a part of your life. I might not like it, or him, but I can accept it. I trust you. Him, not so much."

"Thank you. I know you're not his biggest fan."

"I can tolerate him for your sake. But if he so much as touches you…"

"Will, if he so much as touches me, there won't be anything left for you to pummel after I'm done with him."

"I forgot my girlfriend is such a tough broad."

That word brings a smile to my face. "Is that what I am? Your girlfriend?"

"Would you prefer lady friend? Main squeeze? *Lover*?" he asks that last one in a silly voice.

"Lover," I say in the same voice.

He stops stroking again, but his hands remain in my hair. "Or mate," he says, now serious.

Werewolves, with their keen senses and animal instincts, have an edge when it comes to dating and love. Call it pheromones or connection to the magical, probably both, when they meet "the one," or their mate, that's it. They know. I'll bet their divorce rate is a heck of a lot lower than ours.

"Do you think I am? Your mate?"

"I don't know. I think so. Since we met, I have this…need to touch you. I know I'm in love with you. I just don't know that much about werewolf mating. Even after eight years there's still a lot about this werewolf deal I don't have a handle on."

"We'll figure it out as we go along. Together."

He kisses me again. I don't think I'll ever get tired of those lips of his. "What do you say tomorrow we go out? To a movie or lunch. Whatever you want."

"Are you asking me out on a date? A real, live, honest to goodness date?"

"I promise to be a gentleman."

"I certainly hope not." I tug on the collar of his shirt toward me, kissing him with gusto. His hands rove again, and move south of the border but I push him away with a whimper. "I have to get ready. You have to go. You do. You have to go."

Will extracts himself from my clutches and stands up. I watch with a pout as he moves toward the door. He opens it, smiles, and looks back at me. "Say it again."

"I love you, I love you, I *love* you."

"I love you too." Still smiling, the man of my dreams walks out and shuts the door behind himself.

Happy Birthday to me.

THREE

The Gentleman and the Wolf

After cake and presents, where Will and I can't stop exchanging flirty glances, I climb into Oliver's Aston Martin and make the hour trip to Wichita. The play is awesome, just pure sugar and pink, though not even *Hamlet* could bring me down. I fall asleep on the drive home, but wake up as Oliver carries me up to my bed. The perfect end to a perfect day.

The subject of Will never came up. I wanted to tell him and almost did a dozen times, but the words wouldn't come out. Guess I didn't want to ruin the night. We have this weird relationship that defies definition. Friendship doesn't really begin to do it justice. At times he's my confidant, others a spur in my side. Most of the time he's like a gay husband. We go shopping, to the movies, or just hang out and watch TV. But occasionally, far more times than I'm prepared to admit, something passes between us. A look, a word, and I want to throw myself into his arms. His bed. It doesn't help that he looks like a Disney Prince and on rare occasions acts like one too, saving my life or sanity. He's held me when I cried, suffered torture for me, and at times been my only champion. We'd die for each other, no question, but would he attend my wedding or even offer me congratulations? I truly don't know.

I wake up in the morning, and for the first time in a long while, I don't dread the day. In fact, I can still faintly smell my lover on the pillow and smile almost immediately. Not even here and he brightens my day. My *lover*. I sit up in bed, pick up the phone, and have an hour long squeelfest with April. She doesn't even mind I woke her. I go into detail about *everything* until she has to get the kids ready for school. I'm sure my X-rated escapades will be circulated around San Diego by tonight. I hope to provide her fresh material tomorrow.

At eleven o'clock, while I'm reading one of Emily Bronte's poems to Andrew in the library, Will strolls in. Thank goodness Andrew's blind and Nancy and her tutor Payton are on the other side of the room working on Geometry because with one look I feel myself blush from head to toe. Will's gaze finds me immediately, but *his* face remains neutral. I should have him teach me how to maintain a poker face between our make-out sessions today.

"Morning all," he says, strolling over to Nancy. "How goes the schoolwork, Nance?"

"Boring," Nancy says.

"She's coming along great," Payton says.

Payton, along with the rest of Stoker, KS, believes this is a halfway house/rehab center for people coming to terms with trauma. In a way, not a lie. No one in town asks too many questions, and in turn we sponsor the Fourth of July parade and fireworks show every year. Win win.

I continue reading through the exchange and even as Will crosses the room toward Andrew and I. He stops right behind my chair and puts his hands on the back. "Hi, Andrew. Bea. What are you reading?" he asks, petting my hair with his finger.

"The book Connor sent me," I say. "Bronte poetry."

He parts my hair with the finger and caresses the back of my neck. "Oh. Is it any good?"

"It's beautiful. Vivid," Andrew answers.

"Then I'll have to read it sometime. Or you can read it to me as well."

"Maybe I will."

"You're more than welcome to join us now," Andrew says.

Will pushes himself off the chair. "Afraid I can't. I have errands in town."

Pretty sure this is my cue. "Really? Me too."

"Well, you can come with me. We'll save on gas."

I stand up. "Is that okay, Andrew? We can finish the book tonight."

My friend smirks. I don't think our charade is fooling even the blind man. "That's fine. You two enjoy yourselves."

Will gestures to the door, and I follow him out of the room. As soon as we're out of eyeshot, he takes my hand with a glowing smile matched only by mine. But when Carl comes around the corner, he drops my hand and is all business.

"Give me a few minutes to get ready," Will says when we reach our rooms.

I change out of my sweats into a cerulean sweater and beige wool slacks, brush my teeth again, and fix myself up. I have no idea where were going, but I should be fine. He knocks on my door as I pull on my boots.

My boyfriend—God, I love that word—stands in the hallway in dark blue trousers, dress shirt, and brown suede jacket, holding a cactus in one hand and Kit Kat bar in the other. "I'm here to pick up my date?" he asks as he steps in. He gives me the gifts. "It was the best I could do on short notice."

"I love them. Thank you," I say, setting them on my desk.

Before I can turn around, Will grabs my wrist, spins me around, dips me down, and plants a deep kiss on my lips. We come up for air a few seconds later. "I've been waiting to do that since yesterday. I could taste you on my lips, on my tongue all night. It drove me nuts." I push his mouth back to mine and match the fervor of those words. We kiss like it's going out of style until he pulls away with a groan. "No. We're doing this right. A meal and a movie."

Me and my bright ideas.

The consummate gentleman, he helps me on with my coat, opens the car door for me, and even pays for my ticket and snacks. Call me old fashioned but I do love chivalry. Shows a lady you respect them. He's so respectful the only physical contact is holding my hand in the SUV. At least until the lights dim in the movie theater. Before the trailers end my head rests on his shoulder. By the opening credits, he kisses me and doesn't stop until the end of the movie. I've never made out in a public place before but don't feel one ounce of shame, not even when his hand reaches under my bra. April would be so proud.

We don't make it to the restaurant. On the road, after just a kiss on his cheek, Will whips the car down a desolate dirt road. The moment he puts the car into park, we go at it again. Touching, exploring, kissing. Not near enough. He pulls my sweater off, yanks down my bra down on one side, and roughly kneads my breast until I moan. With the stupid gearshift in our way, we fall into the backseat, him on top of me. He caresses my bare skin with one hand and undoes my pants with the other. Those deft digits thrust inside me again, immediately finding that sweet spot and playing it like a fiddle. I move in rhythm to his fingers until those beautiful sensations crescendo, and the whole car literally shakes. He collapses on top of me, both of us laughing.

"You made my earth literally move," I chuckle.

He kisses me. "Glad to be of service, ma'am."

"And just so you know, I don't normally put out on the first date. I'm a good girl, I am."

"Sorry to corrupt you."

"And everyone thought it would be Oliver."

70

"If it was, it would have been the last thing he ever did." Will pecks my nose. "I love your face when you come. It's just pure bliss mixed with freedom. I spent hours imagining what it would look like."

"And what were you doing, Mr. Price, when you were having these impure thoughts?" I ask in a sultry voice as I start unbuckling his belt and button.

"Let's just say the hair on my palms isn't only because of my condition. I swear, from the second I met you, you've consumed my every thought."

I unzip his pants. "I know. I drive you *crazy*."

My hand finds the edge of his boxers, and I run my finger along his flat stomach before invading south. He's a full salute, has been ever since we got into the backseat. I grip him, running my thumb over his tender tip. He draws a quick intake of breath. "Pretty close to certifiable right about now." My pace quickens along the shaft. He moans. Just like everything else about him I love the feel of him, soft skin over the hard core. We kiss and nibble in time to my own movements. God, I want him inside me.

A guttural, animal groan or really a growl escapes him. All of a sudden Will sits up and scoots away as far as he can from my touch. "What?" I ask.

He shaking and breathing heavily, not in the good way. "Sorry. I…can't do that. Not yet."

"I was just trying to reciprocate," I say as I pull on my bra.

He starts zipping up his pants. "I know. I'm sorry. I hate this."

"What happened? Tell me." He's silent and won't look at me. "Will." I sit up to take his hand. For once he doesn't pull away. "Talk to me. This won't work, *we* won't work unless we're honest with each other. Completely, okay?"

He glances at me and closes his hand around mine. "I felt it coming. The change."

"What does it feel like?"

"Like all of my skin is on fire and electrified at the same time. Then, in the pit of my stomach, it's as if something is trying to claw its way out through my organs, spreading its agony over every inch of my flesh. Of my mind. But that pain's nothing to when I let the monster out. Almost every one of my bones, joints, tendons, and ligaments snap in half before stitching itself back together. My skin stretches and burns and itches at the same time as my hair pushes itself out. My heart feels like it's about to burst out of my chest it has to pump so hard and so fast. I can't breathe a lot of the time, and when I can, I use the air to scream. Sweat, mucous, and ectoplasm coat me. It only takes about three minutes but…if I could, I'd pray for death."

"What about after? When you've changed?"

"I'm in there. Not a lot, not enough I can control myself like a man should, but I can see and feel what's happening. All my senses are heightened. I can see perfectly, hear a half mile away, and smell *everything*. I want to explore, to run, to hunt. It

72

is freeing." He looks into my eyes, sad. "But nothing trumps the blood lust. The savage, raw desire to tear anything weaker than me to bloody shreds and feast."

"Why?"

"Because I'm angry they're in my territory. Because…it's fun. I can't stop myself."

"You stopped yourself with me," I remind him. "In Colorado." On my first case, a necromancer summoned close to a hundred zombies, and Will changed to stop them. Like a moron, I forgot this fact and found myself face-to-snout with werewolf Will. But instead of eating me, he licked me. Our first kiss sort of.

"Yeah," he chuckles. "He likes you. The wolf. Respects you. Wants you. But we can't count on him to always feel that way."

"You're not going to hurt me," I assure him.

"*He* could," Will says as his face falls, no doubt rolling through all the horrible scenarios that might take place. He can't even look at me anymore. The last time he had that expression, he broke my heart. My stubbornness is the only reason we've gotten this far.

I'm not going to let him ruin all my hard work. "Do you trust me?"

"You know I do."

"Then tomorrow night, I want to be on guard duty. From start to finish, all night long."

That melancholy pale is replaced with revulsion. Not an improvement. "No."

"Thought you trusted me."

"It's me I don't trust, Bea."

"That's crap, Will. I fought a hundred zombies. I walked into a room full of vamps and was one of the few to walk out. I can take care of myself." I pause. "You know what I think? This entire thing, this push and pull we've been going through all this time, it's all because you're scared. Scared not about you hurting me, but *me* hurting *you*. You hate yourself, Will. You see yourself as this boogeyman who can snap and destroy all of Tokyo or something. And deep down you're afraid if we get close, *really* close, I'll see that too and go screaming for the hills." I lean across and cup his face in my hand. He still won't look at me, but puts his hand over mine. "That is not going to happen. I could never, ever hate you. Not for that. I've said this a dozen times and I'm going to keep saying it until you get it through your thick skull." I put my other hand on his bare chest right over his heart. "I don't care that you're a werewolf. I don't. And I think the first step to proving that to you is to go through it with you. See you at your worst, your most frightening, and still be there in the morning with open arms. I love you, Will. Trust that. Please."

He closes his eyes to let the prospect sink in. I know I've got him when his shoulders drop and jaw relaxes. "I don't want to ruin this," he whispers.

I rest my head over his heart. As he wraps his arms around me, I close my eyes. "I won't let you."

FOUR

WITH FRIENDS LIKE THESE

Chandler pounces on Will the moment we enter the house just after sunset. Something about a poker game at Rushmore's apartment. My paramour reluctantly leaves with his buddies while I make a B-line to the kitchen. I'm freaking starving. We never did make it to the restaurant, not that I'm complaining. We just talked and kissed then drove around and kissed. If it was up to me we'd be joined at the lips and never leave the bedroom. I think I'll replace food with sex and get really skinny. It may be the first diet ever to work for me. Certainly the most fun.

I'm half-way through my omelet when George walks into our massive kitchen. Just the man I wanted to see. Dr. George Black is the real leader of our ragtag group of abominations. He does the recruiting, the research, and deals with the bureaucracy. At seventy-four he'd had this privilege for over fifty years. He was one of the first parapsychologists to actually earn a degree in it. And he's the man who brought me here. Some days I curse him and others, like today, I want to kiss him. He gets a ginger ale from the fridge. "I've been looking for you," he says.

"Will and I were running errands," I reply.

"I still haven't received reports about Virginia Beach from either of you."

"Nuts. Sorry. I'll do it tonight." I take a bite. "They got her to Montana alright?"

"Yes." He sips his soda. "Did you have a pleasant birthday?"

"It was perfect. And thank you for the book. I didn't know Julian Wilde had a new novel out."

"Well, you are most welcome."

He takes a step to leave, but I pipe up. "George? I need to talk to you about something."

"Okay."

"I, um, want to be the one to guard Will tomorrow night."

He rapidly blinks but shows no other indication of surprise or reprobation. "Have you spoken to him about this?"

"Yeah. He thought it was a good idea." Eventually.

"Well, I'll speak to him when he returns. I personally don't see a problem with it."

"Good. Thank you." I advert my gaze and take another bite of my omelet. And he needs to leave now.

He doesn't. "So, I assume you two are dating?"

"Um," I say into my fork, blushing, "yes. I hope that's okay."

"There are no official rules against it, no."

"Good." Please go away now.

77

"I cannot say I'm surprised. You both seem to care deeply for one another, even during those unfortunate months last year."

"Yeah."

"Just...be careful."

"Like with," I wince, "birth control?"

"No! I mean, yes, of course, but you're both adults, you have that covered I'm sure. No, I was speaking emotionally. Be careful. We've just begun healing as a team and another rift could be disastrous."

I stand up. "I know."

"You know what, Trixie dear?"

George and I turn to the kitchen door where my gorgeous friend fills the frame. He's still dressed in black satin pajamas and holds a coffee cup that has never held coffee. I glance at George who simply sips his soda. "I'll leave you two to talk." George smiles at the vampire as he passes.

Oliver glides over to the sink. "That sounded ominous. What do we need to talk about?"

Like last night, I open my mouth to tell my friend my great news, but the words stick in my throat. Because this will change everything. I could lose one of my best friends. Someone I've come to rely on more than I care to admit. Not yet. Just...not yet. "I was just telling him about the play last night. I had a great time."

"As did I. Though I am afraid I have the opening number repeating through my head."

"Sorry."

"Small price to pay for spending the evening with the most bewitching woman in Kansas."

"You know, when you use that line on every single female within earshot, it sort of diminishes the sentiment."

Oliver, with Grin # 2, saunters over to me, stopping mere inches away. "I may say it to them, Trixie my darling, but I mean it with you." His voice is playful, but his eyes tell another tale. I get goosepimply all over. "So, my dearest darling, what is our destination this evening? We still have not seen that superhero film you spoke of."

"I saw it today." Well, parts of it.

"Then perhaps the pool hall. I promise not to beat you too terribly."

"I think I'm going to have to leave you to your own devices tonight. I have a report to type, and I'm exhausted." And I need to think up the best way to tell you I'm dating your enemy. I put my plate in the dishwasher. "Sorry. But you have fun."

I'm walking out when he steps in front of me. "You do not seem yourself these last two evenings."

"What—what do you mean?" I ask with a nervous chuckle.

"I do not know, but there is something different about you. The word 'distracted' leaps to mind."

"I'm just tired, that's all. Good night's sleep, and I'll be right as rain." I squeeze his upper arm for assurance. "You have a good night."

As I walk back to my room, unease and guilt weigh me down. I just lied to my best friend. The one man I can bare my soul to without fear of judgment. I just can't tell him *this*. Not yet at least. Not until I'm ten thousand percent sure there is something to tell. Because deep down, hidden under the bravado, I have no idea if come tomorrow night there will be.

For all my posturing, I'm scared to death I won't be able to handle it. Knowing the man you love changes into a monster, and watching it from start to finish, then being stuck in a room with the monster all night, are very different things. The last time I saw him changing he punched a hole in someone's chest and tore out his heart. Then he ate it. I didn't stick around for that last part but I heard about it. Saw a picture too. Yet even as I stared at that photo, at the destruction he wrought, I loved him. Still. Doubts are normal, and if I've learned anything from this job, it's to prepare for the worst. If that worst happens tomorrow, and if I tell Oliver about us tonight, I could lose them both. But really, I'm just a coward. I want my cake and to eat it too.

Yeah. That's never worked out for anyone, and I have a horrible feeling I'm no exception. I'll find out tomorrow. I'm already dreading the day.

*

I wasn't lying about being exhausted. I wrote the report, took a shower, and crashed around ten. I kind of expected Will to crawl into bed with me, but when I wake I'm still alone. The game must have gone long. I dress in jeans and black sweater before going downstairs in search of coffee. Fresh pot piping hot. Good omen for the rest of the day. Tonight's the night. I—

"O.M.G! You hooked up with Will!"

I almost choke on my coffee as Nancy pops in and all but shrieks right in my face. The teleporting thing took getting used to, but when she just appears out of thin air inches from me, it still scares the coffee right out of me. Her doe eyes are wide behind her black, cat-eye glasses.

"Jesus! Don't do that!" I cough.

"Sorry. But is it true? Are you two together? Did he propose yet? Can I be a bridesmaid? Does Oliver know?"

"Nancy! Take a breath!"

"I can't! It's too exciting!"

Carl runs into the kitchen, annoyance all over his face. "I knew it. You promised!"

"What?" Nancy asks. "You can't like tell me something like that and *not* like expect me to say something!" The overexcited teen looks back around to me, her black pageboy hair spinning from the force. "So, is it like true?"

I glance at Carl for help, but he seems as interested in the answer as her. "What makes you think we're dating?" I chuckle nervously.

"Last night all the agents totally confronted Will at the poker game. He spilled his guts, then Rush told Carl who told me. And can I say is it is like about time! You two have been like totally in love since you met. Even when you like hated each other, we could all like totally see you wanted to like bang each other's brains out." She gasps as something dawns on her. "That's where you were all yesterday! I totally knew it!"

"You did not," Carl says, saddling up to us.

"Did too! So? Is it true?"

"Is what true?" Agent Wolfe asks as he enters with blabbermouth Rushmore. "The fact Will and Bea are screwing now?"

All eyes jut my way, trapping me. Teleportation could come in handy right about now. "Yes, we are a couple now. For about three days."

"That's it?" Carl asks. "Only three days?"

"How serious is it?" Rushmore asks, face scrunched up.

"Like mega!" Nancy answers for me. "We've all talked about how in love they are for months now!"

"Well, they've been at each other's throats those same months," Carl points out.

"And Will did tell me he couldn't be in the same room as her," Rushmore adds.

"That's because he'd like totally jump her bones if she got too close to him for too long," Nancy informs him. She looks back at me. "So, has he? Jumped your bones?"

"She said it's only been three days," Wolfe says.

"So?" Nancy asks.

"No, they couldn't have yet," Carl says academically. "Too close to the full moon. He'd probably change if they did."

"They can like so do other things," says Nancy.

"I just wish they'd gotten together months ago," Rushmore says to the group, who all seem to have forgotten I'm in the room. "We could have avoided all the bullshit."

Chandler and Andrew walk in, completing the menagerie of my horror. "What's going on?" Chandler asks.

"Talking about Will and Alexander," Rushmore says.

"Oh, that," Chandler says with distaste. He looks at me. "Disaster of epic proportions."

"No, it's not," Carl says.

"Of course it is. Aren't you forgetting someone?" Rushmore asks before turning my way. "Does *he* know yet?"

"Obviously not," Chandler responds for me, though much snarkier than I would have. "Will hasn't been drained of all his blood and crucified on the front lawn yet."

"Oliver would never do that!" Nancy snaps, offended for the object of her crush.

"Then we're not talking about the same Oliver," Chandler says with a scoff.

"And things just got back to normal," Rushmore says to himself. "I'll ask for reassignment before I go through that bullshit again."

"Me too," Wolfe says.

"It'll be worse this time," Chandler adds. "That bastard's going to rain down blood on all of us."

"Hey, *he* didn't cause the rift last time," Wolfe says. "Your boy did."

"It ran both ways, asshole," Rushmore says.

"Don't call him an asshole," Carl says.

Chandler throws his hands up in exasperation. "See? Look what you've done. It's beginning already."

Then everyone takes offense at once, talking over each other but not listening. Nancy defends "my love" but the others just bicker about who started the last war, and what this one will be like. Only Andrew and I keep our traps shut. I'm afraid to move or even blink in case I make things worse. Seems to be a gift of mine.

I breathe a literal sigh of relief when Will appears behind Andrew in the doorway. His brow furrows in confusion at all the commotion. "What the hell is going on here?" he bellows.

"Us," I pipe up for the first time in minutes.

Will eyes all our hostile friends with censure as he stalks toward me. A bit of the wolf peeks out behind his expression, lips pulled back to show his teeth. Jesus, that's unnerving. Don't think there's a single person in this room without chills, myself included. "Us, huh?" He wraps his arm around my waist and pulls me against his hip. A united front. "And I take it they're not happy for us?"

"Nope."

His cold eyes burrow into Chandler's. "And why is that, Paul?" His eyes move to Rushmore's. "Kevin?"

"*I'm* happy for you," Nancy says.

"Thank you, Nancy," Will says, not taking his eyes off the agents. "But why only you? Because when two people find love, their friends should be happy for them, not ripping out each other's throats."

"Couldn't agree with you more," Chandler says. "*Sir.*"

The way Chandler utters that last word makes me want to punch him, and judging from Will's scowl he desires the same. "We never really cleared the air as a team about what happened last year." He scans the group to make sure he has their attention. He does. "I take full responsibility. I let my emotions and prejudice cloud my judgment, and then stood idly by as my poison spread to all of you. For that, you have my most sincere apology. All I can hope for is with time, I can prove myself once again as your leader and regain your trust."

"You didn't do anything wrong," Chandler says.

"Yes, I did. We all did. We're a team. No, we're more than that. We're a family. Whether we like it or not. I made us lose sight of that, but now it's up to all of us to repair that bond. Not just for us, but for the people we're sworn to protect. And I personally vow never to forget that again. No matter what happens." He squeezes me in tighter. "But we're in love. We're together, and nothing anyone says or does will change that fact. As our family, we expect the acceptance and support we would give each of you were the tables turned. And we promise not to let our relationship affect our jobs or the team as best we can."

"Oliver may have something to say about that," Wolfe says.

"If there are any issues, we will deal with them in a way that's best for the whole family," Will stresses. "And I do think he'll surprise us all." Will releases me, grabs the coffee I was preparing him before the Spanish Inquisition began, and takes my hand with the other. "Now, if you'll excuse us, we need to rest for tonight. Enjoy your day." With those final words, he leads me past our properly chastised family. "You okay?"

I shake my head in disbelief. God help us because if that was *their* reaction, when Oliver rises I have the feeling we'll be lucky if it only rains blood. I snake my arm around Will and rest my head on his chest. But he's worth a storm or two.

"Never better."

*

We spend the rest of the day in his bed watching James Bond movies. Not one of my favorite series but I'd watch grass grow if it meant I could be nestled under the covers with Will. 007's adventures do work quite well at keeping my mind off tonight, at least most of the time. When I can't keep the demons at bay all sorts of horrible scenarios have raced through my brain. What if I throw up? Run screaming from the room? What if he gets out? I need to mentally prepare myself for anything. Like if I can't handle the reality of dating a werewolf and this is the last time we're in each other's arms.

As it begins growing darker outside, I sense him getting tenser next to me. The rule is he has to be down there no later than five thirty. At five, I move to get up. "Do you want me to get you something to eat?"

His arms tighten around me. "No. Don't go yet." I settle back onto his chest. He strokes my hair. "Let's just stay like this a bit longer, okay?"

"No complaints here."

As yummy Daniel Craig seduces another chick on another beach, Will twirls my hair with his finger. "Do you remember that day in the car at Christmas? When you asked me to run away with you? I bet we'd be on a beach right now if I'd had the guts to say yes. I wanted to. I almost did."

"Maybe someday we can go. Sail around the world. I've always wanted to go to Australia. And—"

"I'm scared." I look up at him, eyes narrowing in confusion. "Tonight's a bad idea. A *really* bad idea. I'm not going to—"

I touch his face. "Hey. This is it. This is the final hurdle. We survive this, we've done it all. Nothing can touch us."

"Australia, here we come," he says with a smile.

"Exactly."

The smile fades to nothing. "Just know, if tonight changes things, I'll understand. I won't think less of you or hold it against you. I promise."

"Will, all that'll happen tonight if I'll get some reading done and you'll howl a little. And if you get annoying, I'll just shoot you."

"Is that rule just for tonight, or…"

I playfully smack his chest and chuckle. "Don't tempt me, Will Price."

"Why not? You've been tempting me for months. Nothing wrong with a little pay—"

The knock on the door stops our play. "Will?" Carl asks.

Will shuts his eyes and sneers, eyes and nose scrunching in a way that looks almost painful. "I'm coming. Coming."

"I'm being lax in my duties," I whisper.

"Five more minutes?" he whines.

I toss the covers off and sit up. "Nope. Get out of bed, handsome. Jail time." I lead by example. My body's stiff from lying in the same position for so long, I have to stretch and bend. "I'll meet you down there, okay? I got to get some stuff from my room."

After blowing him a kiss, I walk across the hall, and change into my black and green track suit, grab my iPod, book, Kindle, magazines, computer, and DVDs. Should be enough to keep me occupied for the night. I've heard snippets of what happens in that cell and from what I can gather it's about 5% action, 95% boredom. It's not like the wolf can carry on a conversation or juggle to keep me entertained. Julian Wilde and Jane Austen will have to take up that task. On my way down, I stop by the kitchen, retrieving snack foods and water bottles. Kind of feels like I'm on my way to a sleepover, though I doubt the werewolf will let me braid his hair.

As the elevator door opens onto the hall, the gravity of what I'm about to go through hits me like a truck. I'm about to watch my boyfriend change species. The man I just spent all day in bed with will grow claws, sharp teeth, and possibly want to kill me just for being in the room. It's going to be disgusting, smelly, and beyond disturbing. And I have to keep a smile on my face the entire time or I'll fail the test and lose everything.

I take a deep breath and force myself down that hall. I will do this. Heck, it was my idea. And by tomorrow, it'll be over. We'll wake up and officially start our life together. And have sex. Lots of sex. Mind-blowing sex. Multiple times in multiple positions with multiple orgasms. Okay, that brings a smile to my face that I carry with me into the cell.

It's still as bleak and uncomfortable as I remember, but the chemical smell that doesn't quite mask the stench of urine almost brings tears to my eyes. Carl is sticking something in the small fridge and Will, who changed into gray sweat pants, loads the tranquilizer gun with darts.

"Evening, gentlemen." I drop my backpack on the couch in the corner. "What are you putting in the fridge?"

"Meat. You have to feed him at least four times. Just toss it through the bars."

"Okay. What else?"

Will walks over, handing me the gun. "If I get too rowdy, you shoot me once with this."

"The drugs last about two hours," Carl says. "Everything else is pretty straightforward. Just watch him. Make sure he doesn't hurt himself or get out. Coffee's here," he says, hitting the machine. "You'll need it. It's okay if you fall asleep though. He'll wake you up. Hose is over there in the corner. Use it right away or this place will stink to high heaven." Will and I exchange a sheepish look. Normally couples have to be together years before they're comfortable enough to watch *that*. Warp speed ahead I guess.

"Speaking of," Carl continues, "you know where the bathroom is. If you leave, know the door locks automatically behind itself. The code is 2010. And…" he picks up a remote control with a key on it, handing it to me. There's a red button in the middle. "That's the key to the cell and panic button. Keep them on you at all times. He gets free, press the button. The alarm will go off, and we'll come running. With very big guns. The rest, just use your best judgment."

"Okay. Thank you."

"I'll come down and check on you before I go to bed."

"Appreciate it."

90

Carl gives me a rueful smile before walking out. "Have fun you two." The door shuts behind him and the clunk of the lock fills the quiet room.

Will can't look at me. He steps toward the cell. And away we go. "It's cold in here. Sure you'll be warm enough?"

"I have a blanket in my bag."

He turns his bare back to me. "Thought of everything, huh?"

"Sure hope so."

We engage in another of our awkward silences. He doesn't turn around or even move. I slowly walk over and touch his arm. He tenses but doesn't pull away. "This is going to be horrible," he whispers.

"I know." I kiss his shoulder. "But you're worth it."

"Remember that when I try to pee on you." Still unable to gaze my way, he pads into the cell. "Let's get this over with."

"Okay." I shut and lock the door as he turns around. I can sense his fear and sadness from here, though his face remains stone. "Now what?"

"It's better if I bring it on myself."

"Okay."

"I have to, um…take off my pants," he says, suddenly bashful.

"Oh. Do you want privacy?"

Will considers this for a moment. "Um, no. It's okay." Not the time or place I thought I'd finally get to see him naked, but I'll take it. After a nervous, lopsided grin, he yanks his pants

91

down and hands them to me. Damn. *Damn.* I mean that in a good way. I am a lucky girl.

He notices me staring and clears his throat. I glance up, my face so hot an egg could fry on it. "Oh. Sorry," I say.

"I take it you…approve?"

"I think even Ron Jeremy would approve," I chuckle. Will does too. "Turn around."

"What?" he laughs.

"I want the full show. I've shown you mine."

"Fair enough." He spins around. I knew it was cute in jeans but bare is even better. Well rounded and muscular without being fat with dimples in the sides. Sculpted and full, like his thighs. A well put together man. And he's all mine. "Are you done objectifying me? Can I turn back around now?"

"Do you have to?"

He does anyway, stepping toward me with a grin. "This is a lot more fun than with Carl."

"I should hope so."

He takes my hand through the bars and kisses it. "God, I love you. No matter what that thing does tonight remember, *I* love you."

I pull his face to mine for a kiss, the bars cold on my cheek. "Remember I love you too."

After another awkward grin, he backs away into the center of the cell and I toward the couch across. Guess its show time. "It takes about three minutes, sometimes less," he says as I sit down. "Try not to make noise or move for a few minutes afterwards. Don't draw his attention until he's gotten used to his surroundings."

"Okay."

Will sits on the concrete floor. "I'm going to begin now," he whispers a few seconds later. He draws his knees to his head, resting his forehead on them.

I try not to breathe or even blink for fear of disturbing his concentration. Nothing happens for thirty seconds, then his shoulders twitch. Then again. He grunts with the third spasm, this time his whole body convulsing, reaching seizure proportions after only a few seconds. The grunts turn to groans as he curls into the fetal position. Oh God. Oh God. With his back to me, I can see the shining clear liquid coating his tan skin. Ectoplasm to help the magical transformation. Under that the skin looks as if there are worms crawling around underneath. His back unnaturally contorts as if he were hit by a bat. It elongates like a straw, the vertebra popping out like stones. Will roars in agony. I feel his pain down to my bones. I gasp as the cracking of bone and tendon makes me sick to my stomach. I cover my mouth to stop any more sounds and the bile that already stings my tongue.

Brown hair, or rather brown fur, covers the length of his body now, growing from his pores at an alarming rate. Within thirty seconds there's easily an inch or two. He flips over. I drop my hand from my mouth and instantly plaster on my best poker face, though my eyes probably give my horror away. Where there was once a nose is now a snout with jagged teeth inside.

His ears are pointed like triangles. He gets on all fours, hands and feet no longer human. The claws are a stark white amid the darkish fur. Sharp. Lethal. As his joints snap at the knees and elbows, he howls, all humanity gone from his voice. It's over. He's gone. I can breathe now. Huh. That was…huh.

If I didn't know better I'd swear I was staring at a real wolf. The only differences being the eyes and lack of tail. Not that if one was bearing down on you, you'd notice these things. Just the teeth and talons. Transformation complete, Will shakes like a dog, getting off the ectoplasm and sweat off before sitting on his hind legs and howling at the ceiling so loud I cover my ears. The moment the noise ceases he springs up, lunging at the bars. His body smacks against them hard enough to rattle the whole apparatus. He does the same thing on all three sides, growling the entire time. I clutch onto the tranq gun, not sure if now is the time to use it. He tosses his body at the first side again and again. If he keeps this up he'll break a rib. I stare at the gun. I really don't want to shoot my boyfriend.

"Will?" I ask hesitantly.

The wolf's head whips my way, growing so all those teeth are visible while his nostrils flare. Okay, talking was a bad idea. Like the predator he is, the wolf stalks toward me, literally drooling as if I were chicken breast. I've seen enough nature shows not to back down or show fear, so I don't move. I hold my ground. I think it works because instead of lunging again he stops moving and stares at me, nose twitching as those green eyes apprize me. Looking for weakness? Wondering what the tastiest part of me to eat will be? Then he raises his head again, letting out a bellowing howl before sitting directly across from me. Watching. Waiting for me to do something. Okay. Still sitting, I move my upper body to the right and his gaze follows, the same thing happens when I move left. Okay…

"Are you hungry?" I ask. His head cocks to the left. I'll take that as a yes. "Okay, I'm standing now. Don't…do anything." Moving slowly, I set the gun down with the wolf scrutinizing my every move. He sits like a well behaved dog as I walk to the fridge and remove a steak. I'd swear he smiles as I toss the meat into the cage. He trots over to it, lies down, and tears into it. Three bites and it's gone. Guess he was hungry. I sit back down on the couch and he resumes his tranquil vigil over me. Okay, I have no idea what to do now. I was expecting to tranq him and spend the night reading, not being stared at with anticipation. I've never had a dog before. I can't exactly take him out to play fetch. "Um…would you like me to read to you?" I ask.

That definite smile grows, and he even starts panting with my words. I smile back. Beatrice Alexander, tamer of even the savagest of beasts. All that worry for nothing. I passed the test with flying colors. And my reward can't take his eyes off me. The gentleman and the wolf, both mine all mine.

*

95

Will remains a good boy, listening to me read the latest Julian Wilde novel aloud and never removing his eyes from me until Carl brings me dinner. The moment he gets close to me, Will springs up and lunges at Carl, snarling and attempting to claw him through the bars. I grab the tray and rush Carl out. The moment he's gone, Will settles, whining as if I've betrayed him somehow. In my best schoolteacher voice, I chide him about manners. I think he listens.

After another feeding, and after he does his business—I leave the room for that one—he lies down and shuts his eyes. Jeez, it's like I'm sixteen again and babysitting the Riveras children again. I take this opportunity to pull out my laptop and watch *Hello, Dolly!* He wakes half-way through and just paces the cell. Poor thing's bored. He settles in his original spot to stare at me some more. I've gotten used to it so I ignore him. It works because he falls asleep again soon after. I make it halfway through the new version of *Northanger Abbey* before I drift asleep too.

His growling wakes me a few hours later. It's low at first, but by the time I'm fully awake it's downright menacing. His ears perk up and his eyes remain on the door even before the keypad beeps as someone punches in the code. Will's fur stands on end along his curving spine. What the heck? He didn't react like this with Carl until the man was a foot from me. Oh, God. I know who the intruder is before he even steps into the room.

Here we go.

The moment Oliver opens the door, Will goes ballistic. The wolf leaps at the vamp claws first. Saliva pours out of his mouth as his teeth mash in time to those talons. Oliver barely has time to glance at the crazed wolf before I'm up and shoving him back through the door with me behind him. Even in the hallway I can still hear Will rattling the cage and growling.

"What the hell do you think you're doing? You know you're not allowed in there!"

"I had to see it for myself," he says with a small sneer. "You *are* fucking him."

His words are like a slap in the face. "Don't be vulgar."

"But it is true."

I hesitate for a moment before saying, "Yes. We're together."

The left side of his mouth twitches. "Since when?"

"About three days."

The look he gives me, disapproval mixed with fury, makes me feel like I've been caught smoking behind school. "Your birthday. I wondered why you were in such high spirits. And here I believed it was my company, not his." His mouth twitches again. "So, you finally tamed your wolf. And I had to find out from Nancy."

"I wanted to tell you, I did, but I couldn't find the words, okay?"

I touch his arm, but he yanks it away. "You could have said, 'I am fucking the man who made our lives hell for months. Who beat one of my best friends to a pulp. Who toyed with my

97

emotions, made me sob so many times even I lost count. Who broke my bloody heart.' You could have said *that*," he spits out with the venom of a viper.

"You've known about my feelings for him since the very beginning. This shouldn't be a surprise, Oliver. And as my friend, you should be happy for me." I pause. "I love him. And he loves me."

"He may love you, but he hates himself far more."

"We're working on that." I fold my arms across my chest. "Anything else *friend?* Because I have to get back to my boyfriend who you just upset."

I turn to go but Oliver grabs my arm and spins me back around. "We have not finished our conversation, Beatrice."

"You want to finish this conversation? Change your tone and stop acting like a jerk. I'm too tired to fight, okay? And let go of my arm." Still sneering, he releases me. I pull down my hoodie to regain some dignity. "Now, I'm sorry if I hurt your feelings. I don't want to cause you a millisecond of pain, I truly don't. But I'm with Will. I am in love with Will. That isn't changing, and at least from my standpoint our friendship isn't changing either. Unless *you* do something to change it."

"If you truly believe that, my dear, then you are a bigger fool than I thought. Do you truly believe your lover will tolerate my presence in your life when he barely tolerates my presence on this planet?"

"We already discussed it. He's not making me chose. Are you?"

"How long do you think that will last? I cannot envision myself being invited to Sunday supper or playing Uncle Oliver to your offspring, can you?"

I groan in frustration. "What do you want from me, Oliver? What do you want me to say? You're being unfair. If you fell in love, I'd be happy for you. Why can't you return the favor?"

When he doesn't respond except for that icy glare, I throw my hands up and start down the hallway. I don't want to—

I feel Oliver's hands on my upper arms before I see him. I blink and he's pulling me against his body. I'm so surprised, I gasp. Those gray eyes burrow into mine, ice melting to reveal misery. For a moment I think he's going to shake me, strike me, knock some sense into me, but as I stare into his eyes, it's not violence I fear. We've only kissed once, but it was…delicious. And there is a part of me, even now, that wants him to press his lips to mine. For a moment, as I gaze into those glorious orbs, lust strikes like lightening. But only for a moment.

The rattling of the cage and howling on the other side of the door keeps me grounded. "Let me go, Ol—"

A brutal kiss meant to hurt, meant to claim, cuts my protest short. I don't kiss back, instead moving my arms to my sides in surrender. He may as well be kissing a mannequin. I don't give an inch. After a few seconds, he releases me. "You done?" I ask deadpan. His glare answers for him. "Then get the hell out of my sight."

Glaring at him with the same ferocity as he is me, I wipe off my lips and step away. He doesn't say anything as I turn my back on him and punch in the code. Smartest move he's made all night.

I step into the room, replacing one uncomfortable situation for another. In the minute since Oliver arrived, Will's gone from Zen to rabid. His fur is covered with slobber and foam. He bites at the bars, yanking on them to no avail. There are fresh, bloody claw marks on the concrete at the edge of the bars. One of his claws has broken off. Jesus. The bloody paw swipes at me as I enter, its owner snarling and growling like a bear on steroids. I'm gonna have to tranq him. I sigh. I hope he—

"*This* is what you chose?"

Oliver scoffs behind me as he steps in once again. I spin around, eyes wide in surprise and fury. "Get out of here! Now!"

I shove him as hard as I can but I'm no match. Oliver stumbles but grabs my arm once again. This time instead of pulling me toward him, he twirls me around and forces me toward the cell. The only thing stopping me from falling into those claws mere inches from me is his grip. Will's maddened fervor increases two fold. His snout works in tandem with the claws, snapping like a foaming bear trap. He'll break every bone in his head if he keeps hitting it on the bars like that. My body jerks with each banging. "This is your future, Beatrice," Oliver says. "This is who your lover really is. A drooling, disgusting, monster hell bent on killing you."

100

My breath catches from the fear. Not of Will, though. For the first time, I am scared of my friend. I've heard stories about his ruthlessness, his selfishness, his lack of a soul, but I always defended him. That wasn't my Oliver. Not the Oliver who held me as I cried, who endured untold torture to save my life, who makes me laugh, who understands me like no one else. But now... "He's a literal animal," I spit through gritted teeth, "what's your excuse, you bastard?" Oliver doesn't answer, but his grip tightens. With my mind, I push him back. He takes me with him, releasing me. I spin around, slapping his face as hard as I can. "You son of a bitch!"

That exquisite face contorts. He's stunned, either by my slap or his own behavior. I guess the latter because his face falls into confusion and melancholy. "Oh, Trixie, I—"

"Get out!" I scream right in his face.

Flinching, he does as I ask, fleeing like the coward I never believed he could be. When the door shuts, I let out the air I was holding. Though I'm not moving I can't seem to catch my breath. It comes out as ragged as Will's. I have to sit down before my knees give out. He...everyone was right. I just stare at the wolf. Will is still going nuts in an attempt to go after him. To protect me from my friend. His wound has reopened, streaking blood on the floor. I can't take anymore. I pick up the tranq gun and fire. On impact the wolf calms and a few seconds later he slumps to the ground, finally at peace. That makes one of us. I lean back in the couch and let out a fractured sigh. And here I was afraid Will would be the one to scare my feelings for him away. That I couldn't handle *his* true nature. I'm such a fool. A damned fool. I just won one war with someone I care about only to start another.

God, with friends like mine, who needs enemies?

FIVE

COITUS INTERUPTUS

Around six AM the wolf howls his last for the month and transforms back into my boyfriend. It's as painful and sickening as the first time, but when it's over he lies in the fetal position pink as a newborn covered in the mucousy ectoplasm and fur that shed in sheets all over the floor. I open the cage and step in with his sweats as he shivers from either the cold or the adrenaline. I don't know if I should touch him with his skin so raw. He doesn't seem to even register my presence. Regardless I brush the matted hair off his forehead, and he glazes up at me, eyes half closed. The change takes it out of him. He'd probably sleep down here for hours. Without a word I help him up, towel the sticky goo and fur off, dress him, and guide him out of the cell.

We shuffle to the elevator, up the two flights of stairs, and into his bathroom where I sit him on the toilet and start the shower. He smiles as I pull off his sticky sweatshirt.

"You're still here," he says quietly.

"Of course, silly."

The clothes end up in the hamper, and Will in the shower. I'm exhausted after only three hours of sleep. I tried to fall back into slumberland after the Oliver incident but of course couldn't. Every time I shut my eyes, I kept seeing Will's snout and those talons swiping inches from my face. Not even Jane Austen could cheer me up after that.

After I'm sure he won't topple over, I return to my own bathroom, showering as well. I've felt disgusting ever since I set foot in that cell. I let the hot water wash away the grime of the whole experience. I did it. I passed with flying colors. And my reward lies in my bed when I finish my shower.

Will's fast asleep under my pink covers, face so peaceful and handsome he belongs in a painting. There's no trace of the wolf, just the man I love. Quietly I change into my pajamas and climb in beside him, pulling his arm around me. Any thought of Oliver vanishes, and I'm asleep within minutes.

Butterfly kisses on the back of my neck and the throb of his erection against my back draw me from dreamland. A hand reaches under my top and rolls my nipple between its fingers, sending a jolt of liquid electricity through my nerves. I moan softly in pleasure. "Good. You're up," he whispers.

"It appears a part of you is too," I chuckle before flipping over to face him. My mouth tastes of dirty kitty litter and his is probably worse, so I trail his neck then down his chest with kisses.

"What are you doing?" he asks as my mouth continues down. Instead of answering, I kiss around his pajama bottoms while untying them. He gets the clue, turning on his back with a chuckle. "Oh."

I yank down his pants, exposing him. My mouth and hands work in tandem, quickly bringing him blissful relief. Thank you *Cosmo*. As he lies breathless after, I pop out of bed and return from the bathroom seconds later with toothpaste. I climb back into bed, straddling him. He looks on curiously as I line my finger with paste. "Open." He obeys, eyes smiling as I put my finger on his tongue. Playfully he closes his teeth on me. I gingerly smack his shoulder. "Hey! No biting!" He releases me and I eat some toothpaste too. "There." I lean down and kiss him with all my worth. "Good morning," I say after I break away.

"Best damn morning I've had in years," he says.

"Liked that, did you? I figure I owed you."

"Actually, I think you owe me about four more to break even."

I trail my hand down his bare chest. "An Alexander always pays her debts."

He pulls my hand away before I reach my destination. "I'm still exhausted. Give me a few minutes, okay? I'm an old man."

I fake pout before climbing off him. "Good thing I'm so patient and understanding." I settle into bed, lying on my side while staring at him with my head resting on my fist.

He mimics me. "Good thing." He leans forward and pecks my nose, which I crinkle. "You know, you're the best wolf-sitter I ever had."

"Thank you," I say. "It actually wasn't as bad as I thought. You were quite well behaved." Well, except for that one time. "How much do you remember?"

"Parts. I remember you reading to me. Feeding me. Watching you sleep and wanting to crawl up next to you." Will begins playing with a lock of my messy hair. "I also remember what that bastard did to you."

Ugh. Mood killer. "He was upset," I say lamely.

Will releases my hair, face tensing. "That psychopath put your life in danger to prove a point. I know you think he's your friend, but baby I've known him a hell of a lot longer than you. Last night was just the tip of the iceberg of what he's capable and willing to do. I'm scared for you. He thinks you betrayed him. He's hurt, and he will take it out on us both. Probably the whole team. But you especially."

"Oliver—"

"No. Don't you dare defend him, Bea," he snaps. "He's not worth the energy. I don't want you near him, especially alone."

"You never did," I say to lighten the mood.

"I'm serious. You just got a glimpse of the real him. He's been on his best behavior around you, but I think that's ended."

"Will, I just need to talk to him."

Will lies on his back. "No way. He comes within three feet of you—"

"Hey. You're doing that caveman thing that I hate. I'm the one he wronged. *I'll* deal with it."

"But I'm your boyfriend. We're partners now. Someone hurts you, they hurt me and vice versa. And there is *nothing* you can say or do to make me not want to protect you. It's how I'm hardwired and most women would appreciate that."

"I do!" Okay, this conversation is morphing into a fight. That is not happening. No way in heck. My face softens into a sweet smile. "I *love* the fact you care so much about me." I trail my finger down his thick bicep. "I've never had someone so big," I move my finger down his chest, "and strong," to his shaft, "and virile," I take him in my hand, toying with him, "willing to do *anything* to keep me safe. It is such a turn on."

He revs from zero to sixty in a second flat, hard and hot in my hand. He grabs my wrist and rolls over onto me, all but ripping my pajama top off before roughly kneading my breasts. Pinching, pulling in time to his erection grinding against my thigh. This is more like it. The only thing stopping him entering me is the cotton of my pajama bottoms. No problem there. He yanks them down. Common sense, who I so hate at moments like this, sends up a flare the moment his manhood brushes my now bare thigh.

"Wait," I say.

"What?" he asks, physically pained.

"Condom."

But just as I reach for the nightstand, the alarm goes off. No, no, no, no, *NO!*

107

Right above my bathroom door is a tiny white square no larger than an Altoids tin that now emits a huge Claxton sound. I hate it not just for the ear splintering noise but what it means. Duty calls. Monsters to catch. No sex for us.

"Shit," Will says, climbing off me.

Dear God in heaven am I *never* having sex with this man? We could ignore it, but someone would come looking for us. Having no choice, Will and I get out on opposite sides of the bed, collecting our discarded clothes. He rushes toward his room, and I toward my dresser. Five minutes. It couldn't have gone off five minutes later.

I beat Will to the conference room. All the other F.R.E.A.K.S minus the real agents who are on their way and will be debriefed later wait, and I take my usual seat between Carl and Oliver's empty chair. George stands at the head of the table typing on his computer which is attached to the projector. He never puts nice pictures up like puppies or a shirtless Colin Farrell. No, it's always dismembered corpses or scary monsters. Nancy takes out her earphones with a sigh. Nobody likes the slideshow of death.

Will rushes in a minute after me, dressed in dark blue slacks and white dress shirt. He doesn't even glance at me as he sits. When we're at work, we are not a couple. We will not be lovey dovey in public, I will not receive preferential treatment. All business from here on. Professional. God, he looks hot. I just want to run my tongue—

"Okay everyone," George says. He uses the clicker to dim the lights and turn on the projector. "You're going to Appalachia Summit State Park in North Carolina. Nearest population center is Crawford."

"I like North Carolina," Nancy says. "It's pretty."

"What happened?" Will asks.

"The body of an unidentified male was discovered in the park." George clicks to the first photo. Gross. I just love pictures of severed legs. This one also has a raw claw mark on the calf and pitted bite marks along the thigh. At least there's no blood. "This flagged the system. An expert ID'd the wounds and surrounding paw tracks as made by a wolf."

"So?" I ask.

"There are no wolves in North Carolina," George explains. "Not for hundreds of miles. The expert also puts the wolf at six feet long and close to two hundred pounds."

"Werewolf," Andrew says.

We can't help it. All our eyes momentarily dart to Will, whose gaze remains on the screen. "Any idea who the leg belongs to?" Will asks.

"No body. Only the leg so far." George presses the button and a picture of the leg from farther away fills the screen. From this angle I can see the leg was severed at the hip, ripped off at the socket. The bulb of the femur even pokes out of the fleshy mass. "It was discovered by a hiker on one of the paths this morning."

"No ID?" Carl asks.

109

"No. All we know is he's a white male, late teens, early twenties. Nothing more. You're going in fairly blind."

"Any missing persons in the area?" Andrew asks.

"About a dozen in the past year, but it's a college area. Transient. There may be more not reported. But to answer the next question, this is the first reported non-dog mauling in the area."

"Um, does anyone else think it's odd he doesn't have clothes on?" I ask.

"I'm sorry?" George asks.

"She's right," Will pipes in. "Even with the limbs ripped off he should still have on a pant leg or shoes and socks."

"Maybe he was a nudist," Nancy suggests.

"Or taking a bath in a stream when they found him," Carl says.

"Or they made him strip for some weird sex thing," Nancy adds.

"Werewolf sex perverts. You're the expert there, Bea," Carl chuckles. I just roll my eyes, but Will glares at Carl until his smile drops. "Sorry."

Will's eyes move back toward George. "What's our cover?"

"Haven't gotten that far yet. You'll have one when you're wheels down."

"I say we use the same tact as in Cleveland," I say. "Tell them we believe he's one of our open missing person's cases. Worked there."

"I'll have the Charlotte field office begin the paperwork," George says. "As usual cars will be waiting at the airport. The plane leaves in thirty. The others will meet you at the airfield. Good hunting, everyone."

We all rise to leave, but Will's voice stops us. "Pack for outdoors and pack warm. I'll take care of weapons and supplies."

"I'll go load Oliver," I offer.

"Carl, help her. Nancy, when you're done, come find me. Hurry people."

"Don't forget my Bette!" I call after Will.

"Perish the thought."

I don't really need help with Oliver. I usually do this alone but don't protest. Oliver's door is locked and my key is upstairs, so I use my power to turn the lock on the other side. Not the first time I've broken into his room. Even at his most vulnerable he trusts me. That used to extend both ways.

The rat bastard lies on his stomach on the bed, skin whiter than usual against the dark blue sheets. He's dead to the world. Close to literally. I could blast Guns & Roses and he wouldn't even stir. Normally I'd brush that stray strand off his forehead. Now I can't stand to look at him, let alone touch him. We get to work. I pull out his suitcase from the closet, replacing designer chic with designer rustic attire while Carl readies his travel coffin from under the bed.

"So I guess the rumor was true," Carl says.

"What?"

111

"I heard he gave you some trouble last night," Carl says. "Boss man doesn't want you alone with him, even like this."

"How'd you hear about last night?"

"Oliver spoke to Andrew this morning, who told me."

"And you told…"

"No one. And I won't. Chandler and Rushmore would go apeshit. We'd never hear the end of it. Did he really try to feed you to Will?"

"No! He was just…upset. He wouldn't have gone through with it." I don't think. "Really, it wasn't a big deal."

"Bet Will thought it was. Should we be worried?"

"Nope," I say, tossing Oliver's book in his bag. His secret shame. Romance novels. I throw in two more and the last season of *Doctor Who*. We've only finished one disk. Guess I'll have to borrow it if I want to see the rest. Not many TV marathons in our foreseeable future. "Let's get him in."

Carl flips him onto his back. Darn, he's like a three-day-old embalmed corpse with waxy skin, sunken face, and tiny blue veins visible everywhere. I hate him like this. Gives me the creeps. Carl crosses his hands across his chest before the body levitates off the bed then down into the open casket. I can lift him with my mind but not my body, go figure. The casket has its own lift and wheels so we push it out and into the elevator.

"You ever had a werewolf case before?" I ask.

"Twice. Caught them both. As long as we take him in human form, we'll be fine. Probably just some poor guy who thought he'd be okay isolating himself in the woods."

"What do we do then? Arrest him?"

The elevator door opens and we push the casket out. "Depends. If he took proper precautions, did everything he could to stop from hurting someone, we just refer him to the proper pack for guidance."

"He gets a free pass? That doesn't seem fair. What about the dead man?"

He shrugs. "He went out into the woods at night. There's always a chance you'll get attacked by an animal. Don't tell your boyfriend I said that, though."

"I won't."

"And sorry for the pervert joke."

"Don't be. I thought it was funny."

Carl offers to take the casket out to the van, so I run upstairs to pack. Just warm clothes and sneakers. Okay, I do toss in my silky teddy and box of condoms, not that I think I'll get much use out of either. Dead bodies, nasty hotels, and chasing bad guys are all surefire mood killers. Lame. I put on my black jeans, thermal socks, red and black plaid shirt over black long sleeve top and hiking boots still covered in Florida everglades from the Great Basilisk Hunt. Sexy, I am not.

We all ride to the airstrip but have to wait for the agents and Dr. Neill, our medical examiner/doctor to drive in from town. The others arrive a few minutes later, tossing their

113

weapons caches and suitcases into the cargo hold with the rest. When Will boards, he immediately takes the seat next to me usually reserved for Oliver. Chandler, his usual airplane buddy, glares before moving to the back of the plane with Rushmore. New world order, boys. Get used to it.

We take off without incident, me reading my book and Will his. His hand finds mine a few minutes later, but when Nancy rises and kneels in her seat in front of us, he pulls it away. "O.M.G.," she says, taking off her headphones. "You two are like so cute holding hands like that. Why'd you stop?"

"May we help you with something?" Will asks.

"Yeah. So, I've been thinking about the like sleeping arrangements," she says with her usual perkiness. "I figure you two like want a room together for some, you know, bow-chick-a-bow-bow, right?" Will presses his fingers to his temples to stop the oncoming headache. "And I know you don't like me to bunk alone for, you know, like safety reasons, so I was thinking you two can have one room, Andrew and Carl the second, Dr. Neill alone as usual, then Chandler, Rush and Wolfe, then like Oliver and me. Perfect, right?"

I raise an eyebrow. "You and Oliver?"

"Totally! He's like the only one besides you I'd feel comfortable sharing a room with. I can like guard his coffin during the day since you're always making me stay behind. And I totally think he could like use a shoulder to cry on now what with you, you know, like dumping him and all. I'm a good listener."

"First off, I didn't *dump* him," I insist. "For the nine millionth time, we were never dating." Will gives me a sideways glance. "And second, there is no way in heck you're sleeping in the same room as him."

"Why not?" she asks with a pout. "You don't trust him?"

"It's not *him* I don't trust," I say.

"We're keeping the usual arrangements," Will says. "Nice try though."

The teen huffs and falls back in her seat. Smiling, I shake my head. "*Oy.*"

"I hope you don't mind," Will says in a low voice.

"What? Nancy not bunking with Oliver? I don't mind."

"No. Us not sharing the same room. I think we should focus on the case, and I don't want our first time to be in some motel between autopsies and gunfights."

I kiss him. "That's sweet." I wrap my arm through his and rest my head on his shoulder. "And it's nice to know dead bodies don't turn you on."

"Nice to know you feel the same way," he says, locking his fingers with mine.

"Yeah." I gaze up at my boyfriend. "Working with him isn't going to be a problem, is it? After last night?"

"I can restrain myself."

"Since when?" His eyes narrow and lips purse in fake annoyance as I grin. I kiss him chastely again, and again and the third time he deepens it until someone scoffs.

"Get a room."

I shake my head and sit back in my seat with a sigh.

This is going to be a *long* assignment.

SIX

WILDERNESS GIRL

We land and drive to the scene as we've done a couple dozen times before. I used to get nervous on the drive but this is old hat by now. I'm sure there will be plenty of opportunities for nerves and terror during our stay in North Carolina. I've heard it's truly beautiful here, but it being winter the usually lush green of the trees is nowhere to be seen. The hills are nice, though. Even in winter the tops of the mountains are rimmed with blue, hence the name the Blue Ridge Mountains.

Five miles after we turn off the highway, we end up on the two-lane curvy road, then after another turn we're finally at Appalachia Summit State Park. I'm so glad to be off that narrow road without a guardrail for the curves, just rolling hills that dead end at the rapid river a thousand feet down. The park's entrance isn't paved, just gray gravel which kicks up dust behind us. After about half a mile, we dead end at a parking lot where five police cruisers, a Ranger's SUV, and an ambulance sit in the lot. Even without the park being closed only the most hardcore outdoorsman would go hiking today. It's in the low forties, gray as the gravel and windy enough the bare tree branches crackle with every gust. Beats Kansas, though.

The police officers and a Park Ranger with a goatee dressed in a brown khaki uniform and olive green coat, start walking toward the SUVs as we park. I zip up my jacket, affix my professional face, and climb out of the car. Will and Chandler take the lead with me close behind to greet the officers. I've learned a little eyelash flapping goes a long way to quash jurisdictional beefs. Will extends his hand to the state police officer saying, "Trooper Tobin? I'm Special Agent William Price. These are my colleagues, Agents Chandler and Alexander." We nod. "Thank you for waiting for us and allowing us access to the scene."

"I'm Park Ranger Rick Mills," the ranger says, shaking Will's hand.

"Ranger Rick?" I ask as I shake his hand, eyebrow raised.

"I know," he says with a smirk, hazel eyes doing the same. "My friends give me shit for it too."

Will, scowling at the ranger, clears his throat. "Well, now we know who everyone is, perhaps we should get to work." Okay, I must remember not to flirt in front of my boyfriend, intentionally or not. "Walk me through what happened this morning."

"I'm on a week rotation," Mills begins, "but I've been here since four yesterday afternoon. At usual I closed the park at six and there were no cars in the lot. The last group left at five-thirty. I checked the park in my jeep three times last night: after I locked the gate, once at midnight, and finally three hours later.

118

There was nothing out of the ordinary. No cars in the lot, no people camping at the summit, *nada*. I opened the gate at eight this morning and half an hour later a pair of hikers are pounding on my door telling me they'd found a severed leg on one of the trails. I radioed the state police right away and went to check it out. I walked up and down both trails, but didn't find the rest of the body or blood trail."

"One of my colleagues took the couple who found him to our station to give formal statements," Tobin says. "We had cadaver dogs out here, but it was odd. They got about halfway up the trail, then wouldn't go further. I've never seen anything like it."

"Is the search still in progress?" Chandler asks.

"Yeah, but it's slow going. The terrain's steep and dense, and without the dogs it's a needle in a haystack. One of my guys sprained his ankle, and another got a mild concussion when he slipped and hit his head on a tree, and we have nothing to show for it."

"So you've only got a leg? There wasn't any blood around it or detritus?" Will asks.

"Just the leg. If I had to guess, an animal carried it there. Looked licked clean too. Maybe a bear or bobcat, but we haven't had any reports of sightings of either for a year," Rick says.

"What about deaths? Strange, natural, or otherwise?" Chandler asks.

"A man had a heart attack about five months ago, but that's it. This is a pretty quiet place."

"What about other strange incidents? Full set of camping gear found without the owners? Animals acting odd? Reports of dogs or wolves?"

"I mean, we're always finding tents and packs abandoned or just forgotten. Sometimes people aren't supposed to be here and run when we come. That other stuff, no. And there aren't any wolves in North Carolina. Not for five hundred miles."

"I'm sorry to be rude, but why is the FBI interested in an animal attack?" Tobin asks.

Ugh. Every darn time we show up people ask us this question. I just want to shout, "Because we're the mother f-ing FBI and we do what we want, that's why!" It hasn't happened yet. Getting close, though.

"We're investigating the disappearance of Edward Mitchell from Virginia," Will says. "We had reason to believe he was traveling this way. He's an avid outdoorsman and this was one of his favorite parks."

"Oh," Rick says. He turns to me. "So, you're from Virginia? Whereabouts?"

Will clears his throat, and I try to hold in my smile. "I think it's time we got hiking," Will says. "Daylight's wasting."

"Right," Rick says. The ranger pulls out a map from his back pocket, unfolding it on the hood of his car. It's one of those topographical kind, so I have no idea what I'm looking at beyond wavy lines. "There are two paths to the summit, the east and west. The leg was found on the west path. It's the older of the two. Steeper, rockier, only the die hards take it. We've walked up and down both though." He points to the area between the two paths. "We also covered about thirty percent of the woods between east and west."

"Which trail were the dogs on when they freaked?" I ask.

"West," Tobin says, "but the dogs around the east trail, especially the ones in the woods, started whining, and well…" Both he and Rick exchange an uncomfortable glimpse.

"What?" I ask.

"They started, uh, humping each other and the handlers, ma'am," Tobin says. "And all the dogs are fixed, so there's no reason why they'd act like that."

"After we brought them down here, they were fine," Rick adds.

"Okay, give us a minute," Will says as he starts walking away.

Chandler and I follow our leader back to the rest of the team. They're just waiting by the cars, Nancy fiddling with her iPod, already bored. "The thing with the dogs, is that normal with werewolves?" I ask.

"No," says Will. "Frightened, yes. Raging hormones, no."

"Then what does it mean?"

"No clue."

"What's going on?" Rushmore asks, rising from the hood.

"They still haven't found the rest of him," Will says. "So we're going to split into two groups and help with the search."

"What are we looking for?" Carl asks. "If they haven't found anything yet I doubt we will."

"Keep an eye out for claw marks, other dead animals, pools of vicious fluid and fur from the change. We want to see if we can find their trail. For all we know, there might be other victims."

"Do we have to go out there?" Nancy whines. "It's so cold and icky. And aren't there like snakes and stuff? Can't we just let the other police do it? They, like, know what they're doing. We know what did it, we know it's not here, so like what's the point?"

I agree with her, but that could just be the lazy, city girl in me talking.

"The point is, at the moment, we have nothing else to go on. This is a crime scene, we are going to investigate it. Two teams. Me, Bea, and Rushmore will take the west trail and surrounding area, the rest of you the east. Nancy, you lead Andrew as far as he can go up the east. You two don't stray off the path. Radio check every ten minutes. We clear?"

"Yes, sir," we all say.

"Listen and follow the instructions of the other searchers. They have more experience than we do but give nothing away. As far as they know, we're looking for a missing person from Virginia named Edward Mitchell. That's all they need to know. Be safe out there. Good hunting."

After a few more grumbles from the gallery, we start equipping ourselves with walkies, cell phones, guns, and water. Finally, Bette my sheathed machete, takes her spot on my belt. The man did say there would be bears. I add tissues because my nose is already running. The cold and pollen will do me in before the wolves do. Rushmore, Will, and I walk back over to the men, Ranger Rick's smile growing as I get closer. He keeps that up in front of Will, we *will* find a body in the woods.

"The three of us will take the west path. We're the most experienced hikers," Will says.

I suppress a chuckle. Mall walking, yes. Hiking up a mountain, no.

"I'll take the others," Tobin says. The Trooper grabs a portable GPS from the jeep and walks over to Team B.

Rick hands us another GPS. "Are the other Rangers out there too?" I ask.

"There's only three of us assigned to the park. Taylor's in Raleigh for a seminar, and Winsted's been sick all week with the flu. I left them both messages but they haven't called back."

"We'll be fine," Will says.

Rick shuts the trunk and starts toward the back of the lot. Rushmore is close behind, but Will touches my arm to stop me. "What?"

"I'm going to, um, need you to keep him busy and away from me as much as possible."

"Why?"

"Judging from what they've told us, how little progress they've made, I'm pretty sure the only way we're going to find the body or any clues is me."

"You're not going to…you know…wolf out are you?"

"No, but if I do pick up a scent, I'll need to separate from the group."

"Okay, well, I'll use every one of my feminine wiles to distract him. Shouldn't be too hard."

He takes my hand and kisses it. "Just don't be too distracting or I'll have to rip *his* leg off."

With a smile, I roll my eyes and we start into the woods where a chain hangs across the gray gravel trail overgrown by brown foliage and rocks. Ugh. It's all uphill with hanging branches in the way. I'm tired just looking at it, but I still run up to Ranger Rick, all sweet smiles. He grins back, pleased with himself for snaring another one. I know his type. Dating, or mating in his case, is a numbers game. No harm in letting him believe I might become one of his numbers. I'll make things interesting as he's literally carrying me up this massive fraking hill.

I'm the first to admit I'm not in the best shape. There were a few glorious months where I wore a single digit clothing size, mind it was the highest one, but still. I worked out three times a week in our gym and watched what I ate. Then I broke my arm, had surgery, and stayed with my grandmother who loves to cook. In a month and a half, I gained ten pounds. Today is gonna suck.

Ranger Rick takes that trail like the pro he is, and I do my best to keep up, making sure my huffs and puffs remain at a low decibel. Rushmore follows close behind, scanning both sides of the brush for clues. I just see endless dead brown bushes up to my knees and bare trees. Still, it's downright claustrophobic with the trees one on top of another, so dense I can barely tell where one ends and another begins. The last time I was in woods like this I was running for my life, chased by a crazed cop who shot me. Another angry red scar across my bicep added to the collection. I still get nightmares that I'm running and running and can't find the end. Yeah, I hate the woods.

"Have you searched either side of the trails yet?" Rushmore asks.

"The dogs did," Rick answers.

I glance back at Will, whose nose twitches like a rabbit on cocaine. This is not the best look, nostrils flaring and mouth sneering. Okay, it really creeps me out, but I'm sure some of what I do freaks him too. He can't be too happy with falling furniture whenever we're intimate.

"Have you ever been to North Carolina before?" Rick asks me.

"Um, no, but it's beautiful," I say.

"Fall's better. The trees look like a painting. It's the same in Virginia, right?"

"Yeah." I think so.

"So, which office are you based out of?"

"Um..."

"Richmond," Will calls.

I so can't hike and lie at the same time.

"How long have you been with the Bureau?" Rick asks.

"Almost a year."

"A rookie, huh? You enjoying it so far?"

"It has its moments," I say, glancing back at Will who sniffs the air. I turn back around. "How long does it take to reach the top?"

"At this pace? About twenty minutes. Getting tired already?"

My calves are already hard as rocks, and my breath's uneven. We've been walking for five minutes. "I'm not much for hiking. Most of my cardio is done in malls."

Rick grins again. "Then you must shop a lot."

Oh, lord. After you've been flirted with by the master, all the others seem like two year olds just learning to talk. "Enough, I guess." This is wrong. My boyfriend is a few feet away and despite what he says, I know this is bothering him.

"So, you travel a lot?" Rick asks.

"Yeah. We're usually out in the field two or three weeks out of the month."

"That must be hard."

"You get used to it. What about you? How long have you been a Ranger?"

126

He goes on to give me a biography that I barely pay attention to. I nod and smile but am really keeping my eyes peeled for scratches on wood, tufts of fur, anything out of the ordinary. Unless a werewolf pops out onto the path with a bleeding head in its mouth, I'm not going to notice a thing. I see trees, trees, and more trees. Will's our only hope.

"What about you?" he asks.

"Huh?"

"Is being a Federal Investigator a calling or just a job to you?"

"Um, I don't know," I say as surprised by the question as my response. "I've almost quit a dozen times, but I'm still here. Must mean something."

"My sister was a police officer in Winston-Salem. She loved every minute of it, but then she got married and had my nephew, it all changed. Is that common with the bureau too?"

"I guess." I glance back at my boyfriend again, and this time he catches my eye too, smiling. I quickly turn back around, all smiles.

"Well, it must make dating tough. Having such a dangerous job and being on the road so much."

"I do all right," I say.

"Excuse me," Will says. We all stop and spin around. "I think I see a member of the search party. I'm going to join him. You guys keep going."

"Are you sure?" I ask.

"Positive."

127

"I don't see anyone," Rick says.

"You don't?" I crane my neck in search of the non-existent person. "They just went down that slope. Huh."

"I have a walkie, I'll be fine. You guys continue up to the scene." We nod, and Will disappears off the path into the woods. The three of us watch until he's out of sight.

Standing with his hands on his hips Rick seems concerned and peeved. I catch his eye and smile to reassure him. "Trust me, he'll be fine. He practically lives in the woods. Nose and reflexes like a wolf. Come on. Hiking to do."

This time I start walking first, and the strapping men follow behind. Will must have caught the scent of the body or perp. We'll get a call in a few minutes that he's found something, I just know it.

Rick quickly saddles up beside me. "So, how long do you think you'll be in town?"

"Until the case is over."

"Because my friend's band in playing this Friday. They're pretty good. I—"

Will's gone, no reason to continue this charade. "Look, I should tell you, I have a boyfriend."

Rick balks a little, visibly taken aback. "Oh. Is it serious?"

"Yeah, is it?" Agent Rushmore asks behind us.

I shoot my fellow agent a scowl, and he just raises an eyebrow. "Yes." I turn back around. "At least I think so. But thank you for the invite."

128

"Oh. You're welcome."

That shuts him up. We continue up the path in relative silence save for my groans and pants. I hate hills. I'm so missing flat Kansas. We finally stop when we come across a white marker with the number "1" on it.

"This is where the leg was found?" Rushmore asks.

"Yeah," Rick answers.

I start examining the path and adjacent area, as does Rushmore. No blood. He wasn't killed here. The wolf must have carried the leg and dropped it for whatever reason. There are some broken branches, flattened bramble, and quite a few paw prints but no fur, no ectoplasm or anything else.

"Is this where the dogs went crazy?" I ask.

"No, that started back a little ways. But this is where we've been concentrating the search. We haven't even found a scrap of clothing. If I didn't know better I'd say a bird flew by and dropped the leg."

"As good a theory as any," I say.

"Let's continue on," Rushmore suggests.

Fifteen minutes later we're at the top, and it was almost worth the work. Three hundred sixty degrees of rolling mountains, some tinged blue at the tops, others ethereal white from the clouds enveloping them. Depending which way I turn I'll bet I can see Virginia and Tennessee. To the west there is even an entire hillside of Christmas trees. On the drive here, we passed half a dozen of these similar farms. Must be festive around here during the holidays. Even the grass is greener up here. In the distance, maybe a mile away, a farm house with smoke billowing from the chimney sits in the valley. The other sides of this vista are as steep as the one we just climbed but without the trail. It'd be hard but not impossible to climb up here without using the path. If our wolf didn't park in the lot like we did, maybe he left his car on the side of the road and trekked up here. Our victim too. Or the wolf lives nearby and found himself running up here.

"I told you there's nothing up here," Rick says, taking a swig of his water.

"Do you know if the state police have begun searching the vicinity for ticketed or abandoned cars on the roads?" I ask.

"I don't know. I don't think so."

I nod. "Give us a minute," I say to Rick. Rushmore and I saunter away out of earshot. "Okay, so we know there were at least two people here last night: the wolf and the victim. Do you think it's weird there isn't any sign of either of them or their cars? They didn't both walk here. I mean, both of them? And if our victim was here to camp or hike afterhours, there'd be a campsite or backpack."

"Maybe we just haven't found it yet. Or the wolf cleaned up," Rushmore says.

"I guess." I break away, turning back to Ranger Rick. "How far is the nearest house from here? Or road?"

"House, um, three or four miles. Besides Raccoon Road which runs along the north and west of the park, Routes 378 and 585 are three and five miles respectively."

I remove my walkie from my belt. "Trooper Tobin, come in."

"Tobin," he says after a few seconds.

"Have your guys been checking for ticketed or abandoned cars on Raccoon Road, 378 or 585?"

"No, but I'll call it in."

"Thank you." I clip the walkie on my belt again. As I do, I notice a bird streak across the sky landing on the other side of the ridge. Another swoops in from the opposite direction. "Guys?"

They follow me to the spot. It's a lot steeper here, so I scoot down butt first about twenty feet toward the murder of crows picking at the grass beside a huge rock. They fly away when we approach. At first look there's nothing out of the ordinary, no blood at least. The grass is flatter than it should be, but when I look closer I notice a tuft of sandy brown fur and a human fingernail in the crevice of the rock. I also notice a familiar odor, salty and sour like a men's locker room. I spent last night in a room that smelled exactly the same way. "Rush?"

I scoot over so he can examine the scene. "Got evidence bags?" Rushmore asks after taking it all in. Fanny packs are *tres* ugly but very useful in the field. I pull out three baggies and tweezers. He takes care of the rock, and I rip up some grass so we can check for ectoplasm. "Alexander?" He points to his left. I move and see it. Dark brown fur. My stomach twitches. Crap.

131

By the time we're done with collecting that second sample, the crows have returned about fifty feet to our left. Sure enough there's more fur, black this time, and that familiar stench. Rushmore and I exchange a worried glance. This is not good times three.

"What'd you find?" Rick calls to us.

"Animal fur," I say. "No blood, though. He wasn't killed here."

We manage to climb back up. "Let me see the fur," Rick says.

"Can't. Evidence," Rushmore says.

"I might be able to identify it," Rick says.

"It's bear," Rushmore says. "I've seen it before."

"You have?" Rick asks, not convinced in the least.

Rushmore stares him square in the eyes. "Yeah."

I clear my throat. "Um, do you guys mind if we take a few minutes to rest before we rejoin the others? I need to rest." And let the crows do our work for us again. "Rush, why don't you radio the others and tell them what we found?" He nods and walks away from the suspicious ranger as I flop down on a rock and down some water.

A pack. Jesus, one werewolf's bad enough, but three? At least? There are three official packs in America: Eastern, Central, and Western. I don't know much about them or the rules, but I'm positive killing is a no no. Of course it could still be an innocent bystander situation. The pack came here for the isolation, accidently crossed paths with our vic, and are now wracked with guilt over it. Yeah. Right.

The crows return to their original position two minutes later. "There's nothing else up here," I say. "Our vic obviously didn't camp here. I guess we should join the others in the search."

After taking one last look around the summit and finding zippity-do-da, I follow the men back down the trail until five minutes later we spot one of the two men search teams and join them. This is more or less pointless, but I go through with it. There is an off chance we'll find the body, though what it would tell us is negligible. Even if we do recover DNA, until we find the wolves it's moot. We can't run werewolf DNA through CODIS unless they killed him while in human form. Judging from the damage done, that's an unlikely scenario. And unless the werewolves signed their names on the vic's torso, we won't get any closer to finding them. But I go along with it. Whoever our victim is deserves a name and proper burial.

About ten minutes later, and nothing to show for it besides aching knees, calves, and probably poison ivy, Carl comes over the walkie. "Uh, Agent Alexander? Come in," he says, voice uneven.

Rick, my partner in the search at least for the moment, glances at me. I step out of earshot. "Alexander, go ahead."

"Um, Bea…Will's, uh, acting kind of strange. Can you get down here?"

"Strange how?"

133

"He's…just get over here. And hurry. Please." Carl gives me the coordinates, which I punch into the GPS.

Strange. He said strange. Not in pain, not in trouble, just strange. Still. The fear in his voice words makes my stomach clench. I excuse myself, and the moment they're out of sight, I run like hell to the trail and down the hill. A year ago I could barely use a map, now I've mastered latitude and longitude. Survival skill number seven the F.R.E.A.K.S. taught me. All the fatigue from the past hour evaporates as I race down the rocky, uneven path as safely as possible darn near twisting my ankle three times. Three minutes down and five off the path again, I spot Carl hiding behind a tree watching something over a ridge. He hears me approach, concern morphing into relief on his round face. Oh crap. I dash toward him as he rushes toward me.

"Thank God it's you," Carl says.

"What the hell is going on?"

"Honestly? I have no fucking clue. I teamed up with an officer, and we found him like that. After I sent her away, I radioed you."

"What—"

"Just go look. I'm," he throws up his hands, "done."

Great. I take this moment to mentally prepare for whatever is on the other side of that ridge because whatever it is, I am not going to like it. Not one bit. Carl's a few feet behind me as I walk to his observation point. When I get there, I wish I had taken more than a moment.

"Is he…"

"Oh, yeah."

My boyfriend, the future father of my children God willing, is crouched down sniffing a tree and stroking it like a lover. Oh, and he's not wearing pants or underwear. I think he's a millisecond from dry humping a tree. "Oh, lord." I turn away.

"That's not the worst of it."

"How the hell could it get worse?"

"Well, he stopped…you know."

My face falls. "He was…" I grimace.

"Is that what he's into? Trees?"

"Of course not!" I don't think. "Whatever affected the search dogs obviously got to him too. Look, we'll figure out the cause later. We just have to get him out of here before he's seen."

"I tried talking to him, but it was like he couldn't hear me," Carl explains. "Like he was in a trance."

"I'll see what I can do."

Carl bends down to pick up Will's pants, handing them to me. "I couldn't find his underwear."

Great. Of course he couldn't. I toss the pants over my shoulder, take a deep breath, and start walking. If Will hears me approaching, he doesn't let on. I don't exist. There's nothing but him and that tree. As I get closer, I can see he's fully erect. I look away. Him wolfing out I can handle, but this…

"Uh, Will?" I ask when I'm a few yards away. He doesn't respond, just keeps sniffing and rubbing that tree like he did my body hours ago. A crow caws as it flies down to join its

135

many friends in the distance. I think we found our kill spot. Still doesn't explain Will's behavior.

I'm a few feet away, and he still doesn't register my presence. I don't want to touch him. Heck I don't want to be here period. "Will?" His nostrils flare and twitch as he licks the damn tree right over a red spot. Blood. I gag and have to step away. Okay, pull yourself together, Bea. Just get him away from there. I crouch down to his level, grab his shoulders, and shake him. "Will!" Nothing. Having no choice, I slap his face.

That does it. His gaze whips my way, his normally green eyes almost black his pupils have dilated so wide. I barely have time to realize this before he pounces. One second he's there, and now he's here, knocking me down onto the ground. Before I can make a sound, take a breath, Will pins my arms to my sides and forces his lips onto mine. No tenderness, not even passion, just savagery in the act. Our teeth smash into each other's. At first I'm too shocked to move. To fight back. That vanishes a second later, replaced by fear gripping me as hard as he does. He releases one of my wrists, and I try to force him off but it's like a child pushing a two-ton boulder. I start thrashing, digging my heels into the dirt. Nothing. He has me. Panic grips me when I hear the tear in my pants as he rips the front. This is too much like…Leonard.

Instinct intervenes before I have to squeeze Will's heart like Leonard's. Invisible hands lift Will off me, but only for a moment. Still holding my wrist, he yanks me with him. This time I land on top. Be it the surprise of a reflex, he releases my wrist. As fast as possible, I roll off him. I attempt to get up, but a hand clasps onto my ankle and pulls me onto my stomach again. Not good. He's too fast for me again. Grabbing the waist of my jeans, he yanks me toward him again, rocks and twigs scraping my hands. My jeans fall halfway down my hips, exposing my panties. I'm too petrified to think.

"Bea!"

I can't see what happens but thank God for it because Will releases me. I'm free. Though my arms tremble like an earthquake, I crawl a few feet away and flip over. Jesus, Mary, and Joseph. A wild eyed Carl holds up the now split in half branch like a bat as Will, who bleeds from his head, reaches for him. I have no choice. My invisible hands slam Will's head back into the tree once, twice, three times until he slumps into unconsciousness.

Carl and I stay as we are for a few seconds, as if movement or even breath will start the rampage once more. Gasps being the best I can manage right now when I can breathe again, Carl drops the wood and stumbles over to me though his eyes never leave Will. "Are you okay?" He holds out his gloved hand to help me up.

When I take his, my own hand stings. Jesus there's dirt and blood all over them. It's hard to stand my legs are so shaky. My pants drop a few more inches. I snatch my hand away and pull them up. Jesus. Jesus. I don't want to be touched. Actually, if Carl could vanish right now, that'd be the best thing. I just want to be alone and cry.

"Bea…" Carl says in a low voice. He has no idea what else to say after that.

What can he say? There are no words. There never will be.

SEVEN

PROMISES, PROMISES

After radioing him, Chandler finds us a few minutes later to help us lug the unconscious werewolf down the mountain. He takes one look at me, still trembling from the adrenaline withdrawal, and knows to keep his mouth shut. If my convulsions weren't a tip off, he could also take in my dirt caked clothes and hands crusted with blood. I'm still glad we called him because it takes all three of us to get him to the parking lot. We're just in time too. Will starts stirring just as we reach the end of the path. Thank God we always pack a first-aid kit with serious tranquilizers for just such instances. Carl injects him with enough Thorazine to kill a whale. Since I'm the only one who can take on a two-hundred-fifty pound werewolf, which is debatable after what just happened, it's up to me to guard him. Chandler must sense my nervousness because he insists on coming with us. I don't protest. Mobile command is still en route, so having no choice, we take him to our hotel about fifteen minutes away.

George reserved us six rooms at the Hampton Inn, one of the nicer chains. I've become something of a hotel connoisseur during my F.R.E.A.K.S. tenure. I park on the side of the building near a deserted door but still have to face the public. The clerk takes one look at me and grows visibly uncomfortable, even shrinking away when I walk into the foyer from the side hallway. I still have dirt on me from head to toe, but she doesn't say a word beyond the usual checking in formalities. I snag a trolley and push it back to the side entrance. Making sure we're devoid of prying eyes, I use my mind to lift Will's lifeless body onto the trolley, folding his legs underneath him so he can fit. We throw our coats over him and toss some of the suitcases in the back on for good measure. Unless someone really examines us there's no way they could tell there's a man on there. God, my life is weird.

We get him into the room without incident, only a few stares in the elevator by a man and his daughter. I smile, and she looks away. Will remains asleep as we hoist him on the bed. There. Done. After all the hauling, my muscles are locked and aching. I wipe my brow of the new grime covering me, mostly sweat. I really need to get back in shape. Chandler flops into the chair with a quiet sigh. "You should go clean up," he says.

"I don't think I should leave you alone with him."

"He'll be out for at least an hour. Go."

It's more of an order than a request, but I'm too exhausted to fight. Plus I really want a damn shower. I grab my suitcase and wheel it next door. Like theirs, my hotel room has two fluffy white beds, flat screen TV on a large dresser, mini-fridge, desk, and dull artwork. Right now it's heaven. I toss my suitcase on the bed closest to the door, retrieve my toiletry bag, shed my clothes and jump into the shower. My hands sting like a mother but the hot water feels so good everywhere else I don't care. My wrists are just beginning to bruise but otherwise I'm okay. Intact. I—

Out of nowhere, I burst into tears. They start off easy, just stray droplets at first, but within seconds I'm sobbing hysterically, hugging myself even. He…it was as if I was eight again. Leonard was forcing my legs apart as I screamed and cried for him to stop. And Will, if Carl hadn't been there…

"Okay, calm down. Calm down," I order through the sobs.

I take a few deep breaths which always help when I'm like this. After a few seconds I can actually think. Okay. Get a grip. Nothing happened. That wasn't Will back there. He is *nothing* like Leonard. My Will would never hurt me. Never. That wasn't him. It *wasn't*.

I stay in the shower soaping and scrubbing until I'm red. Until I fear I'll draw more blood. I'm as clean as I'll ever be. I put on my blue jeans and dark purple turtleneck, braid my wet hair, and sit on my bed to lace up my sneakers. But I hesitate getting up. I just don't want to. What I want to do is crawl into bed, throw the covers over my head, and never come out. But I have to go back into that room for the very reason I don't want to. I'm scared. I'm scared of the man I love.

It wasn't his fault. I know it wasn't. It was magic or pheromones or God knows what. Will would never intentionally hurt me. Never. It was the wolf. It took over and lost control. I

141

shouldn't have gotten so close. I shouldn't have let my guard down. I won't do it again, not that I'll need to around him. It's over. He'll be fine now. *We'll* be fine now. And we have a clue. Whatever made him attack me has to be related to the murder. How, I have no idea, but I'll find out. Just get off this damn bed, Bea. *Now.* I ball my scabbed hands into fists and force myself to rise. Work. Gotta get to work.

Chandler answers the door with his cell phone pressed to his ear. The agent steps aside without a word my way. My apprehension wavers when I see Will. He's still passed out on the bed and hasn't moved. His peaceful face though covered in dirt and blood seems relaxed. No monster in sight. "No, bag it," Chandler says into his phone, "and get samples from that tree to mobile command. Neill just called. They're set-up now. I'll text you the address. Do whatever you can, but the sun's about to set. It'll be too dangerous out there after dark. Half an hour, no more, okay?" Chandler's quiet and glances at me. "When we deem it safe. I'll see you soon." He hangs up. We stare at each other, more uncomfortable by each others' presence than usual. "Rush."

"Everything okay there?"

"They found the possible kill spot near where Will was. There was blood and torn patches of fur. Looks like someone tried to cover the evidence with leaves. Still no body, though, or explanation as to why he, uh, attacked you. And command's here."

"Good."

"I think we should move him there, put him in the cell," Chandler says.

"No. I don't want him anywhere near Nancy or Dr. Neill until we figure this out." My eyes dart to Will. "We'll wait until the drugs wear off and see if he's recovered."

"Maybe you should wait in the next room. Just to be safe."

"I'm not leaving. If he is still…whatever, I can hold him while you tranq him again."

"Sounds like a plan. If you're okay with it." He pauses. "Are you? Okay?"

"I'm fine," I say quickly. "I'm fine."

"It wasn't his—"

"I know." I'm so not ready to talk about this. "Excuse me." I walk into the bathroom, grab a washcloth, and wet it. I return to the room, sitting on the bed. "Have you ever seen or heard of anything like that before?"

"No. We've tracked werewolves before, and he's never had that reaction."

I begin wiping the dirt off his face. Will doesn't stir. "So maybe we were wrong about it being a werewolf."

"The fur we found is consistent with a werewolf."

"Werewolves," I correct. "At least three if the fur I found is any indication." I wipe his neck, that same damn neck I was nibbling on this morning. "Could there have been something else out there too? Another creature?"

143

Chandler shrugs. "Will should be able to tell us if he comes out of this."

"*When* he comes out of this," I correct.

"Alexander, you need to prepare yourself. If he wakes up violent, we'll have no choice but to dope him and ship him back to Kansas until we find a cure. If there is a cure. For all we know, he had a mental breakdown."

"He didn't have a breakdown. There was something on that tree that, I don't know, drugged him. He's away from it now. He'll be fine."

"Alexander—"

I meet his eyes, mine cold as ice. "He'll. Be. Fine."

Because I won't accept any other alternative.

*

While Chandler channels his inner supervisor, ordering the others around via telephone as I look after the patient. The hits keep coming. If Will is out of commission this case, and Chandler takes over, I will at some point have a hissy fit and smack him. If the calls are any indication he barks orders and expects instant results. At least Will gives us an hour or so to complete the task before he barks again. Chandler's doing this to Wolfe when Will groans beside me. Both of us freeze until he moans again. With a gasp, I leap off the bed and Chandler hangs up, taking a step back as well. Will's fluttering eyes snap us up out of our fear. Action time. Chandler grabs the first-aid kit with the tranqs as I position myself on the other side of the bed right in Will's line of sight yet far enough he can't reach me. One aggressive move, I hold him while Chandler injects him. After that, I haven't a clue.

My stomach clenches as Will continues to fight through the drugs. It's not so much him attacking me again that's causing my heart to beat double. He no longer has the surprise factor that snared me the first time. It's what that attack would mean. That it wasn't the environment. That he could be feral forever. Dangerous. We'd have to send him to Montana doped and alone in a cell until the day he dies. I'd never see him again.

His eyes slowly open and he licks his lips. I don't move. I don't blink. It might change the fate of the next crucial moment. Will rubs his eyes and sighs. "Where am I?"

All the tension and fear evaporate with those three words. For Chandler too. His shoulders slump as he quietly sighs. If Will notices our odd behavior, he doesn't let on. I sit on the edge of the bed. "You're at the hotel."

"Oh." He attempts to sit up but cannot manage it yet. "I'm tired."

"We gave you something to sleep," I say. "You'll be fine soon."

"Good." He closes his green eyes again, nestling into the pillow. He opens his eyes again, smiling at me. I can only manage a shaky one back. He reaches for my hand but the moment his flesh touches mine, I flinch and leap up. "What...?" His face contorts in confusion as he studies mine. I can't hide it.

Heck, I can barely look at him. But as the memories flood back, he shudders and covers his mouth as if he's about to throw up. "Oh, God."

"Chandler, get out of here," I say.

"I don't—"

"*Now!*" As Will buries his head under the covers, moaning as if in pain, Chandler begrudgingly stalks out. The moment the door shuts, I run around the bed where Chandler stood, kneeling down to Will's level. "Baby?" I pull the covers down. "It's okay. You're okay."

His face is red and eyes are rimmed with tears. He flips over to avoid my gaze. Hesitantly, I touch his shoulder. "Don't!" he shouts. I yank my hand away. "Don't touch me."

"Will..."

"I'm sorry. I'm so sorry. I told you. I told you this would happen."

"Will, I'm okay. I'm fine. I promise." I start petting his hair whether he likes it or not. "Baby, look at me. Look at me, William Price." He does, shame brimming from his every pore. I brush the hair off his furrowed brow. "This wasn't your fault. I know that, okay? Do you hear me? I don't blame you so don't you dare blame yourself either."

"I tried to rape you," he whispers. "I-I can't..." He shakes his head and as if he were dangling over the Grand Canyon bunches up the pillowcase with his hands.

"Hey," I say, taking one of those fists into mine. It stings my scabs but I don't let on. "I'm okay. I mean it. *I am*

146

okay. I know that wasn't you. You would never, *ever* intentionally hurt me. This wasn't your fault."

"I'm sorry. I'm so sorry," he gasps with tear rimmed eyes.

Gazing into his eyes so full of pain, any trepidation I harbored vanishes. The man I love is in pain. That cannot stand. I kiss his cheek, then his hair. "Scoot over." He knows me better than to protest. He makes room so I can lie down next to him, our faces inches from each others on his pillow. I cup his face in my hands, wiping his tears with my thumbs.

His eyes dart to the bruises on my wrists. "I hate this," he whispers. "I'm a monster. A fucking monster."

I smile before softly kissing him. He doesn't reciprocate. "Hey. Quit beating up on my boyfriend." Our lips meet again, and this time he responds, kissing me deeply, even wrapping his arms around me. That's more like it. I pull away first with another smile. "I love you."

"I love you too. So much. *So* fucking much. I'd rather *die* than hurt a hair on your head. You have to know that."

"I do. Of course I do."

"I don't know what happened. I caught the scent of the wolves, it led me there, and then...I smelled her."

"Her?"

"She was so intoxicating, Bea. I was just overcome with...lust? Madness? I-I can't explain it," he says with a faraway gleam in his eyes. "I found the tree. She was all over it. Her sex. Her blood. It was...glorious. Heroin mixed with

Ecstasy. And my wolf. It took all my strength not to let him physically push through, but he still overpowered my instincts. I lost myself, baby. He wanted her. More than wanted her. I guess that's when you showed up. A substitute," he says with distaste. "God, what if it'd been Nancy?"

"It wasn't, so don't even go there," I say. "Have you ever heard of or experienced anything like that before?"

"No. Never. I've been around female werewolves before, and nothing like that happened."

"Including the female, how many did you smell out there?"

"Four, I think. I wasn't paying attention after I caught her scent." He pauses. "What if it happens again?"

"It won't happen again."

"No, you don't know that. You *can't* know that." he says, pulling away to sit up. "Listen to me. I need you to promise me something, okay?"

"What?" I ask with trepidation.

"If I ever…become a threat. If I ever lose control or harm anyone, especially you, that'd be it, Bea. The end. I wouldn't want to live. Not for a minute more. Not with that on my head. I *couldn't*, Bea. So I need you to promise me. I need you to promise me that if it gets to that point, you won't hesitate. You will do whatever you have to to put me out of my misery. Just as you would anything else. Will you promise me that? Will you?"

"Will…I-I don't—"

148

He cups my face, drawing me toward his own.

"*Promise* me, Bea," he says through gritted teeth, eyes as wild as they were in the forest. "*Please.*"

What else can I say? "I promise." I nod furiously. "I promise, Will."

He pulls me into a hug, each of us holding onto the other like a life raft during a typhoon. I just swore to kill my boyfriend. Did I mean it? Jesus, could I actually do it? The only thing I know with absolute certainty is I will do anything and everything in my power to make sure neither of us ever has to find out.

That's a promise.

*

As Will showers and changes, I fill Chandler in on the new intel and phone George. He's never heard of a reaction like Will's either but will start researching. He's been doing this job longer than I've been alive, and I've stumped him. This worries me to no end.

We grab some fast food for the team on the way to mobile command. I can tell by his tight shoulders Will's nervous about facing them. Squeezing his shoulder helps his tension a smidge. A blow job would work better, but not with Chandler in the car. Maybe later.

They've set up command in a valley at the outskirts of the park. There's nothing around but a dirt road and field.

Mobile command is a large black RV if an RV was exposed to Gamma radiation. Equipped inside are three state of the art sectors: a small lab, conference room, and medical center with freezer. We do it all from here from autopsies, and blood analysis to dinners, not all in the same room though. Our home away from home.

Chandler parks beside the other SUVs, and we climb out. Food in hand, I lead the way toward the building, but we barely take a step when the door to command flies open. I don't see the person coming out and not only because of the darkness. A sweet smelling breeze blows beside me as at the same time, I hear the thwack of fist against face. Will collapses to the ground.

"You bastard!"

Oliver looms over the prostrate and stunned Will with his fist cocked back for another blow. He delivers it with the force of Thor's hammer to Will's jaw. Then again. And again. Will doesn't move. Doesn't even raise his hands in defense. He takes every blow, blood oozing out of his nose and lip. Chandler steps toward the fray, grabbing Oliver after the fourth punch. The snarling vampire shoves the agent away. Chandler tumbles backwards onto the ground as well. Once again, I have no choice. With my mind, I lift up the insane vamp, sending him gliding into the faraway dark field, buying us all of a second or two. There's barely time to kneel beside the dazed Will before Oliver reappears, beautiful face contorted with intense fury. Bestial almost. My hand instinctively touches Bette's sheath.

"Get away from him," Oliver orders, sounding more menacing than I thought him capable of.

"No," I say.

"Trixie, step away from him *now*!"

"No, *you* get step from him now," I snap through gritted teeth.

"He—"

"Oliver, step away now!" I roar, voice echoing through the air.

Usually I can get a sense of him. His thoughts and motives. We have this uncanny ability to read each other's minds and anticipate the others' move. If I'm in a foul mood, or vice versa, with one look we can glean it and act accordingly, usually doing our darndest to improve the situation. We *know* each other. Or at least I thought we did. It's why we're such good partners. Good friends. As we gaze into each other's eyes, both sets filled with indignation, it's as if that link never was. It's gone. Vanished. If I wasn't so pissed and scared, I'd cry.

With a scowl, Oliver takes a step back. "As you wish."

I let out the breath I held and shake my head. Will groans beside me, then coughs out blood onto the dirt. "Jesus," I mutter under my breath.

Oliver just looms above, watching with disgust as Chandler and I aid Will to his feet. I don't know how long they've been out here watching, probably the whole time, but the rest of the team hangs by the door with mouths agape, save for

Nancy who covers her mouth with her hands. "Are you okay?" Chandler asks Will.

"Fine," he mumbles quietly. Liar. Without a doubt, his jaw and nose are without a doubt broken and his eye is almost swollen shut. He'll heal, but the nose and jaw have to be set, and even if you're a werewolf that hurts like a mother.

"Get him inside and have Dr. Neill take a look," I tell Chandler. "I'll be there in a minute."

Chandler glances at Oliver, who scowls back, before returning his glare my way. "I told you this would—"

"Not now. Just get him inside before those bones begin to heal," I snap.

"No," Will says through the good side of his mouth. "You shouldn't be alo—"

"I'll be fine. Go."

Chandler nods and leads Will toward mobile command. Will glances back at me, and I smile to reassure him. He really must be hurting because he doesn't stop. With the show now over, the others return inside as well. I wait until the door shuts before turning my attention to the still sneering vampire.

"If you think I shall be apologizing to him, you are—"

Literally vibrating with rage, I slap the bastard as hard as I can, my hand raging in pain from the effort. Stunned, Oliver cups his cheek. "*That's* for last night."

"You—"

"No, you do not get to talk right now. All you get to listen." I point my finger right between his gray eyes. "If you ever, *ever* lay another hand on me or the man I love in anger again, I will chop off your head without a second thought. Do you understand me?"

"He—"

"*No. Listen*," I order through gritted teeth. "I know what he did. And I know you know *why* he did it. Which means you just used a horrible experience I had to endure as an excuse to hit him. It had nothing to do with altruism. With protecting me. And regardless what happens between Will and me is just that, between me and him. It is none of your damn business."

"You are my business," Oliver parries. "You are my…friend, and I have vowed to you I shall keep you safe. I will not abandon that vow. I will not. *Never*."

"If you interpret that vow as beating my boyfriend to a pulp for something that was out of his control, then I sure as hell don't want you watching my back anymore. Because I don't know if I can trust you to."

"You do not mean that."

"I do." God help me, I really do. "You know, I really did think we could all be friends. I thought, for my sake, you'd quell your jealousy and selfishness and be as happy for me as I would be for you if the tables were turned. But I was wrong, wasn't I? It hasn't even been a damn day and you're acting like a spoiled child smashing everything in sight when you don't get your way. And I don't have the energy to pick up the pieces. I don't. So if you can reach within yourself, if you can't be the man I know you can be, then you stay the hell away from us, do you hear me? Just stay the hell away, *friend*. We're done here."

With that, I turn my back on my friend and walk away. And damned if it doesn't break my heart. At least I have one.

*

Of course I still have to work with him. I forgot that part. Darn it.

The entire team, Dr. Neill included, sits or stands in the small conference room, and the nervous energy is palpable, like smoke choking us all. No one can look at us three troublemakers. Will sits beside me, face swollen but bruises already yellowing, with his head down. I hold his hand for all to see. United front. Oliver is behind us, out of my sight. Chandler stands at the whiteboard, more than comfortable taking point tonight. He outlines the new information from Will. "So, what have we learned today, people?"

"Sounds like a rogue pack," Andrew says. "One female and three males."

"Sounds accurate," Will says.

"Is there anything else you can remember about them?" Carl asks Will.

"Judging from the smells, the three males hunted together the entire time, then stopped when they reached the female."

"Was she with them? Was she like part of the pack?" Nancy asks.

"I think so. What I smelled was…um…her *sex* on the tree. I think she had sex with one of the wolves there and rubbed up against the tree."

There isn't a face without a grimace in the room. "Gross," Nancy says for us all.

"So is she," I say. "She put the whammy on Will somehow. Whatever affected you probably did the same to them. So, if this isn't normal behavior around a female werewolf what is she besides a werewolf?"

"Another succubus?" Agent Wolfe asks.

"Possible," Chandler says. "We'll start combing reports of odd heart attacks in the area. Other potentials?"

"A witch," Oliver chimes in behind us. "If the reports on the *assault* against Agent Alexander are accurate, it sounds as if Agent Price was bespelled."

I ignore the multiple digs. "A love potion?" I ask.

"Maybe," Will says. "I've been bespelled before, and it was similar."

"We'll contact the local covens and see if they know of any hybrids," Chandler says.

"We should contact Jason Dahl too," Will suggests. "This is his territory. If there is a hybrid or even a rogue pack here, he should know."

"Okay," Chandler says. "So, onto our victim. Andrew?"

"There were a great number of spirits in those woods ranging from Confederate soldiers to Native Americans to the more recent dead. It was a bit overwhelming. Without a name or picture of him, I couldn't tell which if any was our victim."

"That's okay," Chandler says. "Dr. Neill?"

Dr. Lynette Neill, our pathologist/medic, says, "I haven't begun my exam of the leg yet, but from outward appearances I'd agree with the local ME's preliminary findings. Male, Caucasian, six foot, approximate age 19-25, deceased last night sometime between seven and nine. The leg was severed while he was alive, and the wounds are consistent with a werewolf attack."

"There have been no missing person's reports filed in the county today," Agent Rushmore says.

"What about the list of ticketed or abandoned cars around the park?" I ask.

"They haven't e-mailed it yet," Rushmore says.

"We should have them extend the records search to every night of the full moon going back six months," I say.

"Why?" asks Chandler.

"Well, werewolves are territorial, right? The chances are slim that this is the first time they've used the park."

"There have been no reports of strange animals or attacks there before today," Chandler points out.

"This whole thing was way too organized for it to be their first time," I say. "They knew to hide the body, to get rid of his camping equipment, and how to avoid the ranger."

"You think there are other victims in the park?" Andrew asks.

"It's a distinct possibility, that's all I'm saying."

"I agree," Will chimes in. "The way they hunted together takes practice. Experience."

"We'll interview the other rangers tomorrow. See what they recall," Chandler says. "Any other thoughts?"

"Oliver should go to the scene and see if he can pick up the blood trail," I suggest. "Might lead us to the body."

"Good idea," Will says.

"Oh joy and bliss, a night alone in the frigid woods," Oliver says. "Am I the lucky boy."

"The rest of us will continue processing and examining the evidence we already have," Chandler orders. "Carl, you're with Neill on the leg. Alexander, you and Nancy start analyzing the blood and fur we found on the peak. Wolfe, you and Will get on the computers and pull the missing persons and towed or ticketed cars in the vicinity. The staties are taking too long. Andrew, call George and get a list of the local covens and start contacting them. Rush and I will link up with the state police and coordinate with them. That okay with everyone?" We all nod. "Good. Then let's get to work."

Everyone rises, and when I turn around, Oliver has already vanished. I sigh. Will, sensing my displeasure, places his hand on my shoulder. I pat it. No time to mourn a lost friendship. Werewolves to catch. Thank God.

*

Our lab is barely the size of a closet and darn near claustrophobic with all the equipment crammed into the small, windowless space. Under my microscope are epithelial, or skin cells, taken from the tree of doom. These are what caused my boyfriend to morph into a villain from a *Lifetime* movie, and as far as I can tell there is nothing out of the ordinary about them. They're not human, definitely canine, but it's not as if they're glowing with magic. And according to the serology print out of the bark, two male wolves, uh, secreted onto it. This female wolf is quite the slut.

"There aren't any tests to determine if someone's a witch, are there?" I ask Nancy.

She glances up from the computer. "Nope. Just like when they tested us, our DNA came back like 100% human too."

"What about testing for spells?"

"I don't think so."

I slump back in my chair. "Okay, let's work through this logically. It had to be her biological material that caused the reaction in Will. The scent she gave off, pheromones, put him and probably the other wolves into overdrive. So, how do you change your scent?"

"A magical perfume?" Nancy suggests.

"Possible. Or she ingests something. Like when you eat onions and you smell like them for awhile? It comes out of your pores."

"But like, why would she do that?"

"Power. Control. The same reasons you or I would. But it obviously only works on werewolves."

"That we, like, know of," Nancy points out. "Will has super-smell. Maybe the others just couldn't smell it."

And I just sent an enraged vampire with super-senses back there. Crap. I pull out my cell and dial. It rings twice. "What?" Oliver asks, none too pleased.

"I think you need to come back," I say. "We just realized the trigger could be heightened senses. You could have a reaction too."

"Rather slow on the uptake tonight, Agent Alexander," he says. "I knew that before I departed. I have taken precautions, but I appreciate your concern." He hangs up.

I roll my eyes. "Jerk."

"He's not coming back?" Nancy asks.

"No, *he* knows best," I say with a sneer. "Well, if he goes postal there and hurts someone, I'm not saving his butt this time. He's on his own. Hell, I'll wield the stake myself."

Nancy frowns and turns back to her computer. "Whatever."

"What?" I ask as I fold my arms across my chest.

"Can you two just like skip to the part where you make up? Save us all the drama? You so know you're going to. You always do."

"This time's different."

"Why? I mean, you so should be mad at Will, not Oliver. He's not the one who…you know."

"Will couldn't help himself, Oliver could. And this isn't the first time he's attacked Will, okay? You're the one who told me what happened at Christmas, remember?"

"He was like totally worried about you. Like crazy scared. Tonight too. He screamed at Carl. *Carl.* You're like his best friend. I'm surprised he didn't stab Will."

"See, that is not a good thing, Nancy. He didn't ask me how I was, he didn't try to console me, he just tried to kill my boyfriend. And last night, instead of being happy that I'd found someone who I love, and who loves me back, he tried to feed me to a werewolf to prove a point. So no, I do not think forgiveness is forthcoming anytime soon. Sorry."

"He's just hurt," Nancy says quietly.

"That doesn't mean we should all suffer because of it. And that certainly doesn't give him the right to physically harm anyone, no matter the circumstances."

"So you're like no longer friends? Just like that?"

"Until he can be happy for me and act like a grown-up, yes. The man is over five hundred years old, he should act like it. And this conversation is over." I stand up. "I need to use the bathroom. Excuse me."

I really go outside to gulp in some fresh air no matter how cold that air might be. I am beyond sick of being in that lab. It's my least favorite part of the job, which is why I'm so crap at it. And that's when I'm on my A game. Tonight I'm barely on my D game. My hands hurt, my wrists ache, and now I have to worry about a pissed off vampire making all our lives a living hell, not to mention the fact that I'm chasing some creature that makes my boyfriend literally lose his mind. This is supposed to be the happiest time of my life, and I'm struggling not to burst into tears. Again. Story of my life.

It's not supposed to be like this. I shouldn't have to stop my boyfriend from raping me. I shouldn't have to shun my best friend because he's being a jealous idiot and lashing out like a toddler. I should be cuddling up on the sofa with Will watching *Glee.* I should be driving around with Oliver complaining about our co-workers. We should all be out playing pool and shooting the breeze, not beating each other bloody. Is it so wrong to want my boyfriend and best friend to get along? Is that too much to freaking ask?

I swore I wouldn't choose. That I would find a way for us all to get along come hell or high water. That I wouldn't lose either of them. I didn't expect them to be best friends, but I thought at least the physical violence had come to an end. Okay, so I really thought all the crap everyone told me about Oliver had been magically cured by my friendship. That I'd quelled his tortured, selfish soul and he could be Uncle Oliver to my kids. Yes, I'm delusional.

As I'm staring up at the thousands of twinkling stars, hugging myself against the cold, I hear the door opening and shutting but don't turn around. A moment later, the interloper places a big coat over my shoulders and wraps his arms around me, pulling me against him. "You're so cold," Will whispers, breath hot against my ear.

"I'm better now." I stare up at his still bruised face and half smile. "You look like hell."

"I've been beat up twice. It has not been a good day."

"Does it still hurt?"

"Not too bad. You kicked my ass a lot harder than he did." Will kisses my forehead and hugs me even tighter.

We stand there gazing up at the starts in silence for a few seconds before I say, "I hate this."

"What?"

"Why can't people just be happy for us? Why does everything have to be so freaking hard?"

"You mean Oliver," he says. "Bea, I'm not going to lie and say I'm not thrilled you've finally removed those rose colored glasses but…I know how much he means to you, and I'm sorry you're hurting. I really am. If I could wave a magic wand and make it right, I would."

"He shouldn't have attacked you like that."

Will pauses, then says, "Baby, if the roles were reversed, I would have killed him. Without a moment's hesitation. I almost did, remember?" he asks, caressing the scar Oliver gave me on my first case.

162

"That was different." I turn around to face him. "I don't have rose colored glasses about Oliver. I really don't. I see him for exactly who he is. I don't know if it's a vamp thing, but he has this deep darkness inside that scares the hell out of me, and I see it creeping to the surface. It was in his eyes last night and here again tonight. I refuse to be the excuse for him to unleash it. And if that means turning my back on him until he comes to his senses, then I will. But I…we have this connection. We do. I can't explain it, heck I barely understand it myself, but I won't completely abandon hope that one day…he'll be the man I know he can be. And when that day comes, I just hope *you* can embrace him too."

Will takes me into his arms, squeezing me tight. "He doesn't deserve you. Neither do I for that matter."

"Well, you've got me, and you're stuck with me now."

"Promise?"

"Promise."

EIGHT

ATTENTION DEFICIT DISORDER

Everyone was exhausted, so we cut the work short around midnight and retreated to the hotel for some much needed sleep. My head hit the pillow, and I was out like a light. The ringing telephone beside my head wakes me way too soon. It's Chandler with a gruff, "Good morning, and get out of bed." Nancy groans in the other bed and removes her hot pink eye mask. I've been her hotel mate for almost a year so I know she's not a morning person. Hoping to avoid the gripes and snotty comments, I quickly climb out of bed, grab my clothes, and hide in the bathroom.

Make-up does a fantastic job of covering the dark circles and bruises. Since the plan for the day, at least mine, calls for no trips into the wilderness, I throw on my best suit, black with ruffled pink dress shirt opened enough to show off my golden compass. Since Oliver gave it to me at Christmas, the only time I've taken it off was when I had surgery. *"To always find your way back to me."* The man gives good gift. I also fasten the charm bracelet my mother gave me when I was a child, my most prized possession for years, lost then found by that same vampire. Crud, I'm getting misty just thinking about it.

164

I don't know how one man can be so wonderful one minute and the next grow horns and a tail. Thank God for work. Solving a murder should be a great distraction.

I leave Nancy to get ready and go down to the lobby for my complimentary breakfast. The men, devoid of a necessary beauty ritual plaguing us gals, are already mingling with the suburban tourists, who steal glances at these handsome men in suits packing heat. My handsome man sits at a table reading a newspaper with three Danishes piled high. He is damn delectable himself today in a dark blue suit, striped tie and white shirt. I'm a sucker for a man in a suit. "Good morning," I say before giving him a quick peck on the lips. I can't believe I finally get to do this every morning from now on: kissing, goo-goo eyes, eating a breakfast together just like a real couple. Oh my God, we're a real couple!

"Morning," Will says, beaming up at me. Guess he can't believe it either.

I swipe a blueberry Danish before sitting across from him. "How'd you sleep?"

"Like a rock. You?"

"Would have been better if you were there."

"Well, that goes without saying," he retorts with a smirk.

Chandler steps over to our table, once again ruining the mood. "Good morning, Alexander," Chandler says with his usual stony expression.

165

"Agent Chandler, how are you this beautiful morning?" I ask with my brightest grin.

"Fine," he says dismissively. "Will, you should get going. It's almost an hour drive to Charlotte."

"Just going to finish my coffee," Will says, holding up his cup.

"Good. And Alexander, you're on evidence until it's time to interview the Park Rangers. And keep your phone on. I may need you to run down more leads as they come in."

"Sir, yes, sir," I respond with a salute. He is not pleased. His thin lips purse with disapproval before walking over to Rushmore's table. I roll my eyes. "Can you please get your job back from him? Orders sound much sexier coming from you."

"I'm planning a coup as we speak," Will says with a smirk.

I stuff a piece of Danish in my mouth. "So, what's in Charlotte?"

"I got in contact with an old friend at the Bureau who agreed to help me cull through missing persons reports."

"An old friend?"

"Yeah, he was one of the FBI liaisons when I was at Metro P.D. We sometimes went rowing together, out for drinks, stuff like that."

"When was the last time you saw him?"

"About a month before the attack. We took our wives to a Chris Isaak concert."

"Are you nervous about seeing him again?" I ask, stuffing more Danish in my mouth.

"A little. I mean, I don't think he'll take one look at me and think, 'That guy's a werewolf' or anything. We've e-mailed once or twice through the years. I just hope I can keep my lies straight."

"Do you keep in contact with a lot of people from DC?"

"No. Everyone sort of gave up trying after a year of me not calling or writing back. Not that I blame them. I just, I wasn't in any shape to handle their pity and questions. I severed all ties and didn't look back," he says with a hint of regret. "Even with Mary's parents. They tried for years. I handled the whole thing so badly. I just…vanished."

"It's never too late," I say. "I'm sure they'd love to hear from you."

"Maybe. We'll see how things go with Jonesy first. And speaking of…" He downs the rest of his coffee and stands. "I better get on the road." He takes a step and kisses the top of my head. "See you tonight. Love you."

"Love you too," I say as if I've been doing it for decades.

Giving me a boyish smile, he runs his hand over my hair and walks off. Wow. Anyone who was watching us would think we were an ordinary, boring couple together for years. I used to be so envious when I'd see a couple like us, just this cohesive unit with eyes only for each other as they shared a meal. Let me just say finally being on the inside looking out totally rocks. Envy away outsiders.

Nancy and the others join the breakfast brigade after I'm on my second Danish. Before they can grab a bite, Chandler is upon them with orders of the day. Nancy is back on lab work, Andrew is on communication with law enforcement and George, and the rest are on park duty. At least I won't be stuck in that trailer all of today. In my tenure with the F.R.E.A.K.S. I discovered I'm a natural interviewer. Something about me just puts people at ease and makes them want to tell me all their secrets. Oliver's better at it, especially with women, and when we're together we're unstoppable. We just have this rapport, instinctively playing off each other. Crap, I'm doing it again. Stop thinking about him. He is *persona non grata* until he apologizes, and that includes thoughts. The band has broken up. I'm a solo act now.

We all finish breakfast, go back to our rooms to retrieves our kits, and drive to mobile command. First up, I telephone the other two rangers, Adrian Winsted and Kyle Taylor, and set up appointments. I have a bit of time before I have to go meet Winsted so I skim the report Oliver wrote last night. Despite his personal faults, the man is a good agent. He tracked the four wolves from the summit where they changed. He located some spoor spread out down the mountain, but the scent was gone until a blood, tissue and fur trail began about a hundred yards from where Will flipped out. It ended where we found the pool of blood hidden under leaves. Per the report, he had no reaction at the site, nor did anyone else, which led him to conclude that she had ingested a mild potion to amp up her pheromones to a level animals can sense and thereby turn the wolves into horn dogs. And every woman knows the best way to control a male is through sex. Yes, he wrote that in the report.

I find it odd that there's no mention of the victim in the report. Oliver spent all night combing the woods, at least according to this, and found nary a trace of human blood except for at the kill spot. It's as if our mystery man plopped down from the sky in the very spot he was attacked. The blood trail continued sporadically to the spot on the trail where they found the leg. I thought for sure that he'd find a trace of the victim. A piece of clothing, a wallet, body parts, something.

These people are good. Through. They had to have planned this. Where the heck is the rest of this guy? Did they bury him? Pack him in garbage bags and haul him home? Even if they ate him, there would be bones. No, I'll bet they dug the grave ahead of time. Graves. Oliver marked spots where he sensed bodies around the park, about ten of them. Guess we'll have to dig those people up. I just hope I don't have to be there when we do. Interviewing park rangers is more my speed, thank you very much.

There were no further developments in the night, so I join the others in the war room. They've read the report too and are speaking to the state police about digging up those bodies. We may have an ID by tonight. Wolfe drew short straw, as he usually does when up against Chandler and Rushmore, and has

169

to coordinate at the park with the staties. Ten bodies to be excavated, examined, photographed and that's before they bring it out of the grave. I hope all aren't victims of the wolves, but I'd bet money one or two are.

Dr. Neill is in her sanctuary, throwing together her kit with the assistance of Carl. Busy day for them. We're going to be knee deep in corpses tonight. Since I'd rather visit the dentist than the lab, I check our e-mails and faxes before my appointment. George faxed a list of telephone numbers and names of local witches with Mona McGregor circled. She lives in Goodnight, Virginia, wherever the heck that is. The town's name is familiar for some reason. It takes a second but it does come to me. About six months ago I met another witch, Anna West, who was involved in a triple murder in Goodnight. Her vampire lover and two others killed an entire family after she ran away from him. Vamps really have to work on their jealousy issues.

It's rather early, but I call McGregor anyway. Life and death and all. Someone picks up on the third ring, though I can barely hear over the commotion. "Cora, just put on your flipping shoes like I asked," the woman on the other end shouts. "You'll miss the bus!"

"But Aunt Mona," a little girl, I assume Cora, whines, "I—"

"Just do it! Now!" Mona snaps. She sighs then says, "Sorry about that. Hello?"

"Um, Ms. McGregor?"

"What's left of her after this morning. May I ask who is calling?"

"My name is Special Agent Beatrice Alexander. I got your name from George Black?"

"Oh. So how can I help the F.R.E.A.K.S.?"

"We've come across what we think is a werewolf using love potions to control her pack."

"What makes you think that?" I tell her about Will's reaction, and while I do I swear I feel his hands pawing at me. My wrists even ache where he held me. "Hell's bells," Mona says when I'm done. "Well, it doesn't sound like a love potion or spell I've ever heard of. They're more directed. You can only target one person. It sounds more like a lust amplification potion since it comes off in biological material."

"What?"

"She pumped up her womanly scent to make men go bonkers when she's around. You say only werewolves are affected?"

"And dogs."

"Then she's probably using a low level dose but still. The potion is short term, a day or two at most until it's worked out of the system. She'd need a steady supply. If you're in North Carolina we're the closest supplier for magical ingredients, and I haven't seen anyone buy the stuff for that potion. You need worm root, which I get imported from India, and black toadstools. I haven't sold either in awhile."

"Do you know of any witches in this area?"

"One or two, but once again they buy from me for the most part, and that spell's illegal. Anything that takes away a person's free will is. I can ask around to other suppliers. Whoever this witch is, she could be buying from multiple suppliers so she wouldn't arouse suspicion."

"Could you also send the names of every known witch in a hundred mile radius? I have George's list, but you might have some names we don't."

"Look, I know the ones closest to where you are. They're good women. Besides, it'd get real expensive real fast just due to the illegal factor. Black toadstools are very rare and forbidden in witchcraft. They're only used in black spells."

"Is it possible the witch and werewolf are one in the same?" I ask.

Her end is quiet for a second. "I've never heard of a witch/werewolf hybrid, but stranger things have happened. It's possible. Jason Dahl would know more about that than me. Werewolves are big on population control and keeping track of their wolves."

"Yeah, we have a call into him as well. Is there anything we can do to counteract the lust spell?"

"Not really. It changes her body chemistry. There is a magical element to it so maybe a charm to shield from magic, but I doubt that would completely negate the biological factor. Just keep your agent away from her. Listen, I have to go get the girls to school. I'll e-mail George the stuff you wanted, and you can call if you have more questions, okay?"

172

"Thank you."

"Good luck. Bye." She hangs up.

Well, that could have gone better. Diddly bubkus. Maybe the list will prove more useful. I just have to wait. So not my strong suit. Distraction time. Rangers to interview. Kyle Taylor is still at his seminar, but we have a Skype conference set-up in three hours. Adrian Winsted is up first. We have an appointment in over an hour, but I don't want to wait that long in this metal box with nothing to do but stare at blood. The element of surprise is a useful interview technique anyway. The target doesn't have time to work on the lies. A good excuse as any to get the heck out of here. I hop back into my car and punch Winsted's home address into the GPS. Hopefully I'll open the door, and he'll blurt out not only the names of the werewolves but where they live. We'll arrest them with no fuss, and Will and I can go home and finally have that wild hot monkey sex we deserve. It could happen.

Yeah. Right.

*

Ranger Winsted sure does love nature. One would think he'd get enough of that at work. Nope. Half mile from the neighbors, his domicile resembles a tree house, a two-story wood paneled home that could very well be built into the hill behind it. I park behind the red Ford Focus, only one of the five cars in the gravel driveway. A full house.

Just as I climb out of my SUV, the front door opens. An African American man, a dead ringer for a teenage Idris Elba (swoon) complete with muscles in a tight white shirt and jeans steps out, followed by a woman fiddling in her satchel. Not his mother as she's Caucasian, though I judge her old enough to be. Early to mid-forties but gorgeous with wavy dark brown hair framing her round face. That's not the only round thing about her. She has curves to die for, like Marilyn Monroe or an earth mother. Full breasts and large hips but all in proportion. The green dress she wears brings out the green in her large gray eyes that instantly begin to appraise me. "May I help you?"

"Yes. My name is Special Agent Beatrice Alexander, FBI. I have an appointment with Adrian Winsted?"

"Your appointment isn't for another half hour," the woman says.

"I was in the neighborhood," I say, walking up to the duo.

The man, and I use the term loosely because he looks barely twenty, moves right to the woman's side. "Jamal, go wait in the car please," the woman says, squeezing his hand. Jamal nods and starts toward the Prius. "We're just on our way to school. Adrian's still in his pajamas, I'm afraid. He's had bronchitis for over a week, the poor lamb."

"Well, I promise to go easy on him," I say with a smile.

Her smile melts ten years off her face. "I'll hold you to that. Let me show you in."

174

"Thank you." God, she even smells good, like cinnamon and apples. Great, now I'm hungry. I follow her inside the tree house. Damn, it's like a museum in here with wooden totems from Africa and Asia complete with large heads and phalluses on every surface. Even the furniture is earthy, mostly wood in dark greens and browns, antiques I think. Does need a dusting though. There are several bare spots on the walls and surfaces where paintings and more statues used to be. Mrs. Winsted must notice my furrowed brow because she says, "We're remodeling in a week. I just started boxing everything up. It's going to be a nightmare. Would you like some coffee or…"

"I'm fine, thank you."

She gestures to the hard green padded futon couch for me to sit, which I do. "Let me go rouse Adrian." After another pleasant smile, the woman leaves the room. Okay, snooping time. I rise from the couch and begin by the sideboard. More knick knacks like flutes adorned with feathers or animals carved in wood and stone. Lots more bare spots. Okay why—

My cell buzzes in my pocket, and I pull it out. Oh, how sweet! A text from Will. "*Miss U already. Luv U.*"

Smiling, I text back, "*Ditto. In Charl yet?*"

A second later, "*Bad traffic. Where R U?*"

"*Ivew. Luv U Luv U Luv U. TTYL.*"

A man's coughing and footsteps make me slip my phone away. Mrs. Winsted and a man still in his brown pajamas and sipping a water bottle pad into the living room. Trooper

175

Winsted is rather non-descript medium height and weight, with the same dark color hair as his wife receding at the temples. His frameless glasses can't hide the red rimmed eyes. Even his skin shouts "sickness" with its waxy pallor. "I'll leave you both to your interview," Mrs. Winsted says. "It was nice meeting you, Agent Alexander." She kisses her husband's head. "Be good." With a wink my way, she departs toward the front door.

"I apologize if I woke you," I say. "I found myself in the neighborhood sooner than I expected."

"It's fine, I just," he coughs, the deep rattling kind, before sipping his water. "Anytime is a bad time with bronchitis. I need to sit down."

"Yes, of course." I sit in the chair and he the futon. Not far enough away for my liking though. Those coughs of his make me squirm. "I just have a few quick questions. I'll keep this as short as possible. You have a lovely home," I say as I pull out my pad and pen for notes. "Very interesting knick-knacks."

"Yes," he chuckles. "Patsy's an anthropologist. We've traveled the world. I—" The thump upstairs draws both our gazes toward the ceiling. "Just the dog. He jumps on people. Patsy indulges him."

"It's fine. As I said on the phone this morning, a body, well part of a body, was discovered in your park yesterday by your colleague, Trooper Mills."

"It's unfortunate, but it does happen. People aren't meant to be in the park after dark for a reason."

"We've since found ten more bodies at various locations within the park."

Winsted's bloodshot gray eyes grow behind his glasses. "Really?"

"Our forensics team is excavating them now."

"That's...disturbing," Winsted says before coughing phlegm onto his sleeve. Gross. "Sorry. Any idea who they are? The victims?"

"Not yet, but we have reason to believe a group of people, possibly with attack dogs, are hunting people in your park, primarily on full moons."

"Um, I'm sorry, Agent Alexander but that sounds kind of farfetched." He coughs again, for several seconds this time. Ugh. Poor guy. "Sorry."

"It's okay." I rarely get sick beyond allergies, but this man's about to topple over. He's definitely not a werewolf, that's for sure. "It's just a theory, but all the evidence is pointing that direction. So, have you seen or heard anything suspicious at night in the past year or so? Howling? Campsites or cars left abandoned? A group of people, primarily men, you didn't later see or appeared again the following morning?"

"No, none of that. I mean, there's been the occasional abandoned tent or article of clothing, but in the spring and summer the homeless take to the woods and run when they see us coming. I really think you've got this all wrong. I've *seen* bears in those woods, ma'am. They've attacked before."

"And buried their kills?" I counter.

"All I know is I've never seen or heard anything like you've described. But it is a big forest," he concedes.

Time to switch tactics. "What about the other rangers? Taylor and Mills? Anything strange or off about them?"

"I don't really spend much time with them, just when we switch off shifts. They seem solid enough."

"Do either have a girlfriend or wife?"

"Taylor does. A wife. I don't know anything about her though." Winsted begins coughing again, this time for a full thirty seconds.

I try not to cringe. "Are you sure you're okay? Should I—"

He waves me off. "I'm fine. I'm fine."

This is a waste of time. He doesn't know anything, and the longer I spend here the bigger the chance I'll catch pneumonia. Plus he's about to collapse in that couch. In this state he's not going anywhere. I pick up my purse and rise. "Okay, Mr. Winsted, I'll let you get back to bed now. Thank you for your time."

"That's it?" Typhoid Larry asks as he coughs again.

"For now. If I have any follow-up questions, I'll call."

"Sorry I couldn't be more help right now. If I think of anything useful, I have your number," he says through more coughs.

"Thank you. I'll see myself out. You get some rest. Feel better."

With one final smile, I walk out with about as much info as I had before, nothing except the need to bathe in hand sanitizer for an hour. As I hustle out of the house, it occurs to me that maybe this murder was a one off. That the bodies they're digging up could be decades old. With the pack running wild, the rangers *would* have heard something at some point. Or the men are lying. I couldn't get a read on Winsted with the illness factor. I'll have to do more digging on them all. Today's interviews are really just to get a sense of them. All I gleaned from Winsted is he needs more Vitamin C and Zinc in his diet. With a sigh, I climb into my car. I hate this part of an investigation. All we have are a million puzzle pieces with no clear guidance how to assemble them into a full picture. It's frustrating and annoying and never, ever easy to assemble.

My cell buzzes again, and I retrieve it. "Oh," I coo. Two texts, both from Will.

"*Luv U more.*" Then, "*Counting the mins til Im xxxing u again.*"

I grin from cheek to cheek. At least now at the end of an aggravating day at the office his arms are waiting to embrace the ickyness away. I'm counting the darn minutes.

*

"So you never heard any howling? Never found any wolf tracks?"

On my computer screen Ranger Taylor does a double take. Skype is a miraculous invention, no question, but I prefer the personal touch. Mostly because I can't feel emotions through a computer screen. The ranger is a robust man with tan skin, graying brown hair, and a wide face. The outdoors agree with at least two of the rangers, save for poor Winsted. "Wolves? There are no wolves for hundreds of miles. People bring their dogs to the park a lot. As far as I can recall, no one's reported any attacks. This is actually the first death in over a year, and the last poor soul died from exposure, God rest him."

I'm not really paying attention. He knows nothing. None of them know a thing. A broken record played from three separate mouths. Bo-ring. I've spent the last minute planning Will's and my dream house. Near Nana and April definitely. And the beach. Not on it, but within a few minutes. Minimum four bedrooms and a big backyard. We'll have to build a panic room for full mo—

"Agent Alexander?" Mills asks.

"Huh?" I ask, head whipping up to the screen. "Oh. So, nothing out of the ordinary?"

"Um, as I said before, no."

"What about your co-workers? Either of them acting oddly?"

"We don't see much of each other. When one shift's over, another begins."

Yep, waste of time. "Okay, well, thank you for speaking with me."

"That's it?"

"For now. Enjoy the rest of the conference. Bye." I end the video chat.

Useless. Heard nothing, saw nothing, knows nothing. It is a big park. Or someone's lying. Just can't tell yet. Really, judging from our preliminary findings, there's nothing out of the ordinary about any of the men. No criminal records, no citations, no complaints. We're still waiting on their financials just in case the wolves were bribing them to look the other way. I just can't focus. Maybe I need to step away for a moment. Or a week.

Dr. Neill and Carl don't have the luxury of focus problems. They already have a body, or what's left of it, with nine more on the way. When I stroll into medical, they're hard at work on the first, which is little more than bones they're assembling like a puzzle. "The neck bone's connected to the shoulder bone," I offer with a smile.

"It's called a clavicle," Carl says.

"I was kidding." Neither cracks a smile behind their blue surgical masks. Tough room. "Find anything useful yet?"

"Can't tell much from this one," Dr. Neill says. "Per the field report she was buried in pieces. See these indentations in the femur?" She points to the leg bone. They're faint but I do see what look like pores. "Probably bite marks. So far I've found them on the tibia, radius, and cervical vertebrae. Rib cage has been cracked as well."

"How long has she been dead?" I ask.

"Best guess is two to three years. We do know she was in her late teens, early twenties and most likely Caucasian with platinum blonde hair. Nancy is analyzing her personal objects from the scene. They found a bracelet and pieces of clothing. And this girl had a rough time before she met our wolves. Multiple healed fractures, bad teeth, and she's had at least one child. We're just about to do the dental impressions."

"What about the most recent vic? The leg? Anything to run down there?"

"There was one odd thing," Neill says. "The claw mark on his calf showed signs of healing, as if it had been made a day or so before death, but not where the leg was severed. That was perimordum."

"Which means what?" I ask. "They chased him the day before too?"

"It's just a theory but…I think our latest victim had a rapid restorative capability consistent with a lycanthrope."

It takes a second to wade through the medical jargon. "You're saying he was a werewolf."

"Give the lady a prize," Carl quips.

Well, that's a horse of a different color. "They turned on their own pack mate. Could explain why there's been no missing person's report, and why he wasn't wearing clothes when he died. But why would they do that?"

"I'll let you run with that one," Neill says.

"Can do. Thanks guys. Keep up the good work. If you need help, let me know."

I walk out and toward the lab to check on Nancy. She's hard at work with her iPod on and magnifying glass running over the scrap of red cloth on the table. She looks up when I step in and yanks out her ear buds. "Oh. Hey."

"Did you hear? That our vic may be a werewolf?"

"Yeah. Toates weird, huh?"

"What about you? Got anything for me to run down?"

"Just that this chick had like totally horrible taste in clothes and jewelry. It's like all cheap and plastic. And who throws together red vinyl and leopard print? I don't know. Maybe we can like ID her from the jewelry or something but I totally doubt it. That stuff is so from Claire's."

"Who is on missing persons cases besides Will?" I ask.

"I was before I like got pulled again for lab work. Rush and Chandler are on the bodies and Wolfe is taking Andrew around the park again to see if he can find any ghosts to talk to before we get totally swamped here."

"Then I guess it's me. Unless you need me in here."

"Later totally. I'm good now."

"Okay, e-mail any pics of the clothes and jewelry to the meeting room terminal. I'll update and call Will. Get me when you need me."

When I reach the terminal, I access my e-mail first. Mona McGregor works fast. There's a list of twenty names and addresses. I'll work down the list, checking for criminal records after I phone Will. I forward the list to George and Jason Dahl as well in case a name raises a red flag. Getting names for our first

183

John and Jane Does is top priority though. Will picks up on the second ring.

"Hi, beautiful," he says chipperly.

"Hey," I say, matching his tone. "How's Charlotte?"

"Dull. Culling through hundreds of missing persons cases. Missing you."

"I miss you too. I can barely concentrate on anything."

"I know the feeling. How'd it go with the rangers?" he asks.

"Dead ends. Know nothing, saw nothing. And I probably caught the plague from Winsted. He is for sure not a werewolf. Did you hear our male victim might be?"

"No. He was?"

"Yeah. But why would they turn on their own?" I ask.

"He could have invaded their territory. Insulted one of the pack. Wanted to leave. My guess is as good as yours. There is a reason I'm a rogue."

"Well, the semi-good news is that the first body they dug up seems to have been another of our victims." I give him her general description and send Nancy's photos.

"Give me a second," Will says. I hear him typing away. "Jackpot. Lindsey Amber Gerber, reported missing two years ago by her friend Naomi Ash in Boone, North Carolina. Last seen wearing a red vinyl skirt and leopard print top getting into a red four-door Sedan. She was a working girl. Witness didn't get the plate or see the driver. No leads, no suspects."

"When we have them, I'll send the dentals for verification," I say. "And I'll go interview Naomi. Talk to some of the other girls on Lindsey's corner. Maybe other girls are missing too. At least we know this pack's been here for at least two years, and they pull people off the street to hunt. I'll bet all our vics end up being pros or drug addicts. Less chance that their disappearances will draw attention."

"They are smart, I'll give them that," Will says.

"That they are." I pause. "So, how's your friend? Just like you remember?"

"Balder but yeah. Ray's good. He invited me to dinner over at his house tonight. Don't know if I'll go though."

"Why not? Can't bear to be away from me a moment longer than necessary?"

"You read my mind, sweetheart. I keep staring off into space thinking of your birthday, the truck, the movie theater...I can't stand up without getting embarrassed," he whispers that last part.

"Get your mind out of the gutter, Agent Price or I'll have to give you a good spanking," I say seductively. "Multiple times."

"I thought teachers weren't allowed to administer corporal punishment."

"I'll make an exception for you, Agent Price. You've been very, *very* naughty after all. I may even have to pull down your pants, exposing you, and—"

"Ahem."

185

Oh, crap. I was so into my fantasy I didn't notice Nancy step in. She's barely controlling her giggles. And...*there's* the mortification right on schedule. "Sorry to interrupt, but I found fur on the clothes. Just thought you'd like to know. Carry on with your phone sex." She releases the giggles and walks out again.

"We weren't..." I call but stop myself. We so were. "I, uh—"

"Yeah, me too," Will says. "I'll see you tonight."

"Yeah. Bye." I hang up and thump my head on the keyboard.

Okay, I've been a slave to my hormones and unfulfilled sexual tension almost non-stop for close to a year. I should have developed an immunity to it by now. But no, the madness has grown way *way* worse in the past few days. This itch of ours needs to be scratched post haste or pretty soon it'll become all consuming. There are monsters to fight. I need to get laid to find them, end of story.

Oh, what a wonderful problem to have.

NINE

ALPHA MALES

The dead will still be dead in the morning, but if I have to examine one more piece of disintegrated clothing, I'll be joining them. We often work twelve to twenty hours when on a case, but I'm usually on the move, interviewing people or chasing down leads out in the field. Seven hours in the lab testing and combing the objects of the dead, sometimes literally with a fine tooth comb, seems like an eternity. Wish I was out interviewing hookers again. Strange how a year ago I wouldn't know a prostitute if she was standing under a neon sign with "Hookers For Rent" on it, now I've made the acquetiance of a dozen. Today's weren't as helpful as others have been. No one could tell me anything new about Lindsey or the SUV that picked her up. If the wolves picked up any others from a red light district, the girls didn't know or wouldn't say. "Hos come, hos go," I was informed, including Naomi Ash. Poor girl. OD'd six months ago. Bye bye lead.

When I returned to mobile command from my ho run, Nancy was swamped in the lab with the arrival of bodies two and three, later four, so I jumped in. For forensics work an investigator needs an eye for miniscule details and the patience of Job, which is why I absolutely hate doing it, now more than ever. I examine the same piece of clothing three times without even realizing it. There could be DNA coating everything, and I'd miss it all. Okay, I'm not that bad. The ripped clothes have tons of canine DNA from three, sometimes four different wolves. No visible fingerprints though. By hour seven my eyes are so gummy you could make bears out of them. Time to call it a day.

Nancy, who shockingly said nothing about my earlier inappropriateness, gathers our things as I power down the machines. There'll be no more bodies tonight. The searchers at the park left at sundown but will continue tomorrow. Like Nancy, Carl and Dr. Neill jump at the chance to finish for the day. While I wait for them, I retrieve my cell phone from the meeting room. I know me. If it was nearby I'd be checking it every ten seconds for one of Will's texts. I missed three. *"Thinking of U." "On my way back." "Luv u."* I coo as I read each of them. He is so thoughtful. I text back, "Coming home. Counting secs until—"

"Ahem."

Once again I'm so into my thoughts, I fail to realize there's someone behind me. Not a good trait for an officer of the law. Especially when I spin around and find it's a vampire who gotten the drop on me. Well, he's already done the damage back there. I can still sense the knife he planted between my shoulder blades. Oliver's gone causal tonight with black cargo pants, black sweater, and hair pulled back in a small ponytail. I'm not sure what I should be feeling after last night, anger and sadness I guess, but the usual lust peeks out instead. If I have one addiction besides *Turner Classic Movies* it's to eye candy, and this man is instant diabetes. "Oh. Hello."

"Are you leaving for the evening?" he asks, stiff as a board. "I came to see if you required assistance before I ventured to the park in search of more victims."

"Oh. That was thoughtful of you."

"How kind of you to notice, Beatrice."

Oh, he used my full name. I used to hate when he called me "Trixie," now my full name seems unnatural coming from those red lips. He only uses it when we're about to stare down death or I've insulted him so harshly he wishes death had won. Our recent divide is his fault, yet I want to throw my arms around him and beg forgiveness. I won't though. He gets no reward for bad behavior from this girl.

"Well, we're swamped in the lab. Any analyzing you can do would be appreciated." I slip my phone into my purse and start walking. "Have a good night, Oliver," I say as I pass.

"He attempted to rape you," stops me dead in my tracks. "To *rape* you. He knocked you into the dirt, held you down, ripped off your pants, and tried to force himself upon you. Forgive me if I…saw red. But I will not apologize for caring for you. For wanting to protect you. I have *earned* that right."

I literally turn on my heel and fold my arms across my chest. "And the night before? Trying to make me werewolf chow? Did you earn the right to do that too?"

"I was angry. I committed a foolish act, one foolish act, and I am sorry for that. From the bottom of my heart, I am so sorry, Trixie. But after all we have been through, it takes only one idiotic mistake for you to terminate our relationship? Do I truly mean so little to you that you will not forgive one minor indiscretion committed whilst I was facing my greatest fear? Losing you? Are you really so cruel?"

Fudge. Fudge. Fudge. How does he do that? How does he always know the exact right thing to say to make me so weak in the knees? To blow away all the anger I have every reason to feel with a few choice words? I should have an immunity to him by now. Yet I succumb every time. *Don't give in. Don't give in...* "I accept your apology," I say emotionless. Okay, I'm such a softie. But not a pushover. "As will my boyfriend when you apologize to him."

He sneers. "Never. I would rather—"

"We're a package deal, Oliver. You want me, you take him too. Either accept it or..." I shrug. "Night, Oliver."

When I step into the hallway I find Nancy pretending to examine her cuticles. She needs to work on her eavesdropping skills. They're slipping. I pull her out to the car and wait for the others. Before Nancy works up the nerve for her trillion questions, Carl and Dr. Neill come out so we can leave. Hallelujah.

I don't go to my hotel room with Nancy when we arrive. She chuckles as I continue two doors down to knock on Will's door. The moment he opens it, I launch myself at him lips

190

first. Swathing me in his arms, he kisses me back with equal vigor. Oh that is a million times better. But not good enough. Still kissing, I back him inside his room. I've waited all day for this. I—

"Ahem."

Again? Frigging *again*? We break the kiss to turn to the source of the snooty noise. Chandler, in his pajama bottoms and white shirt rests in his bed, remote in hand. Guess it's true: when in love you only have eyes for one man. I take a step back with a nervous chuckle. "Sorry. Hi. Chandler."

"Alexander. Don't mind me, continue with what you were doing. It'll save me money on porn."

Will shoots his friend a fierce glare to which Chandler responds with one of his own. Yeah, one friendship's already been destroyed by our relationship, don't want a second. I take my boyfriend's hand. "Let's talk in the hall." I flash Chandler an apologetic smile, garnering an eye roll for my effort. Jesus, it was just a kiss.

"He *really* doesn't like me, does he?" I ask when the door's shut.

"Who cares? I like you," Will says with a seductive grin. Smile still affixed, he leans down to kiss me again. A slow, lingering kiss that makes my toes curl. God, this man can kiss. "I missed you today."

"I missed you too. I could barely get anything done. All I could think of was…"

"This?" And he goes in for round three. K.O. on impact. I'm lost in all these glorious sensations this man inspires in me. Tingles, warmth, raw lust. Heroin has nothing on Will Price's lips. I instantly go through withdrawal when he breaks away. "I was thinking of using the hot tub downstairs. Join me?"

"Heck yeah. Meet you down there." I give him a little peck before practically skipping to my room. Nancy's already claimed the TV, The Real Housewives of Wherever per usual. Thank God for my boyfriend. I couldn't stand another catfight. I change into my bathing suit in the bathroom as the insults fly. Oh, I do wish I had a body for a bikini but the red one-piece with tummy control will have to do. My roommate is so engrossed in her program she doesn't even ask where I'm off to.

Our first luck of the day, nobody's downstairs in the pool area. Will's already relaxing in the bubbling water with a serene smile on his face. It grows when I walk in. "How's the water?"

"Perfect."

I remove my towel, setting it next to his on the white tile floor. I wade into the water, and he is right, it is darn perfect. With a contented sigh, I slip into my nook against his almost nude body, resting my head on his shoulder as he wraps his arm around me. Okay, *now* this is perfect.

"Oh, this was a good idea. The stress is just soaking out," I say. "It has been a long, long frustrating day with nothing to show for it."

"Same here. I hate this part of the case. Questions only leading to more questions, the entire world a suspect. And God knows how long this has been going on under all our noses."

I kiss his bare shoulder. "You are not responsible for all the ills of the world, lover. We'll find the beasts. We always do. Not many can claim they lead a team with such a high clearance rate. You're like super-cop."

"Well, I have been on the job for over thirty years. Longer than you've been alive."

"Thinking of retirement, Agent Price? Taking up golf? Gardening?"

"Never really gave it much thought. Always…kind of assumed this job would kill me." I stare up at him in confusion. "What? I did. I've been beaten, shot, maimed, burned, and blown up. I've fought trolls, vampires, giant snakes, ex-boyfriends," he says with a smirk. I don't return it. "After Mary, I wouldn't say I was chasing death, but I sure as hell wasn't chasing life."

"And now?"

"Does San Diego have nice golf courses?" he asks, smile growing.

"Best in the world," I say, returning the gesture.

"Good to know." Will lowers his head again for a quick kiss. Then another. Then a longer one. Deeper. Oh, I love to kiss this man. I really, *really* do. I like it even more when he rounds second base, rolling my sensitive nipple in his fingers in time to his kiss. Oh, God. "We need to get our own room," he whispers between the kisses.

"Hell yes."

Will unfastens my straps before taking my free breasts into his hands, rolling my nipples, pinching them as the kisses down my neck. I wrap my legs around his hips. Not surprising he's hard as a rock, almost bursting out of his swimsuit. I reach into his trunks, hopefully giving him the same pleasure he's providing me. Okay, we need to get a room NOW! Before I forget all propriety, and...oh come on.

Come on!

When I open my eyes, two men are walking into the aquatics center. Five minutes. We can't have five fraking damn minutes alone? Really? "Will," I gasp as I push him away. His eyes narrow in confusion before I signal behind him. He stands and turns around as I press myself to his back to hide my still bare breasts. Not that it does much good. The men locked their gazes on us the moment they entered, the one on the left staring with sniper like precision on us. Even with Will here I'm uneasy with that man in the room. Sharp cheekbones and nose, blonde hair slicked back, ice blue eyes, and muscles for miles. Would not want to meet him in a dark alley. Don't want to meet him *here.* His companion is a head shorter with buggy blue eyes, floppy light brown hair, and a nice smile he's trying to contain.

"Jason? Adam?" Will says in shock. "What...?"

Oh God. I've just flashed the king of the werewolves and his number two. Perfect. Great. Kill me now.

194

"We thought you weren't coming until tomorrow," Will continues. I pull up my top and fumble with the straps. How can two strips of fabric be so complicated?

"We wanted to get here before the trail went cold," Jason, the scary one, says. Even his tone is sharp and mean. "We would have been here earlier but we had a contract to complete. Not to mention we weren't informed of the attack until last night."

"We were handling things," Will replies.

"Yeah, that was, uh, quite apparent when we walked in," Adam retorts, not even bothering to reign in his smile. "Sorry to interrupt. Agent Chandler told us where you were."

Oh, I'll bet he did. Thank God, I've got the straps done. "It's fine. Um, may-may I present, um," Will says, scooting away from me to wade out of the tub, "Special Agent Beatrice Alexander. Bea, this is Jason Dahl and Adam Blue."

"Hi," I say with a little wave as I get out of the water too. "Nice to, uh, finally meet you both. Heard great things." I quickly wrap the towel around myself.

"Us too," Adam says.

"You never said she was psychic," Jason says with disdain as if I were a stripper or something.

"Didn't think it mattered," Will says.

"Only if you're pack," Jason says. "Or ever want to be."

"Think you know my views on that already," Will responds.

Okay, I don't like where this is going. Manners to the rescue. "It's wonderful you've come to help us. We can certainly use it. Right, Will?"

Will's glare never moves from Jason as he says, "Yes."

I take Will's hand to draw him out of the visual pissing contest I'm witnessing.

"And we're glad to be of assistance," Adam says, touching his friend's arm to do the same. "So, what can you tell us?"

"We've found several more bodies we suspect are also victims of this pack, but—"

"They are not a pack," Jason snaps, "don't call them that. They are rogues and a hybrid abomination."

"Don't speak to her in that tone," Will warns.

"It's fine," I say, squeezing Will's hand. Lord save me from another Alpha male blowout. I haven't recovered from the last one. "Look, whatever they're called, at the end of the day they're killers. They're the enemy, can we all agree on that?" Only Adam nods. Ugh. "Have you two checked in yet?"

"No," Jason says.

"Why don't you do that while we get dressed? Go from there? Is that alright?" I ask.

"Sounds like a plan," Adam says.

"Fine," Jason says.

The men all nod before our new friends skulk off. When they're out of earshot, I let out a sigh. Chandler so sent them down here to ruin our night. I want one person, just one

196

person who is happy for us. Who isn't trying to sabotage us. One. Even strangers like Jason Dahl seem pissed we're in love, and I just met the man. "That guy's a jerk."

"You don't keep dozens of werewolves in line by being Mr. Congeniality. He is in rare form tonight, though. I had half a mind to punch him in the nose for being rude to you."

"We need him, right? I for one am still glad they're here. We now have three werewolves to their four. So no punching." I lean up and peck his cheek. "Kill him with kindness, love."

"Don't know if I can tonight. I'm beat."

"Then send them to the park to search for more bodies. Let Oliver deal with them." Serve him right.

"Maybe."

"Up to you. Just make sure they avoid that spot. I, for one, am going to take a shower and crawl into bed."

"Wish I could join you. God do I wish I could join you. I wish…everyone would just go away. Leave us alone for one damn night."

"I know. It'll happen." I peck him again. "Just not tonight." Another peck. "You want me to help you with the welcoming committee?"

"Probably not a good idea, but I appreciate it." This time he kisses me. Deep. I have to pull away or we'll end up shaming ourselves again. We both chuckle. "One for the road. Love you."

"Love you too."

With one final grin, Will follows his friends out. Alone again. Damn. Not even the killjoys lowered the buzzing in my body from our hot tub session. I drop my towel and leap into the pool, letting the cold water crystallize my lust to be thawed later. Whenever later is. I let myself sink underwater with my eyes shut as tight as my lungs. It's peaceful down here. As if I'm alone in the universe. I fight the pressure, the pain, the panic as my lungs ache to expel the sour air filling them. I hold it in as long as I can before screaming out all my frustration, sexual and otherwise, so no one can hear me. Spent, I launch myself to the surface, huffing and puffing until I feel fit for society again. Just get through the case, Bea. Get through the case. Ignore the snotty vampires, werewolves, and federal agents. Concentrate on finding the big bad wolves because then our lives together can finally begin. I'm not giving up. Do you hear me, universe? Keep throwing me those hurdles. I'll leap every one until I reach the finish line where my Prince Charming awaits with open arms.

Look out, wolves. I'm about to huff and puff and blow your damn houses down.

TEN

TIGHT SHIPS

Nana always said life's small problems can be wiped away with a good night's sleep. As with most things, she was right about that. Nine hours of slumber does a wonder. I wake rested, get dressed in my smartest beige wool suit, rouse a grumpy teenager, and drag our butts to mobile command. Per the night's report, Oliver found two more bodies. We're up to an even dozen now. The others woke at the crack of dawn to continue excavating the park and examining the bodies. With two extra sets of hands, us lab and medical monkeys get extra help with Rushmore in medical with Neill and the bodies, and Wolfe on analysis with us. In the space of two hours we find traces of fur on three more victims.

With three cooks in the kitchen, the lab is cramped. So since I loathe lab work almost as much as I loathe running, I put myself back on missing persons. Those potentials Will and I found in our research are mostly transients and hookers from around the area. I input the descriptions of what's left of the five, then six people we've excavated already and their personal belongings into NCIC and CODIS. *Nada.* When their DNA gets processed they should hopefully be ID'd.

Since I've found myself at yet another dead end and *really* hate that lab, I decide to collect my thoughts. The whiteboard has helped me crack many a case before, don't fail me now. Okay, four werewolves, including our witch and possibly the victim. With the two new bodies we dug up today, we now know the "pack's" been active for at least six years, but only half the bodies have been dug up, so it's possible they could have been active for decades. Judging from their clothes and the condition of their teeth, all but our recent victim were on the fringes of society. No one to love them, no one to notice they're missing. Our werewolf vic could be a hobo or something too, but we won't know until we discover the rest of him.

Next comes motive. Why kill at all? Duh, they're evil. *The Greatest Game* and all. They obviously don't hunt humans every full moon or we'd have a mountain of bodies. So what happens when they're not treating themselves the nights of the full moon? I write, "check amt animal carcasses reported at park." Maybe not just that park. Is it their only killing grounds? They're smart, maybe they rotate parks. It might explain why the rangers never heard wolves. I scribble, "check records every park w/in 50mi radius for maulings/wolf sightings."

Now onto the big bad wolves. If I had to guess by Will's reaction, I'd say the female is in charge, using lust potions to keep the others under her literal spell. She's the Alpha. If she wasn't homicidal and basically raping the other wolves, I'd be impressed by this accomplishment. I scribble, "witch/wolf mix?" Since the head witch and werewolf were unaware of a chimera like her, maybe she's just buying the potion. It'd be costly but possible. I write, "e-mail Mona and Anna to ask around witch communities re: black witches." I also scribble, "Mona covering for witch/self?" Doubt it but possible. For all we know it could be her sister. Or her. Staring at the board, I frown. That's it? I thought I'd come up with more potential avenues. The park and vics should be our main focus. In my gut I know the last victim will bust this thing wide open. Find out his identity, find our wolves. We just have to find *him* first.

As I stare at my handiwork, the door slides open and our new ally, the nice one, steps in. He's not as put together now as he was last night with armpit stains and dirt covering his white shirt. "Hey. You're tracing the bodies, right?" Adam asks before handing me an evidence baggie. "This should make your job easier. Found an ID with the corpse I just brought in."

"Thank you," I say, taking the baggie. Victim # 7, come on down. I examine the dirty ID. From Crawford College, student ID of Imelda Solis Villa. Awesome. "No problems at the park?"

"No. We stayed away from…that area."

"Good."

I move to the computer and punch in Imelda's data as Adam fixes himself some coffee behind me. Her file pops up immediately in NCIC. Reported missing almost a year ago by her roommate Anika Rister. Last seen leaving her poetry class at 6:15 PM and was meant to be at work across town at seven. Car found on campus so whoever grabbed her did it between 6:15-

6:45 at the college. No one saw the abduction. Like she vanished into thin air. Ex-boyfriend Timothy Acker was lead suspect despite a verified alibi. Anika, co-workers, other friends also investigated and discounted. Anika did receive a text from Imelda's cell a week later claiming she was on the road with a band and not to worry. Nothing since.

"Mona McGregor isn't covering for anyone."

"I'm sorry?" I ask, spinning in the chair to face Adam and the whiteboard.

"I can personally vouch for Mona McGregor. Jason and your supervisor Dr. Black will too," he says with a hard edge.

I think I've offended him. "I was just brainstorming. I mean, from what I understand, the witch and werewolf communities are kind of small and tight knit. The fact that neither head of those factions ever heard of this woman is strange."

"We thought of that. Jason e-mailed every pack head in the world asking if any know of a female hybrid. *Any* hybrid is extremely rare."

"Mona McGregor sent a list of names of known witches. You or Mr. Dahl should review it. See if anyone strikes your memory bell. Maybe we'll luck out." I turn back to the computer to jot down names and telephone numbers of the lead detective and important witnesses. I need the full case file though. My Spidey sense is tingling. This still seems like a random grab, but compared to the others, it was a heck of a lot more brazen. "The clothes with the body, were they blue jeans,

202

fucia sweater, gold cross with a diamond in the center, and a white puffy jacket?"

"Sounds about right," Adam responds. Good enough for me. I collect my things and skedaddle from the room. "Good hunting!" Adam calls.

"You too."

We have a lead! About damn time.

I stop by the lab for my purse, coat, and Imelda's cross to verify with Anika before commandeering an SUV. Before I start the car, I phone the lead detective Hill Cleve who agrees to meet with me straight away. I put the car into gear, and to the police station I go.

Seven minutes later I'm shaking Det. Cleve's hand in the small Crawford P.D. lobby. He's a detective out of central casting with a huge belly, rumpled suit, jowls, and shock of white hair. He ushers me into the back of the station. We've taken about half their personnel for our forest project so most desks are deserted.

"I worked this case for a full month," Det. Cleve says as he passes me the box and file across the conference table. "In my gut I knew the ex had a hand in it. The kid was nervous as hell. Even brought a lawyer with him during questioning. We couldn't break his alibi though. He was in a study group until nine. The five students and TA verified it, not to mention we have him on video surveillance. He didn't even leave to go to the bathroom."

"Even with that, you still think it was him? Why?"

"They'd been fighting. He'd gotten distant then broke up with her a week before she vanished. The roommate said Imelda thought he'd been cheating."

"Who with?" I ask.

"She didn't know, and I never found anyone. The kid had no life outside of school and the girlfriend. And I've kept tabs on him off and on. He goes from home to school to back home, though the roommate Anika could answer that better. She probably sees him every day. But if Imelda was found with all the other corpses, hell maybe I was barking up the wrong tree. I heard you've pulled half a dozen bodies already. Dismembered and all chewed up. Can't believe this was going on under our noses all this time," he says, shaking his head. "Y'all sure Imelda, hell all of them, were killed by the same man?"

"Looks that way. We are going to hold off on family notifications until the DNA and dental reports. Should be a day or two longer."

"We won't say a word until you tell us to. I just got assigned a robbery. If you need me…"

"Thank you."

As I open the file, the detective leaves me in peace. Thank God. Some detectives become like helicopter parents, hovering over my shoulder and second guessing my every move. So annoying. In solitude I skim the file and examine what little evidence there is in record time. No forensics, no witnesses, no wonder they never found her. Random grabs are like that. Still, due diligence is required. I whip out my cell phone and call the roommate Anika, who agrees to meet me at the Crawford College food court in half an hour. I also leave a message for the ex-boyfriend Tim Acker before heading out again.

Crawford College is just five miles down the road but it takes twenty minutes to find parking, and even then I may as well have walked straight from the station. After checking the map in the quad, I stroll toward the food court. I do miss college. The carefree days, the parties, the community, the…oh, who am I kidding? I went to class, I went to the library to study and work part-time, I went home. I was never invited to a single party, was offered zero drugs, and only had sex three times, and that was with my student health counselor before *he* ended our sessions. Still. As I amble through the campus past co-eds texting or joking with their equally cheery friends, I can't help but grin too. They have their whole lives ahead of them. They have no idea what's around the corner and the feeling of invincibility youth provides makes them not care. I do remember that. Jeez, I've been out of college almost five years and it's as if it's been quadruple that. Facing life and death situations sure has aged me.

The campus is minimalist, maybe three city blocks, with brown and white buildings close together, the tallest no more than four stories. There are a few grassy knolls with the odd tree where students sit in groups talking or eating. I locate the student union building hiding behind another. The food court inside is about half the size of my old elementary school cafeteria, though it didn't have a Pizza Hut or Chick-Fil-A like here. Since I don't have a clue what Anika looks like, I call her cell and as asked she rises from her table by the window. Pretty girl. Medium brown skin, full lips, curly hair piled atop her head with an actual bow that matches her dress. She reminds me of Irie, may she rest in peace.

"Hi. Thanks for meeting me on such short notice," I say as we sit.

"I have like an hour before my next class. It's cool. So, the FBI's taken over Melly's case? That's good, right? You have like new leads or whatever?"

"We are pursuing new leads, yes." I reach into my purse and remove the evidence baggie, handing it to Anika. "Can you identify this as belonging to Imelda?"

She studies the jewelry, face contorting in disgust. "Yeah. That's her cross. Her grandmother gave it to her for Communion. She never like took it off like ever. Does this mean that…" Anika slides the bag back. "You found her?"

"We're awaiting DNA confirmation, but we believe so. Yes. I'm so sorry."

The girl falls back in her chair and stares down at the table to process this new information. I wait for her to speak, which takes about ten seconds. "I knew…I mean I like figured she was dead, but…how?"

"She was discovered in a local park along with several other bodies."

"A, like, serial killer? Oh my God. How'd she die?"

206

"I can't comment on that." Really I just won't. This girl doesn't need the visual. "In the police report you said you suspected Tim Acker. Why?"

"Because it's always like the boyfriend or husband, right? They'd just like broken up the week before, and he'd been weird for a few months before."

"Weird how?" I ask.

"I don't know. Distant? Always making excuses why they couldn't hang out. Projects, studying, stuff like that. Then there were like two weeks where he didn't return any of her texts or show up to school at all. They went from Siamesetwinville to on different planets."

"Did he give a reason why?"

"He wanted to focus on school. Getting into a Ph.D. program. I mean, you know, that happens and stuff, but he breaks up with her and a week later she disappears? Yeah, he was suspect number one even without me even like pointing him out."

"Was he ever violent or did he hang out with violent people?"

"God no. I mean, I like only see him in passing now, but when I knew him he was totally sweet. More than sweet. Always did whatever Melly wanted. I was like so jealous of them." The girl instantly regrets those words as her mouth snaps shut, and she starts picking at her salad. "They were totally in love, is all."

"Did he seem upset when she vanished?" I ask.

"Yeah, he uh helped me put up fliers and stuff when I asked him to. Like I said, I barely see him and from what I've heard he is a total nerd now. It's all about school." She shakes her head. "Really, like deep down if I'm honest, I didn't think he *really* did it. I mean, he used to paint her toenails. But if not him, then who, you know?"

"What about people following her? Did she mention that or have any run-ins or arguments with anyone that got heated? We believe there's a group of people involved, three men and one woman. Did she ever mention anything along those lines?"

Anika thinks for a moment. "No. You think they were stalking her or whatever?"

"We just don't want to leave any stone unturned," I assure her. And I'm sensing another dead end here. Wrong place, plus wrong time, equals dead co-ed. Nothing more to the story. "Well, if you think of anything, no matter how small it may seem, please call me."

"I will. I'm sorry I couldn't like be more help."

"You were plenty help," I say with a smile before standing. "We'll contact you when we have official confirmation about Imelda, but until then please don't discuss anything I've told you today."

"I won't," the girl says.

"And if you see Tim, please tell him to give me a call."

"Oh, he's in the library or was like twenty minutes ago when I left. You can probably still catch him. He was in the front carrels."

"Thank you. And I'm sorry about your friend."

The girl simply nods. I give her one last sympathetic smile before rushing out. I want to catch Tim unawares before he can plan what to say. A rattled perp is an easy perp. I hustle to the library, only getting lost once. The ground floor of the two-story library is mostly tables and plywood study carrels where only about half the kids are studying with the others texting, talking, or both. I shake my head. In my day if we said one word inside these hallowed halls the librarian kicked our butts to the curb. Whatever happened to respect? One of the few with his nose actually in a book is Tim Acker, who I recognize from a picture in the file. Good looking boy. A bit on the thin side with a more feminine face than even mine. Delicate cheekbones, full lips, big brown eyes though he has cut his sandy blonde hair so it's almost hiding them. Studying must be as boring now as it was in my day because almost the moment I walk in, the kid clocks me. With each step toward him, despite my smile, those eyes grow until they're the size of saucers. How does he know who I am? Maybe I just give off the law enforcement vibe. That'd be *awesome.*

"Tim Acker?"

"Yeah?" the boy asks, closing his anthropology book.

"I'm Special Agent Beatrice Alexander. I've left you a few messages about Imelda Villa?"

"I-I'm sorry. I haven't checked my messages in hours. What-What about Melly?"

The nearby students stare at me, and one even texts, probably my every word. "Why don't we talk outside? You look like you can use a break."

"I...guess. Okay." He grabs his gray hoodie from the chair before standing. He trails a pace behind, fiddling with his cell phone as he does. When we reach the entrance, he stops. "Hey, um, can I use the bathroom first? I've had like a ton of coffee."

"Of course," I say with a fake pleasant smile. "I need to go too."

"Uh, sure. It's this way," Tim says, gesturing behind us.

Test one passed. Not even a moment's hesitation agreeing to my request. If he planned to escape, he would have made excuses or become flustered. I know from experience. Since it's not a foolproof indication, I position myself right beside the men's room door and wait. Good time to check my messages. Oh, a text from Will. Part of me, the smart focused side, screams, "Don't open the message idiot! Eyes and brain on the case." Of course I ignore her. She's such a nag.

"Where RU?" Will texted.

I text back, *"College. Ivews. U?"*

Within thirty seconds I get back, *"Lving_mobile. Another body. Need help?"*

This time I listen to the nag. *"Almost done._Dead ends. Miss U."*

"Me 2. Luv U. CU 2nite. Stay safe."

"Luv U 2."

I slip my phone back in my pocket just as Tim steps out of the bathroom. "Better?" I ask.

"Yeah. Thanks," slipping his hands into his pockets.

We find a bench just outside the library. I study my quarry as he sits beside me. His face is a little tight, especially his lips, so I know he's uneasy. Even without my newly acquired powers of deduction I can sense the nervous energy wafting from him almost to the point I have pains in my stomach. Nerves. Could just be because I'm law enforcement. Time to find out.

"I'll try to make this as quick and painless as possible," I say with a grin.

"Do you have new leads or something about her? Melly?"

"Um, yes. We believe we may have found her."

"What? Is she alive?" he asks, perking up.

"I'm afraid not. I'm sorry."

The boy's eyes avert down to the ground. "Oh." A pause. "That sucks."

That sucks? I just told him the girl he loved is dead, and that's the best he can do? There isn't a whiff of sadness radiating from him. Hello suspicious behavior. "You don't seem too broken up about it."

"Guess not. I just kind of figured she was like dead for the past year. Or she ran away to frame me for murder or something cause we broke up. She could be a vindictive bitch like that. I forgot our half anniversary once, and she started telling people she found me making out with some guy. It got around school. And when she disappeared…" He shakes his head. "Everyone acted like I was Hannibal Lecter. They'd give me dirty looks or even avoid me. I had to move off campus and everything. No one cared I had like five people as my alibi. No one. So yeah, it sucks she died. Maybe it'll hit me later or something, but I'm not going to lie and say I'm devastated or whatever. Besides, if I did, you wouldn't believe me either. That's why you're here. The boyfriend's always the first suspect. The police like ripped my life apart, examined everything, and found nothing because there was nothing to find. I didn't kidnap her and I have five people and surveillance video to prove it."

Either this kid's an acting major or he's telling the truth. I read the report. The police tried and failed to break his alibi. The study group members had no reason to lie, and there was the surveillance footage. He didn't leave the library until after nine. And he gets points for honesty. If he's been a blubbering mess, making the girl into a saint, my antenna would be swirling like a cyclone.

"Was there anyone else who Imelda may have angered?" I ask.

"Like I said, she could be a bitch but not like *that* big a bitch."

"What about people following her? Did she ever mention being scared or feeling like things were out of the ordinary?"

"We weren't talking so no. Look, I can't help you. I wish I could, I do, but I don't know anything." For the first time a glimmer of sadness flits across his brown eyes. "How did…did she suffer or whatever?"

"I'm not at liberty to discuss particulars, I'm sorry."

"Well, do you have any suspects? I mean, besides me? Was she found in that park?"

I raise an eyebrow. "How did you know about that? The park?"

"It's a small town. Even smaller campus. Everyone knows you're digging people up there. It was even on the news. They said it was a serial killer and something about dogs or something."

"Then…can I go? I have an anthropology paper due."

"One last question." I pull out the photos of the other victims we've identified and my business card. "Do you recognize any of these people? Are there any Imelda may have known?"

He studies the photos, shaking his head each time. "No. Sorry."

"Long shot anyway," I say with a smile. After collecting the photos, I rise with him following suit. "Thank you for your time. My number's on the card. If you remember anything, no matter how unimportant you believe it may be, please call. I mean anything."

"Yes, ma'am," he says, pocketing my business card. "Good luck."

The boy politely nods before returning to the library. When he's out of earshot, I let out a long, aggravated sigh. Fudge. Double fudge. Nothing, nothing and more nothing. I want to bang my head against all the dead ends. These wolves are good. Damn good. Experienced. Probably been doing this kind of thing for decades. Heck, even when the crime appears random, like now, the baddies leave a trace. Fibers, DNA, one of the group starts blabbing to others of their deeds. *Something.* Whoever this hybrid is, she runs a very tight ship. She even keeps them in line as a werewolf so they don't stray toward the Ranger's station. If she weren't a mass murderer, I'd almost respect her.

There's one last stop to make before I tuck my tail between my legs and head back to mobile command empty handed. Imelda was leaving her poetry class in the English building at approximately 6:15 PM. I locate the currently dark, empty classroom on the second floor. Okay, per the file she said good-bye to her friend Hayley when they exited this building. Per Hayley, there was nothing out of the ordinary when they parted, Hayley walking to the left and Imelda to the right toward her car. As I take the route to the parking lot, I examine the surroundings. It would have been dark, just past twilight. I pass through the open quad, just a vast flat space with sidewalks, where two students remember seeing her. Once again, nothing suspicious was noted by either of them. No one obviously following her or paying attention to her, but both insisted it was dark and they weren't really paying her any mind. These two were the last to see Imelda Villa Solis alive.

About halfway through the quad, I veer right toward the three-story buildings as it's the most direct route to Lot C at least per the map I check. The sidewalk cuts between two buildings, social sciences and mathematics, in a narrow alleyway with trees inside concrete enclosures every few feet. Downright claustrophobic. Even now, with the sun shining above there's an air of un-safety, like a rapist's hiding behind a tree trunk, bush, or pillar. Per the police report, this is where it's believed she was grabbed. After subduing her, the assailant raced up to their waiting car and drove off with their prey. But as I stand here, I flashback to my not so long ago college days and recall how skittish I was walking to my car from my one night class. Staring at every bush as I rushed past it, darn near leaping out of my sneakers when I heard footsteps behind me. Lights and people, every girl knows at night if you're not with a group you stay near lights and people. This place may as well be named, "Rapist's Alley." Imelda didn't come this way, at least not regularly. I often went through buildings, especially when it was cold and dark, but the police canvassed both buildings and those inside that night neither saw nor heard her. There was no trace of her in this alley either, nothing left behind, but if this was a random grab, the wolf could have been patiently waiting for

215

some idiot co-ed, and Imelda was the unlucky one. Wrong place, wrong time. Makes sense. Fudge. I can feel this case growing colder by the minute.

As it stands now, I have a 100% clearance rate. I always get my man/woman/vampire/ whatever. I often have to reach the precipice of death to get them, but I do get them. This time I'm not so confident. We usually have more evidence by now, a grasp or at least a direction to continue in. I thought Imelda would speak to me, provide me a compass heading, but she's as silent as her grave. With another long sigh, my millionth this case, I turn back the way I came. Not the first walk of shame this campus has seen, but definitely the most shameful.

ELEVEN

A MARVELOUS NIGHT FOR A MOONDANCE

"So...*nothing?* We still have nothing?"

"We're still waiting for about half the packs to respond, but no. Nothing yet," Alpha Dahl responds.

Of course. I should be at least a little content not to be the only one trapped in a maze of dead ends. That I'm not the only incompetent one, but it's cold comfort. I just want out of the damn maze.

"Send another e-mail to those who haven't gotten back to you and press upon them how important it is they do," I say.

"They will respond. A situation like this impacts us all. We want to locate the rogues even more than you do, Agent Alexander."

"I very much doubt that, Mr. Dahl." I stare at the murder board with our victim's pictures, a map of the park, and my scribbles from earlier, a frown forming on my face. "Have you ever seen anything like this before? Any insights you want to share with the class?"

As he steps beside me, his icy blue eyes scroll the board. I don't like him standing so close to me. Every nerve ending is on high alert when he is. I hope this isn't what Will feels when he's near me. "I find it strange the park rangers never heard a single howl or discovered a body until now. After a change, we're exhausted. We can barely walk or think. Yet these wolves manage to clean up all the mess—the limbs, the blood— and dig a grave before the park opens?"

"They could have dug it beforehand," I suggest.

"True. But still there would be several odds and ends to clear up. There's also the fact even the most feared of pack leaders can lose control of a subordinate, especially in wolf form. As a wolf you want to run, to hunt, to howl. They would have periodically strayed from her designated territory. Unless she used a barrier spell."

"We haven't found any crystals or sigils in our canvasses, but it is possible," I say. "And if she did use one, why not on this last hunt? Years of going to this park, possibly every month, but at least twice a year for sure, without a single mistake. What was different this time? Why wasn't there a complete clean-up? We know they weren't interrupted."

"The victim was a werewolf himself," Dahl points out. "He may have sniffed out he'd walked into a trap and escaped before the barrier was up."

"And the leg? Were they so upset in the morning having killed a fellow wolf they got sloppy this *one* time? They obviously buried the rest of him or someone would have sniffed out the rotting carcass by now."

"Is your doctor positive he was a werewolf?"

218

"As close to positive as she can get. You guys do change back to human form when you die, so it's not like we found a wolf's paw."

Alpha Dahl's cell begins chirping "Someone To Watch Over Me" and a flash of a grin crosses his sharp face. So he *can* smile. "Excuse me, it's my wife. I need to take this." He removes the phone from his belt and walks out of the conference room. "Hi, love. How are the kids?"

At least our talk was marginally helpful. I add, "barrier spell" and "park rangers lying?" on the board. I circle that last one. The park. The killing fields. The victims are leading us nowhere, maybe it's time to shift focus. We have the dates the vics were grabbed. It'll be easy to cross reference those full moons with the ranger's work schedules. See if one was working all those nights. My money's on Ranger Rick. He did report the leg, and he has been helpful the past few days, but it could just be a cover. He overlooked the leg, civilian witnesses reported it, and he had no choice but to phone the police. I jot this theory on the board too before e-mailing the Forestry service again for copies of the work schedules. I've e-mailed them twice and haven't gotten even a form letter back. It's past eight so they probably won't get this e-mail until tomorrow. Tomorrow and tomorrow and tomorrow. Always tomorrow.

I swivel my chair back around to the board, re-reading everything in the hopes something new will magically present itself, but my eyes stop at Imelda's photo. One of these things is not like the others for sure. This pretty English major rests

219

among a drug addict, a prostitute, another homeless man/drug user, and two others never reported missing. Why her? Why risk the exposure? Why—

My concentration breaks when the door slides open again, and completely shatters when my gorgeous boyfriend steps in. Oh, he is especially yummy tonight in khakis, the blue fleece sweatshirt I got him for Christmas, and hair wet yet full. Heck he even smells divine, like shampoo and Calvin Klein cologne. If the man is attempting to torture me it is so working. "Thought you'd be in here," he says with a smile before moving behind me.

"Where else would I be?"

Will begins rubbing my shoulders which sorely need some TLC. "Been busy I see."

"Yeah," I sigh. God those hands feel good. "Bees got nothing on me. Of course they have something to show for it at the end of the day. I've got bubkus. A million theories and no proof. The dots are all there but I just can't connect them. I just feel like…I'm missing something obvious."

"This doesn't all fall on you, babe. We got over a dozen people on this."

"But they're not me."

He kisses the top of my head. "I know." He kneads my knots out in silence for a few seconds before saying, "You working on anything that can't wait until tomorrow morning?"

"Not really. Why?"

"I have a surprise for you. Get your purse."

I do love surprises.

I collect my jacket and purse before following my guy out of mobile command. Of course we're stopped halfway to the exit as Wolfe steps out of the lab. Gives me a chance to slip on my coat. "Will, do you know when they're bringing in the next body?"

"I just spoke to Chandler. Should be here in an hour or two."

"Well, when can you—"

"I can't. Whatever you're about to say, no. Bea and I are off the clock for the rest of the night, alright? We'll have our phones on but only call if someone's dying. And I don't mean bleeding, I mean literally dying. And spread the word."

"You're just…taking off?" Wolfe asks, glancing at me. I shrug. News to me.

"Yep. While Chandler's in the field with Oliver, you're in charge here. If you want to send everyone home, by all means. Everything will be here waiting for us tomorrow. Have a nice night."

"Um…"

Will grabs my hand and pulls me toward the door before Wolfe can finish his protests, of which I'm sure he has many. He probably thinks Will's lost his mind. Never, *never* has Will just abandoned a case for the night with so much still left to do. The man I love cracks the whip until we're all bleeding. I'd say something, but if it means no more work tonight forget that. And I really do love surprises.

221

Dahl's still on the phone when we get outside. Without breaking our fast stride to the SUV, Will calls, "See you tomorrow, Jason!"

Even in the darkness I can see Dahl's eyes narrow at us in confusion. But we're too quick for questions. We climb into the SUV and shut the doors. "What is going on?" I chuckle.

Will starts the car. "Thought it was obvious. I'm kidnapping you for the night," he says with a wicked grin.

"We're playing hooky? In the middle of a case? Everyone's right, I am a bad influence on you."

"The worst, babe." He takes my hand and presses it to his lips. "The absolute worst."

*

"Seriously Will, where are we going?"

I have no idea where we are. Not a clue. Outside Crawford somewhere in the freaking woods. There are barely any cars on the two lane road, no lights from houses, only the outlines of thick trees on top of more trees. If he really has lost his mind, this would be the perfect spot to dump my body.

"I told you, it's a surprise," he chuckles. "One I hope you appreciate. It was a pain in the ass to put together."

Before I can hassle him further, my phone begins playing "The Stripper." Oliver. Crud. If he's at the park it might be important. I reach down to retrieve it from my purse. "Don't," Will snaps. "Bea…"

"They could be under attack or something." I accept the call. "Hello?"

"I am phoning to inform you we have uncovered another body. A fresh one. We believe it is our Werewolf Doe. We should have him to mobile command in two to three hours."

"They found the dead werewolf," I tell Will who has gone all scowly again. "Does he have ID on him or—"

Out of nowhere, Will snatches the phone from my hand. "Unless lives are in immediate danger, you are not to call either of us until tomorrow morning. I mean it. Do not call again." As if squishing a bug, Will stabs the end call button before handing it back to me. "Don't answer it anymore."

"Okay…" I slip the phone back into my purse.

"Jesus Christ, the man's twenty miles away and still manages to ruin this!"

"He hasn't ruined anything," I lie. The temperature is certainly about twenty degrees chillier in here. I take his hand off the wheel to hold mine. "Not if we don't let him."

Will glances over again, his scowl morphing into an apologetic half smile. "I just…want everything to be perfect."

"It is perfect." I press his hand to my lips. "I love you."

"Even though I'm a grumpy, ornery old werewolf with a short temper?"

"Well…there's always obedience training for those types of things," I say with a smirk. "Should take about forty, fifty years of living with you day in and day out, but I'll crack you eventually."

"Forty to fifty years, huh?" His smile grows to match mine. "You're up for that kind of commitment, Agent Alexander?"

"I think you already know the answer to that, Agent Price. The question is, are you?"

He opens his mouth to respond, but something catches his eye on the left side of the road. He releases my hand, returning it to the wheel. "We're here."

We turn down a gravel road, driving about a quarter mile into the woods, surrounded by bare yet dense trees and nothing else until we reach the end where a little lonely cabin sits. It's cute, a one-story made of actual logs with a wraparound porch complete with rocking chairs. "Are you taking me to the Love Shack, baby?" I ask.

"I am told it is where it's at."

The first thing I notice as I climb out of the car, besides the cutting wind, is the sound of running water to my right. With my better than average night vision I can make out a rapidly moving creek about ten yards away. I'm sure this spot is beautiful in the day but right now all I care about is getting inside and not just because I'm freezing.

After retrieving an overnight bag from the backseat, Will rounds the SUV, throwing his arm over my shoulders and pulling me in tight to his side as we hurry to the cabin. The butterflies begin fluttering from stomach to brain as he unlocks the door. This is it. This is really going to happen. I'm going to make love to my dream man. God, please let it be like riding a bicycle. Please let our bodies fit well together. Most importantly, please don't let me kill him. *Please.*

The door swings open to a living room bathed in soft orange light from the crackling fire in the far wall. Aww, he must have come here to get everything ready before he picked me up. My mouth literally drops open as I step in. It's so homey. One large room with a futon couch, table, chairs, kitchenette, quilts like Nana makes hang on the walls, and two doors that must go to the bedroom and bathroom. It's…perfect.

"Like it?" Will asks, shutting the door behind us.

"I love it," I say breathlessly. This moment has literally taken my breath away. I twirl around and throw my arms over his shoulders. "I love *you*. I love you so much."

I kiss him. The moment our lips lock, we have liftoff. Literally. He scoops me into his strong, comforting arms to draw me in closer, hoisting me off the ground. I wrap my legs around his waist. Lips, tongue all play in a frenzy as he moves us toward the fire. The bedroom's too damn far away. May as well be on freaking Mars. He lowers me onto the sheepskin rug. Clothes. We have way too many clothes on. The kiss breaks as we struggle with jackets, shirts and pants. He beats me in the naked race, and I take just a second to appraise his amazing body. All his strong contours glow in the firelight like some mythical creature out of a fairy tale. And he's all mine. Every last huge inch of him.

As I rip my panties off, he reaches into his discarded pants pocket, removing a condom. I never minded those things before but tonight I do. Screw caution, screw consequences, I don't want anything separating us. I want his flesh touching mine, inside mine with no barriers. We've had enough barriers already. But he rolls it on anyway. Without hesitation, I open my legs to allow him to crawl between them. I'm ready for him. My whole body's ready for him, literally quivering in anticipation, especially the tender, wet flesh between my legs. But he doesn't take advantage. Instead he hovers over me, gazing into my eyes as he draws his fingers down my cheek, my neck, the slope of my exposed breasts. I suck in my breath as he trails over my nipple, which puckers and tightens at this touch. That breath comes out as a shiver as those same fingers press into me. His thumb circles my clitoris as he teases that sensitive spot inside, every one of my nerve endings firing with every stroke. And I was worried about exploding *his* brain.

"You're so wet. You're so beautiful," he whispers. "I love you so fucking much. I love you."

It's unbearable when he removes those expert digits to grab my leg and position it over his hip. If he doesn't—

Holy shit!

He thrusts into the very end of me with little grace. It's been years since that final Saturday night with Steven, so having anything there is kind of a shock to the system, never mind something so large. I force the pain from my mind as best as I can as he pulls back only to slide a little gentler this time. By the fourth time I begin to catch his rhythm, my hips dancing with his, and by the sixth nothing remains but pleasure, the divine

226

pleasure radiating from where we're connected. Where we're one. We rock harder, faster as I cry out into the silence. Whimper. Moan. I dig my fingers into the flesh of his back, that butt I adore so much. With each thrust that heat, that tension mounts inside me. It's freaking brilliant. I wrap my legs around his waist, drawing him inside me deeper. Deeper, until it almost hurts. As deep as the kisses, the deft strokes of his tongue playing with mine. He's everywhere. Filling me. Loving me. Where he belongs. Worth the wait. This was so worth all the pain, the heartbreak, the longing, the—

"Oh, God!" Will calls.

He shudders on top of me, inside me, as with the one final thrust he breaks, collapsing onto me, into my arms. His manhood becomes as limp as the rest of him, spent from the last far too few minutes of bliss. I'm spent too, my breath ragged but equalizing as he rolls off me onto his back. I close my eyes to gain control, but I'm still just a jangle of open nerve endings, especially down below where I'm literally aching, hell downright *burning* for deliverance. I was close. Very close. God, I hate being a woman sometimes.

We lie shoulder to sweaty shoulder with nothing but our heavy breaths and the crackling fire for a soundtrack until we catch our breath. "I'm sorry," Will says after about thirty seconds.

"Why?"

"It's been over eight years. I was a little trigger happy there."

227

"It's alright. I'm not even sure I can that way. I never did before. Some women—"

He shifts beside me, and I open my eyes just in time to watch him take position between my legs again, erection at full salute already. I think I'm going to love and hate having a lover with supernatural recovery time in the coming years. This time he slowly enters me, gliding in like silk, while positioning my legs around his waist so my hips once more lift off the soft rug. "Tell me when it feels good," he whispers into my ear before kissing the lobe. I shift to the left, then right as he adjusts as well. The moment he hits that sweet spot my eyes all but roll into the back of my head. Oooh, golly! Undiscovered country located, he picks up the pace, this time following my furious arching, forcing him in deeper and deeper until he reaches my very end, pleasure and pain as entwined as we are. Over. And over. And over. Sharper. Tighter. Tenser. Growing behind my eyes, in my toes, all-encompassing and astounding. Nerves, soul on fire until…until…

Kaboom!

I literally scream as the spasms, both of ours, shatter this very world. In the afterglow, the crash from the couch falling from the ceiling onto the hardwood floor doesn't even startle us. How could it? There is nothing in this universe, in heaven or hell, but he and I. The psychic and the werewolf, the freaks, who finally found each other among the dead bodies and pain and misery and loneliness life keeps throwing at them.

Thank you, God. Thank you for this man. Thank you for his love.

"Thank you."

TWELVE

THERE'S GOT TO BE A MORNING AFTER. DAMN IT.

So much for the theory that if we slept together I'd be able to focus on the job. As we drive to mobile command on this beautiful sunny day all I can think of is getting him naked and inside me again. He may as well be. I can all but feel him still. This is my favorite kind of sore though. Five times in one night, six if I count the fireside as two will do that to a gal. From the floor we moved to the couch. Then the floor again. Then we finally made it to the bedroom. Finally, I woke at dawn to find him gone. I wrapped myself in a quilt and joined him on the back porch to watch the sun rise over the mountains. He pulled me onto his lap in the rocking chair, but I took charge from there. Slow but sweet. It would have been a true five but I was so spent I refused him entrance to my shower. Go willpower!

I'm exhausted, sore, and have been shattered and reassembled multiple times. I've never been happier. But the real world calls with all its problems and concerns. Of which there is one that overshadows them all, one even more pressing than murderous werewolves.

"Have you seen a pharmacy around here?" I ask my lover.

"There's a CVS near the hotel. Why? Are you okay? I didn't hurt you, did I?"

"No! No, I just…we didn't use protection the last time. I should probably, you know…morning after pill? I'm not on anything. Yet."

"Oh. That didn't even occur to me. We can swing by." He pauses. "Or…"

"Or…" I prompt.

He shrugs. "I mean, you know, would it be so bad? Really?"

Is he…does he mean what I think he does? I glance over and darned if he isn't smiling at the prospect. When he catches me looking, he raises an eyebrow. Holy Hannah, he's serious. I quickly do the math. Auntie Flo's a week away, we should be safe, but barely. But would it be terrible? Heck no. I've wanted his babies since the first day we met. "No," I say with a matching grin, "it wouldn't."

"Okay then."

Okay. We drive in silence for a minute as the wheels in my mind spin, inevitably landing on Realityville for $100. "Are we moving too fast?" I spurt out.

"Bea, we can go to the pharmacy. It's okay."

"No. Maybe. I don't know. It's just…we've only officially been a couple a week. We haven't even known each

231

other a year, Will. Now we're seriously talking babies. It's like warp speed ahead. It's not normal."

"Babe, you said it yourself at Christmas: *we're* not normal. Forgetting all the psychic/werewolf bullshit, you and I have endured more than most people do in three lifetimes. We know how fragile this life is. We know how rare it is to find someone to connect to, really connect to. I've loved you for months, hell practically since I first met you, and I almost lost you half a dozen times. I wasted so much time fighting it, fighting you, I don't want to waste another damn second. I love you. You love me. We want the same things out of life. We respect each other. We make each other happy. Most couples can't claim one of those damn things. So to outsiders, yeah, we're moving fast. But fuck them. All that matters is what *we* think. And for me, if anything, we're moving too damn slow. If I had the balls to tell you how I felt nine months ago, six months, hell two months ago, we'd already be back from our honeymoon or painting a nursery. I love you. I want to spend the rest of my life with you. I want you to be the mother of my children and wake beside me every morning. Do you feel the same?"

"You know I do."

"Then there you have it. We found each other. We found happiness. We're just not used to it, that's all. Stop trying to put holes in this. I've done that enough for the both of us for months. I almost sank the damn ship because of it, so don't you start." He flashes me a smile to show he's joking, and I return it. "Besides, I'm almost eligible for AARP membership. I want to have children while I can still play with them. And have the strength to throw our daughter's boyfriends out of damn windows."

"Ha ha," I quip.

Oh, crud. I can see the turn for mobile command and grimace. Our night of debauchery is officially over. Dead bodies and murderers ahoy. Yet I feel something akin to relief. I'm too tired for this life changing conversation. "Let's table this, huh? Bad guys to catch. Need our heads in the game."

"That is going to be damn difficult, Agent Alexander. It's taking every ounce of willpower not to turn this car back around, lock the doors to the cabin, and not let you leave. I have the cabin rented for the week.

"Pretty sure you just described kidnapping, Will," I chuckle.

"Twenty years in the clink would be worth it," he says with a grin. He pulls up to the trailer. "We'll just have to catch these bastards real fast, or I might just lose my damn mind." He shuts off the car. "I love you."

I lean across to peck his lips. "I love you too."

This time he kisses me. *Really* kisses me. Another of his toe curling, ambrosia from the heavens, caresses I don't know how I lived without until this point. "Just think about what I said, okay? I meant every word." He smiles again, then sighs. "Come on, Agent Alexander. You're late for work."

"Good thing I'm sleeping with my boss then, huh?"

Carl, Nancy, Agent Chandler, and our new werewolf pals have all beat us into the office this morning. At least we're in time for the morning meeting in the conference room. Not sure if that's a good thing though. The way they look at us, or in Chandler's case how he refuses to, I can tell they all know what happened last night. I have the strongest urge to just get it out there. To shout, "Yes, we had sex! Lots of sex! Multiple times in multiple positions! Sex, sex, sex, sex, sex!" but do refrain. Instead, I plaster on my nicest, sweetest smile. "Good morning!"

"Morning," Adam says.

"Glad you could finally join us," Chandler responds with a scowl directed my way.

"It was my fault," Will chimes in. "I lost track of time."

"I'll bet," Nancy chuckles.

"We're here now," says Will. "So, what did we miss?"

"We found the remains of Werewolf Doe last night," Chandler informs us.

"Well, what was left of him," Carl adds. "The meat was literally ripped from his bones. Arms, legs, torso, head decapitated and missing chunks like they…"

"Ate him," Jason cuts in. "They more than likely did."

"Lovely," I say.

"He was found in a shallow grave like the rest of them," Carl says. "But his clothes were completely intact, like he removed them himself."

"Gives credence to the theory he was a werewolf too," I say. "They invited him out for a moonlight run then for whatever reason they turned on him."

"That would be consistent with the remains. Werewolves change back to human form when they die—they're no longer linked to the magical source—but as with the leg, he already showed signs of healing in multiple places," Carl explains.

"And he reeked of ectoplasm," Jason adds. "He was a werewolf, no question."

"What about an ID?" Will asks.

"Several of his teeth were missing so dental won't work," Carl says. "His fingerprints and DNA are filtering now, but if he's never been arrested…" He shrugs.

"Then let's hope he was a bad mammajamma," Adam says.

"Well, Carl and I can do our…thing," I suggest. For whatever reason, if I touch Carl while he's using his empathy gift, my own connects with his and we can actually see through the victim's eyes in his or her last moments. That's how we caught the succubus so quickly.

"No, I tried on my own," Carl says. "He's too long dead."

"You should have thought to do it the day we arrived with the leg," Chandler says.

"*You* didn't think of it either," I snap back.

235

"Well, it's moot now," Will says. "So what else do we got?"

"Of the eleven bodies we've recovered so far, eight have wounds consistent with werewolf attacks," Chandler says. "We have IDs on all but three of the eight, including Werewolf Doe. Doc puts the first victim in the ground about six years ago. Judging from the pattern we've established, they killed about twice a year."

"So we're missing bodies," I point out. "Four."

"Oliver spent the last two nights searching that park," Carl says.

"Then he won't mind going tonight as well," Will says. "These people deserve to be found. They *need* to be found."

"The ones you've ID'd since last night," I say, "what do we know about them?"

"Jackson Markus had four arrests for heroin possession and no fixed address, and Enrique Martinez appears to be an illegal from Mexico. His fake passport and driver's license were buried with him."

"Any indication Werewolf Doe was a transient as well?" Will asks.

"His blood work showed no drugs or alcohol in his system, but that doesn't mean much with a werewolf metabolism," Carl says.

"He's still an outlier," I point out. "Him and Imelda. They're the keys, I can feel it."

"We read your report," Chandler says. "You learned nothing to indicate her abduction was anything but random like the rest of the victims."

"The girl still doesn't fit the pattern," Will says. "Bea's right."

"Of course you'd think that," Chandler says.

Will stares at his best friend, eyes slowly narrowing. "You're right, I *would* because as far as I can tell, we have dick else. And I don't hear anyone else coming up with sound theories."

"Well, maybe if everyone on the team weren't too preoccupied—"

"This helps nothing," Jason booms. "We've wasted enough time, don't you think," he asks, glaring at Will and me. "I want to find these fuckers and go home to my wife and kids before the next Ice Age, so we need to focus. No more infighting and no more fucking around."

God this man makes me feel about three feet tall and on the verge of being squished. Someone *married* this man? She must have a heck of a backbone or is certifiably insane.

"Well, have you heard anything?" I ask. "This is your world. From what I gather a witch/werewolf hybrid is about as rare as a unicorn. None of your cronies have anything to add?"

"I'm still waiting on a quarter to write back," Jason says, "but according to the oldest pack leader living, there have only been three witch hybrids born worldwide, all male and all from one line in Germany. On the planet today there are two, both of whom still live in Germany and are under constant supervision."

"Why so few?" I ask.

"Because before about 1930, any known werewolf hybrid offspring would be executed," Adam explains with a grim expression.

It doesn't hold a candle to mine. My mouth drops open and teeth clench. "That's barbaric!"

"That's survival," Jason counters.

Jesus Christ. A chill snakes down my spine as his cold as his arctic eyes. A hundred years ago Will's and my children would have been smothered in the cradle without a second thought or worse by this man sitting across from me. And I didn't like him to begin with.

"But now they're just monitored," Adam adds. "They can never join a pack, their parents either, but they're allowed to…exist."

"Oh, because *you* deem it so?" I spit out at Jason. "How magnanimous of you."

"We're veering off topic again," Carl cuts in.

"He's right," Chandler says. "The politics of pack policy discussion should be tabled for now. So the gist is no pack is aware of our female hybrid, correct?"

"As I said before, from those who have returned my calls and e-mails, no," Jason says.

"That they're aware of," I say. "I can't exactly see anyone lining up to disclose that sort of information to you."

"Or she like could have been bitten or whatever and didn't know she had to like register," Nancy adds.

"Both valid theories," Will says, "but they won't help us locate her. We go with what we have: the park and the victims. Where are Rush and Wolfe?"

"Asleep at the hotel with Andrew. They were at the park all night," Carl says. "The doc too. I was just about to join them."

"Then go. Get some sleep," Will says. "Anyone else who pulled an all-nighter too. The locals can continue excavations without us for a few hours with the bodies Oliver already marked. There's nothing to do until he rises and does another sweep." He stands. "The rest of us will process whatever evidence remains and continue gathering information on the victims. Dismissed."

Jason and Chandler's noses scrunch up almost in unison with displeasure at this order, but like a pimp Will ignores the other Alpha males and strolls out. That's one way to put the bastards in their places. I follow close behind into the lab next door. "Can you believe the fracking nerve of that bastard?" I ask.

"You weren't helping matters, you know," Will chides.

"They invite themselves on our case and do fudge all but judge us. And what is that crap about murdering babies? You know it was directed at us."

"It wasn't," Will insists. "And even if it was, who cares? I never wanted to join the pack anyway, even before I met you."

239

"But you heard them. They're still going to keep tabs on you and our children forever. One slip, and they'll kill them."

"That's not going to happen."

"It could! And what if our children *want* to join the pack? They'll be told they're freaks among freaks. Abominations. I—"

"Hey," Will says, pulling me into a hug. He just holds me for a few seconds, all but sucking out whatever poison just infected me in that meeting. I'm working myself in a frenzy for nothing. We don't even have kids yet, and I'm already overbearing. Here I thought Will would be the overprotective one. "Maybe you should go back to the hotel too. I didn't exactly let you get much sleep last night."

"And give them anymore ammunition? Hell to the no." I extract myself from his arms. "By the power of Greyskull, I *will* be the one to find these wolves."

He kisses my nose. "I believe you. Just please, play nice with Jason. He's a powerful ally, but God help us if we get on his bad side."

"I'll do my best." I peck his lips. "I'll continue on Imelda. Maybe interview the rangers again. Werewolf Doe is all yours and your new best friends. Play nice for the both of us." One more peck and I side-step out of the room before I lose my willpower. Points to prove, werewolves to catch. Today's the day. I can feel it in my bones. Of course I also felt it yesterday…

There's a copy of last night's report in the near deserted conference room. Adam smiles sheepishly before slinking out.

240

Nothing we didn't cover in the meeting. What…oh, fudge. I forgot to write my official report on Imelda. They had my notes, and I really didn't find anything, but my fellow bureaucrats thrive on our paperwork, so I have to waste time reviewing my notes and typing it up. I'm actually shocked Chandler didn't chide me when I walked in the door. He, along with the others who filter in and out of the conference room, have decided to go the passive aggressive route instead, glaring or in Nancy's case staring in an attempt to have me provide the X-rated details of last night. That particular honor is reserved for April only. I'm dying to call her and give her the literal blow-by-blow recap later. She'll help me solve my morning after pill dilemma as well. I have seventy-two hours to decide. More pressing problems to sort out right now. I need the frak out of this trailer before I start screaming at people. "I'm off," I tell Nancy in the lab. Time to fill in some gaps.

The ranger service still hasn't sent over the schedules, so my first stop should kill two birds with one stone. Appalachia Summit State Park has been closed since we arrived, so I have to flash my badge to the State Trooper to be allowed down the road. The press descended like vultures the day after we arrived. I count seven news vans, and I think Paula Zahn, Nana's favorite, is among them. They shout questions and shove cameras and microphones at my window as I pass. No sound bites from this gal, through Nana would flip if I were featured on *Dateline*. It's her guilty pleasure show. I used to like it too until I started this job. My days are filled with crime, I don't need my free time tainted with murders as well.

It seems the whole of the North Carolina State Police and forensics squad are camped out here as well. Three forensics van, close to a dozen squad cars, the ME's van, two ambulances, even a fire engine. I have to park on the side of the road itself and walk past uniformed officers and forensic analysts changing out of white space suits. One such astronaut holds the door to the Ranger station for me as he leaves and I enter. Ranger Rick stands center stage by a large map tacked onto a bulletin board surrounded by men and one woman dressed for a hike but all sporting badges and guns on their belts.

"...no, they searched this quadrant already," Rick says, pointing to the map. "If it's got lines across it, it's been covered. They said to focus on *this* area today." He taps a blank spot on the map. "According to the FBI, there might be another body there. They haven't been wrong yet."

"How many more do they think are out there?" the woman officer asks.

"We don't know," I answer. All heads pivot my way. "Best guess, at least four. We're assuming they've been active for six years with two kills a year, but that's really just an educated guess."

"Is it true this is a cult thing?" another officer asks.

"That's one avenue we're investigating. And I'm sure no one's said it, but I just want to thank you all for the hard work you and your fellow officers have put in on this case already. I know it's cold and kind of treacherous out there, but with each body we uncover we come that much closer to finding these monsters. You should feel proud for what you've done and are doing here."

"Thank you, ma'am," the woman says.

"No, thank *you*." I catch Rick's eyes. "Um, Ranger Mills, if you could spare a few minutes?"

"For you? Anything," he says with a smile. "I'll catch up when I'm done here. Just watch out for poison ivy. There isn't a person here who isn't covered in it." The searchers all nod as they pass me out the door, which I return each and every time. One should always show respect when it's due. When the last one files out, I smile at the ranger. He appears as exhausted as I feel with dark circles under his eyes, limp hair, and rumpled uniform. "So what can I do for the FBI now?" he asks with a yawn.

"We've been running you ragged, huh?" I ask.

"I haven't slept more than an hour or two since I found that damn leg. I tried to get Winsted out here to help, but he's still sick. Thank God Taylor gets back today. He can take over hand-holding duty. I swear, about half the people here have never set foot in a damn park before."

"Present company included," I say.

"That why I haven't seen you in days?"

"Pretty much."

"A damn shame. Not to talk out of turn, but your fellow agents leave something to be desired in the friendly department, especially the blonde one and your bloodhound."

"My who?"

"Sorry. That's what we've been calling Agent Montrose since, you know, he's found so many bodies."

"No, it's…very accurate." More than you know. "Just between us, we think he's a little psychic, if you believe in that sort of thing."

"Anything's possible, right? I mean, if you told me last week we had some fucked up cult chopping people up in the name of Satan or whatever in this park, I would have laughed in your face."

"It is pretty unbelievable," I concede, "especially since it all happened under your nose."

"Yeah. I guess."

"So you really didn't hear anything once in six years? Nothing suspicious at all?"

"I have been asked that question by three of your guys, two of the state investigators and myself once every hour. You have to understand, they did this shit in *my* backyard. I want to find them more than anyone else here. I've been wracking my brain trying to figure out how this happened for so long. How they pulled this off. People keep asking about howls and animal carcasses, but we're in the fucking woods. There are going to be dead animals. How was I supposed to know humans did it instead of animals? And I know I'm a suspect, which quite

244

frankly, pisses me the fuck off. I'm working my ass off for you people when I'm not supposed to even be here, and despite what Agent Montrose says, you think I'm an accomplice."

"You are one of only three who work here. And, to be honest, it *is* odd after years of them being active here, you saw nothing, knew nothing. We have reason to believe they were here every month for at least six years. How long have you been stationed here?"

"Eight. Since I got hired."

"And your colleagues?"

"Taylor's been with the service for fifteen years, Winsted about seven. Taylor was assigned here about a year after me and Winsted six months after him, but he's a floater. He rotates around three parks as needed."

"What can you tell me about them?" I ask.

"Not a hell of a lot. We just see one another when we pass the baton. This is a small park, only one guy on duty at all times."

"Based on what you do know, do you think either of them—"

"Could be in a cult? Hell no. Winsted's afraid of his own damn shadow, and Taylor is a bible thumper. I can't imagine either of them involved in mutilation and organized murder. Hell, I can't imagine them getting a damn parking ticket."

"Just because someone loves Jesus doesn't mean they're not able to take bribes for looking the other way," I point out.

"Last summer Taylor's church went to Africa for a month to help build houses or some shit. He's a do-gooder. I'd believe Jesus himself was involved before Kyle."

"What about Winsted? What makes you say he's a wimp?"

"There's two types of rangers: the bold and the beautiful. Rangers have the highest injury and mortality rate of any law enforcement agency. People come here to grow pot, to bury bodies, you name it. We have to fight man and beast." Sounds like being a F.R.E.A.K. "Now, I love nature. Always have, but I applied because I needed a job. I've grown to love it, especially busting people and saving lives. Winsted, though, he's more beauty than bold. He took this job to commune with nature. He has a Masters in Botany of Ecological studies or whatever. He's always doing these experiments or cataloguing plants. Even makes his own new agey salves, and they're damn good. I mean, he does the bold stuff, otherwise he'd be fired by now, but just judging for our few interactions, and how his wife treats him, if he is involved it's passively. Like if he did hear howls he'd be too shit scared to go investigate. I mean, his wife all but grabs my crotch at my Christmas party, and Adrian just rolls his eyes. I think I could have laid Patsy down on the floor and screwed her right there and then, and Adrian wouldn't have batted an eye. His wife still cuts his damn meat for him like he's

246

a fucking child. So, out of the three of us…yeah, me. But it isn't."

And I believe him. Be it the sincerity in his voice, the way he meets my eyes, or experience hard earned, I believe him. "There is one way to prove it."

"Anything."

"Your superiors have been slow to send us your schedules. We know when the people were abducted, approximately when they were killed, it's a simple cross-reference."

He nods. "I think I can help you there, actually." He moves toward the desk and sits in front of the computer, clicking away. "Our HR department is massively understaffed after all the government layoffs. That's why *we're* down to two permanent and one floater. There's my girl," he says with a grin. "Been meaning to call her anyway." He picks up the telephone and punches in the number. "A temp in HR." He listens for a few seconds. "Hey, Kayla. This is Ranger Rick Mills. How you doing, pretty lady?" He listens. "I know, I'm sorry. I've been working around the clock. One of the reasons I'm calling is to remedy that. I got two tickets to the Trace Atkins concert next week. Wanted to know if you want to go with me?" He listens. "Well, who doesn't love him? You better wear your best badonkadonk shorts though." Rick chuckles. "If you got it, flaunt it, baby, and boy do you got it." Dear Lord he and Oliver probably get along like a house on fire. Mills chuckles again. "Can't wait, babe, because let me tell you, things are nuts here.

The damn FBI won't leave me alone. They keep bothering me about my schedule and if I was working the nights those people were killed. I thought you guys were gonna fax them to the agents. I just don't want this hanging over my head, you know?" He's quiet again. "Oh, babe, that'd be great. You got their e-mail?" A second of silence. "Can you do it right this second? Just for my own peace of mind?" Another second. "You're an angel. I'll pick you up next Wednesday. Can't wait. Bye." Mills hangs up. "She's sending it now."

"Thank you."

"Any chance you might want to show your gratitude by buying me a drink?"

"Only if my boyfriend can come too." I grin. "Enjoy Trace and Kayla."

"I will do my damndest," he says as I step toward the door.

My smile grows when I step outside. That was worth the trip. I hope. I wait until I'm safely out of the park—it's like a damn obstacle course with all the cars and people—before I pick up the phone and call mobile command. Unfortunately, Chandler is the one to answer. "Agent Chandler," he says, already displeased with me.

"It's Alexander. I just left the park."

"What were you doing there?"

My job, jerk? "I wanted to re-interview Ranger Mills."

"Why? Oliver cleared him two nights ago. Glamoured him and asked point blank if he was involved. He wasn't. Do

248

you really think we'd let him work this case if we weren't a hundred percent sure he wasn't our perp? It was in Oliver's report. Did you even read it?"

"I…" Skimmed it. Maybe.

"Jesus Christ, Alexander. What—"

"Before you yell at me, just go check the e-mail in-box. The ranger's schedules should be in waiting in there. Ranger Mills called in a favor."

"I'll check." And he puts me on hold. Oh God, I need to stop giving this guy ammo to rake me over the coals. He thought I was a problem before Will and now probably believes I should be riding the short bus. Maybe I should. I really should have just read the damn reports. "Got them. Finally." He pauses. "Thank you."

"Just doing my job. Do you need me to come back? I was going to return to the college to pull Imelda and Tim Acker's transcripts. Maybe—"

"Sounds good. If we need you, we'll call." And he hangs up on me.

"Jerk," I mutter before throwing my phone onto the seat. Fine then. I'll stick to my plan. Got to college, re-interview Anika and Tim, interview Imelda's professors, campus security, then if there's time, ambush Adrian Winsted and Kyle Taylor when he gets back tonight. Heck, maybe it won't be necessary. With any luck the park records will lead us to the wolves accomplice, and I can be back in Kansas by tomorrow.

At the first stoplight a few miles from the park, I have to wait across from a Walgreens. Ugh, just what I need. More reality. I sigh. I *really* should stop and get the pill. I mean, a baby? How is that a good idea at this time in your life, Bea? We've been together less than a week. We have a dangerous job. We live with monsters. Heck, we practically *are* monsters. There is absolutely no space in our lives for a child. It's irresponsible and just downright insane. You know that. Despite what Will thinks, we are moving too fast. According to *Cosmo,* you should be in a relationship at least two years before progressing to the next level. You can't fully know a person in less than a year. Of course I was with Steven for two years and had no idea he had psychopathic tendencies, so strike one for *Cosmo*, but still. What do I truly know about William R. Price?

I know his favorite movie is *Patton*, his favorite color is blue, he's smart, protective, considerate in bed and out, he cares about things more than he lets on, he'd be a wonderful father...and I love him. I love him so darn much. *Cosmo* also said before taking that next step the most important things you need to know are how he is with money, if you're sexually compatible, if your life goals are the same, and if he'd make a good parent. In those respects, he earns an A+ in each category. And he is right on one front. Life is so precious. It's a crime to waste even a second of it. And—

A car horn knocks me out of my head. Oh fudge, the light's green. I turn the wheel and drive on. Jesus, if I were any more distracted a werewolf could transform right in front of me and I wouldn't even notice. Just as it takes me several seconds to realize the Walgreens fades away in my rearview. Huh. Guess my subconscious made the decision for me. Am I okay with it? As the pharmacy disappears, a smile creeps across my face until my stretched lips can't move any further. Guess so. Okay then.

Let forever begin.

THIRTEEN

BITCH FIGHT

Next stop on the "Bea Ties Up Loose Ends Because She's Been an Ineffective Lust Crazed Moron" tour—the name needs work, I know—is Crawford College and Tim Acker. Despite the airtight alibi, he deserves a second look. Due diligence requires I interview those in the study group and his friends. Maybe they've remembered something new in the past year. Heck, maybe he could have had someone else abduct her. Like a pack mate. I stop dead in the middle of the college courtyard as this realization smashes into my consciousness. Motherfu… I fall in love and lose a hundred IQ points.

Tim Acker could be a werewolf. Easily. What did Anika say? Really, I can't remember so I have to sit on a bench and check my notes. Here we are. Became secretive a few months before, then broke up with Imelda a week before she vanished. Goes to class, goes home. All about school. Thought he'd been cheating. Yeah, okay not a lot screams, "Here's a werewolf!" I didn't get that vibe from him either but that means precious little. Unlike werewolves us psychics don't have preternatural radar. According to Will, whenever he's around me he can literally feel my power prickling his skin like ants on the march. He's either gotten used to it or has hopefully grown to like it, as if I'm licking him. Like last night. Oh, I can still feel his tongue slowly trailing down my flesh and biting my...okay, there I go again. I've morphed into a crazed, hormonal teenage boy. Head in the freaking game, Alexander. Head in the game.

I phone Tim Acker, but once again it goes to voicemail. Avoiding me? Not for long. I have to ask two students, and still get lost, but do eventually find the Administration building. After a short wait, where I get to hear student after student whine about their grades to the attendant, it's my turn. The student aide prints out Tim and Imelda's class schedules and transcripts. The power of an FBI badge and threat of a warrant. As they're printing, my phone plays, "Hips Don't Lie." April.

"Special Agent Beatrice Alexander," I say.

"You had sex!" my best friend shouts over the phone.

The aide must have heard, heck people two buildings over probably heard, because she chuckles while handing me the transcripts. With a nervous smile, I take my papers and scuttle away. "Will you keep your voice down? I don't think they heard you in freaking Canada!"

"But you got laid! Finally! It's been years. I was worried you'd forgotten how."

"No, it was just like riding a bike." I bite my lip before gushing, "A flipping amazing, earth shattering, I'm surprised I can walk bike that I would sell my soul to be back on right this moment." I step out into the sunshine and hustle over to a bench. "He rented us a cabin. We made love in front of the fire on a sheepskin rug. Then the couch. Then the bed. Then in a rocking chair as the sun came up."

"Holy shit. It *is* a miracle you can walk. But was he good? Did you...shatter the furniture?"

"There wasn't a lamp left in the joint," I chuckle. "I never knew sex could be so...yummy. With Steven it was always so mechanical. I mean, it wasn't terrible, but I could have lived without it."

"Well, he was a psychotic asshole. Making sure you reached the end zone probably never crossed his mind. Which is why he burns in hell now." She pauses. "And, you know, for all those people he fed to that troll." She pauses. "So where are you now? Not in Kansas if you needed a cabin to sneak away."

"North Carolina. Wolves, witches, drama at every turn. Oliver beat up Will, I smacked Oliver, everyone hates me again, Will sort of proposed, I—"

"Okay, wait. Stop. Back up. Start at the beginning where everyone beats everyone else up to holy shitballs! You're getting married?" she shouts again.

I unravel the whole sordid tale, minus the attempted rape part, instead whitewashing it to a simple assault, all the way to the traffic light. The other end is silent for several seconds, then several more. "April? You still there?"

"I'm here. I just...don't know what to say."

"You're happy for me? You'll help me plan the wedding?" I suggest.

"Bea, of course if I'm happy…you're happy. But, I just," She pauses, "I think you need to slam the brakes a little here," she chuckles. "You've been a couple less than a New York minute. Three months ago you were at each other's throats because he was acting like a jealous asshole for absolutely no sane reason."

"We settled all that," I snap. "And I thought you liked him."

"I barely know him. Hell, *you* barely know him. And the majority of the time you have, you didn't particularly like him. He treated you like a child, your words, not mine. Not to mention all the practical shit you haven't considered. Have you discussed where you're going to live? What you'll both do for work? How you'll handle his not so little condition?"

"You're being a real big buzz kill right now, you know that?"

"No, I'm being your good friend, Bea. If I came and told you I was actively trying to get pregnant with a man I'd only been with for a week, you'd lock me in a closet and lecture me for a day. I'm going easy on you here." She pauses to calm herself down. If she's half as pissed as I am right now, it's gonna take her a year to cool off. "As long as I've known you, all you have talked about is having a family. A husband and babies and a house on Pooh corner. Even with Steven you very seriously considered his offer, remember? You didn't love him, but you were still a hair's breadth from moving in and having children with him."

255

"But I didn't because when it came down to it, I didn't love him. I love Will."

"That is not enough, Bea. Not by a long shot. At the end of the day, you dumped Steven because he wasn't your friend. You had no similar interests, you didn't have fun together, and you had nothing to talk about. He bored you to death. What do you and Will have in common? Does he make you laugh? When everything goes to absolute shit, can he be trusted to have your back? Be your champion when no one else will? Smack some sense into you even when he knows you won't speak to him for days after, like I know you're not gonna speak to me after this call? Can you, at this moment, answer 'Absolutely yes' to all of those questions?"

"Um glass houses much? You were only dating Javi four months before you got pregnant," I spit out.

"Yeah, but I'd known him since I was ten, and *you* were the one who asked me those exact same questions. And *I* could answer yes to them all." She sighs. "Look, I'm not saying break up with him or anything, just slow down, Bea. Please. If it's meant to be it will be months from now too."

My teeth are clenched so tight I could very well chip one. God, I so want to reach through the line and throttle her. I thought she'd be happy for me. The one person who would be. Is that so much to ask? One freaking person to congratulate us? Share our fraking joy for even a minute? What the hell is the matter with everyone?

"I have to go now. I'm working a case." Really I have to get off this call or I may begin shrieking at her and saying things I can never take back.

"Oh, don't do that. Don't you *dare* be pissed at me for telling you the truth. I—"

"Talk to you later. Bye." I hang up, fall back against the bench, and sigh.

She doesn't know. She can't know. She lives in the boring little ordinary world. With all that Will and I have seen and endured together, it's the equivalent of knowing one another since we were ten. We've seen each other at our best and worst, and I still love him. As for mutual interests, well I'm sure he'd spend the weekend marathoning *Doctor Who* or going to a karaoke club just like I'd suffer through football and war movies. When you've stared death in the face as many times as we have, it becomes infinitely clear you have to *carpe* some *diem* while you can. There *is* no time to waste.

And thinking of…

No more distractions. Tim Acker, where are you? According to his schedule he's assisting a teacher in the Social Sciences building. Intro to Anthropology. Yeah, that'll be useful in the real world. The class should just be ending. I hustle across campus, not easy in heels—Will would have packed my sexiest three inchers—but judging from the mass exodus through the doors, all classes inside have ended. I don't see him among the crowd, so on the off chance he's stayed late, I make my way to the second floor where a few stragglers remain in the halls. Okay, if Tim's not here, I'll try calling—

When I step inside the small, nearly empty classroom and see who stands at the desk packing her belongings into her satchel, my body realizes the severity of the situation before my brain catches on. I stop dead in the doorway, and my mouth even drops, but I don't know why the sight of this woman incurs such a reaction. I know her, I just don't know *where* I've...oh, God.

"Agent Alexander!" Patsy Winsted says with a smile. "Hello."

Park Ranger Adrian Winsted's wife. Who apparently Tim Acker works for. All those puzzle pieces suddenly fit together in the blink of an eye, even the ones I hadn't really noticed. All those cars in their driveway. The missing knick knacks. Anika's comment about how Tim suddenly got obsessed with school. The Social Sciences building beside where Imelda was thought to have been abducted. Mills' statement about Winsted being into plants and new age medicine. I'm a moron. If I'd asked more questions, paid more attention, I would not have just blindly walked into an empty room with a woman who can kill me with one word if she doesn't decide to just rip my limbs off with her bare hands.

I lose precious seconds assembling the puzzle, seconds the werewolf uses to study her prey. Once again my body is quicker on the uptake than my mind, plastering a grin on my face. I need to get the hell out of here. Wait for back-up to apprehend her, and by back-up I mean Oliver. The wolves can't get near her in case they go full horn dog, and the others don't stand a chance against a damn werewolf. But if I wait until nightfall, she could run. Of course if I take her now, it all ends. She goes to the Facility, I go home with Will. Shoot, I don't know—

"Are you okay, dear?" Patsy asks.

"I, uh, yeah," I say, shaking my frazzled head. Jesus, pay attention, Bea. "I'm sorry, I just, I know I know you but…" I fake groan in frustration.

"Patricia. Winsted. We met briefly when you interviewed my husband."

"Right! Oh my God, my ditz moments are growing more and more frequent. I'm surprised I can still tie my shoelaces. I'm so sorry. How is your husband feeling?"

"Not well at all. His fever was almost at a hundred and four this morning. We think its pneumonia, poor lamb. I was just on my way home to check on him."

"Oh, don't let me keep you. I-I'm actually looking for Tim Acker. His schedule said he'd be here."

"You just missed him," Patsy says.

"Do you by chance know where he went?"

"Why?" she asks, perfectly pleasant.

"Just need to ask one or two more questions to put him to bed as a suspect."

"Yes, he told me you'd interviewed him yesterday." Yeah, he probably called her while he was in the bathroom to ask how to behave during the interview. "He was most upset to have all this resurrected. I remember when that poor girl went missing. The whole of the campus treated that boy as if he were The Yorkshire Ripper."

"I'm being discreet, I promise," I say with a sweet smile.

"Well, if anyone knows about being discreet, I suppose it would be you, wouldn't it?" she asks with a matching smile.

"I'm sorry?" I chuckle.

Patsy fastens the strap of her satchel across her ample chest. "Of course, after watching this, I'm *shocked* you haven't been found out by now," she says, smile never wavering.

My stomach clenches. "I don't—"

"The F.R.E.A.K.S. really should make their agents take acting lessons before putting them in the field," she says, the grin slowly dropping. "Perhaps they wouldn't have such a high mortality rate then. But let's cut the shit, shall we?" She plops down into her chair with a sigh. "You've caught me. Intentionally or not. *Not* judging from that stupefied expression on your face when you walked in and your lack of back-up, which more or less puts us on an even playing field as my boys are absent also. It gives us each a sporting chance, which, as you've seen firsthand, I am largely in favor of."

She's also in favor of toying with her prey before devouring it judging from that speech and the fact she hasn't tried to kill me yet. "Is that what you gave to Imelda? And Jackson and Enrique, and countless others? A sporting chance?"

"They had the time it took us to change to flee as far as they could get. Some even made it to the ranger's station."

"Where your husband turned a blind eye to their screams," I finish for her.

"*Son.* Adrian is my son. Everyone just assumes we're married, and it's easier to let them go on thinking that. Second best age remedy besides vampirism, lycanthropy. Adrian was five when I accepted the gift. Guess how old I am. Really guess," she insists.

"You don't look a day over fifty," I say with a cruel grin.

"I look thirty," she says with a sneer.

I suppress a scoff. "Of course you do. Gals who look thirty often have to resort to lust potions to keep the boys interested."

Her sneer blooms into a full blown scowl. "Women have only two weapons in their arsenal when dealing with men: a keener mind and what's between their legs. Any one of my boys could easily win against me in physical battle, which in the patriarchal misogynistic lycanthrope world is all that matters. I have established that need not be the case. In fact, I believe my little experiment has proven what history has shown already. Matriarchal societies thrive better than male dominated paradigm. There has never been a female Alpha with a pack before me, little girl, and mine *is* thriving. My boys all have college degrees, they give back to the community, and are gainfully employed. To achieve that, to lift them to reach their fullest potential, to guide them, one does what one must."

So she's basically roofieing boys and murdering innocent people to strike a blow for the feminist movement. It has nothing to do with the fact she wants to bang hot guys to feel young and desirable again, and the fact she likes killing? Please.

"And what? Your last victim dissed Gloria Steinem so you decided to eat him? Or maybe he just decided he didn't like being your sex toy anymore and was leaving the Mason Family pack?"

"Loyalty and trust are paramount to the functionality of any society or even the smallest of social groups. Lars questioned my leadership. I gave him the most precious of gifts, vitality and strength while connecting with any animal's basic animal instinct, not to mention entrance to my body whenever he desired it. And what did I receive in return? He spread discord through my pack. He even threatened to inform the Eastern Pack of our existence. I did only what was necessary to protect me and mine as any good leader would."

Yeah, he was so dumping her and she couldn't just go the Hagen Daas and crying during a Jane Austen marathon like a normal gal. "Well, it didn't protect you, did it? Your son's being arrested as I speak, and Jason Dahl's been begging for all your heads for his trophy case. You surrender, come quietly, I can personally guarantee the physical safety of your pack. If you care about them, truly care, all you can do is—"

As fast as quicksilver, Patsy raises her finger up at me. *"Excessum!"*

Base survival instinct twirls my body sideways into the hallway to use the door as cover. The door frame where I stood a millisecond ago scorches black as if hit by a blowtorch. The power of a magical curse. Jesus Christ. I take one second to let my brain catch up with my body. She just tried to kill me. Guess playtime's over. I remove my gun, take a deep breath, and peek around the corner.

"Excessum!"

I take cover again. There isn't time to aim. Fine, two can play at this, beyotch. Ready…set… I poke my head around the corner, and her mouth opens. *"Excess—"*

Never bring a curse to a psychokinesis fight. Before she can get the third syllable out, the bitch lifts off her feet, flying backwards. Unfortunately, even after a year of training, I still have little control over my strength and aim. To both our horrors, Patsy shoots straight through the big bay window, glass shattering around her, and falls out of sight. Her scream cuts short a moment later after a thud. Oh crap.

I sprint across the classroom, glass crackling under my heels, and peer out the window. Patsy lies unmoving on the sidewalk two stories down, blood already seeping from the dozen cuts covering her from head to toe. The worst of the blood pours from underneath her head where she must have hit it. Students already run toward the unconscious woman. Double crap.

Running as fast as possible in heels, I dash out of the classroom and down the hall and stairwell. Halfway down, I pull out my cell phone. I have a voice message. No time. "Did you get—" Chandler begins.

"I need back-up at Crawford College ASAP. Patsy Winsted just tried to kill me. Get here. *Now!*" Line still open, I slip the phone in my coat pocket and continue down the first floor hallway and out the door.

I lose another second to gain my bearings, but veer left and continue around the building. The crowd's grown larger, about ten people now stand around chattering, but the source of the commotion is gone. Glass, blood, bystanders, no evil werewolf. Crap. Crap! "Where'd she go?" I shout.

A girl with purple hair points across the grassy commons. There's only one figure running and pushing people out of her way. Damn she's gotten far, about fifty yards. Flipping werewolves. Running. Why did it have to be running?

I kick off my heels and start after her as fast as possible, which after almost two months of recovery from surgery and daytime television, isn't that fast. The only thing I've got going for me is she's limping and decades older. That almost evens the playing field. Almost. "In pursuit of suspect," I huff into the phone, "toward the Admin building and south parking lot. Excuse me. Excuse me," I say to the students I brush past. Okay, I all but body slam them which just slows me down further. Patsy glances back a few times, and must see me coming because she picks up her pace. I attempt to do the same, somehow getting a second wind. Soon the gap between us grows smaller and smaller, forty yards, twenty-five. I can even see her frightened, round bloody face as she glances back again. She should be scared. With a thought, I knock her aside onto the grass to slow her down. Of course once I reach her, I'm not sure what to do next. I could shoot her—boy do I want to shoot her—but I have silver bullets in here. It could kill her. I—

Wham!

It's as if a freight train knocks into my back, sending me toppling sideways to the ground. The air is forced from my lungs at the same time my legs give out. Instantaneous pain begins in my still tender elbow before I even hit the grass. When I do, agony spreads to my knees, my other arm, for a second everywhere. When I realize what happened, that someone body slammed me, that same someone grabs my hair and flings me onto my back. My head hits the pavement so hard I blink back tears. Fudge. Tim Acker looms above me, panting as hard as I am. The fuzz just begins to clear as Tim bends down to pick something up. I don't grasp that it's my gun until the instant that steel weapon's pointed right at my face. My genius body reacts again. As trained, I sweep his legs with my own. The boy falls onto the grass in front of me. He fires but the bullet hits inches from my head into the concrete. Damn, the ringing in my ears is downright agonizing, but I still manage to lift up my leg and bring it down as hard as possible against Tim's stomach. He drops the gun and curls into a ball, twitching as he tries to draw breath. Down for the moment.

When I sit up, the now familiar spins begin, but I struggle through. Another damn concussion. Wonderful. I don't attempt to stand—learned that from experience—and instead get on my knees and crawl toward Tim. He's reaching for the gun, but I get it before him. "You're under arrest for assault and accessory to multiple murders. You have—"

His fist comes out of nowhere, smashing right into my ribs. I don't hear a crack, damn tinnitus, but judging from the white hot searing pain, he's broken at least one. I shrink in anguish and collapse in on myself into a heap. Tim leaps up, grimacing the whole time. I guess since fight didn't work out for him so well last time, he chooses flight this go round. Still clutching his stomach, he staggers the way Patsy fled.

Oh, hell no.

With all the gawkers standing around, even recording this madness with their phones, I can't shoot without risking hitting one of them. Option B it is. As best as I can, I focus on his head, his brain, imagining all the blood vessels snaking around those little gray cells. I squeeze one, a dozen, I don't know, but it works. Tim howls in misery and stops his dash to grip the back of his head, even clawing at his hair and skull. Not good enough. I literally rip the vessels apart. The shriek the werewolf lets out is as inhuman as he is. The boy collapses in a faint. He'll heal. Maybe.

I somehow rise to my feet and stagger toward the unconscious undergrad. Blood pours from his nose and ears as he stares up at me with vacant, bloodshot eyes, but he's breathing. Well, one down. I gaze up where Patsy was but of course she's gone. Ran to save her own butt. So much for loyalty. With a sigh, okay more a pant than a sigh, I sit beside the boy, shaking my head. Looks like she wasn't worth it, kid. But nothing and no one is *ever* worth your soul.

FOURTEEN

EMERGENCY CARE

"...discharging of weapon in a crowd, use of ability in public, not properly identifying yourself as an FBI agent, and let's not forget failing to wait for back-up, oh, and letting the suspect get away! Could you have created more of a clusterfuck?"

"Paul, enough!" Will snaps at his friend.

"No, you are done, *done* protecting her, Will," Chandler snaps back. "I swear to Christ you both have literally fucked each other's brains out."

I suppose I should care I'm being berated by my boss, huh, that sounds funny "being berated by my boss," but yeah, pain killers are awesome. And I suppose I should care I have a broken rib, mild concussion, and scraped everything, not to mention I'm in the hospital. *Again.* But...Demerol. I love you. And I love this man holding my hand so damn much. He smells great. And he's defending me even though he shouldn't be. And he really, really shouldn't be.

"Don't you speak to us that way, Paul or so help me—"

"No, he's right," I chime in. "Not about, you know, f-ing my brains out because that's like physically impossible or

268

whatever, but…yeah. I messed up a little. But I mean, we got here, we got the bad guys eventually, right?"

"What have we got? Patricia Winsted is still in the wind with at least one other murderous werewolf, if not a dozen more. And we don't *know* because *you* didn't do your damn job. You should have spent more than five minutes interviewing Adrian Winsted and the other rangers. You should have noticed Tim Acker *lives* at the same address as Patricia Winsted. It's right there on his current driver's license and transcript. You should have interviewed his alibi witnesses, most of whom were students of Winsted, including her former TA Lars Tinning, our latest victim, who by the way, also has the same address as Patricia Winsted! Or maybe if you had just answered your damn phone, or listened to your voice mail, you would have known we were about to apprehend Adrian Winsted and wouldn't have walked right up to his mother and almost gotten yourself killed!"

Will places his open hand on Chandler's chest and lightly pushes him back. "I'm serious, man, back the hell off her right now," my boyfriend snaps. "She admitted she messed up. It's done. All we can do now is move forward."

"Don't you ever put your hands on me, Will," Chandler growls right in Will's face.

"Or what?" Will growls right back.

For whatever reason—drugs!—I start giggling. "You two look like you're gonna kiss." Both men glance at me. "Don't-Don't let me stop you."

Chandler rolls his eyes and takes a step back. "Adrian Winsted has pneumonia and will remain here at least overnight until he's out of the woods, then we'll take him to mobile command. Not that he's talking. The doctors couldn't find anything wrong with Acker, so they're working on his discharge papers. Dahl's with him now. She's," Chandler says nodding at me, "in no fit state to help anyone, can we agree on that at least?"

"Absotootly," I say.

Chandler rolls his eyes again. "We'll have them sedate the hell out of Acker, and you can transport him and her back to mobile command. You have a problem with that, Agent Price?"

"I think we can handle that, Agent Chandler," Will replies with the same snooty tone.

"Me too," I say.

"Fine." Chandler throws open the curtain and with equal frustration closes it. Thank God he's gone. He was totally harshing my buzz. And making my head ache with his anger, though that could just be the concussion.

"Asshole," Will mutters. "He's acting as if you were the only one working the case. *He* didn't notice any of that shit either. None of us did."

"But I should have. It was right in front of me, all of it, but I just didn't notice. And people could have died. Heck, I could have died. Like two times today."

"I know," Will says quietly.

"And I fought with April, and I let a psycho get away, and I'm in the hospital again, and I lost my shoes, and I guess it's a good thing we had sex last night because it looks like we won't be for a super long time because I suck so bad, and everyone thinks so, and they're right, and…I'm sorry."

"It-It's okay," he says. Yeah, so don't believe him. "I'm going to work on getting us out of here. You rest, okay?"

Will kisses my forehead before leaving. Oh, I do so love him to bits and bobs and turtle nobs. I lie back down on the gurney, wincing the whole time down. Even with my eyes closed the world spins. Yeah, I think I need to lay off the drugs from here on. I've messed up enough. Time to make up for it. And there's a lot of work to do now. While I was gabbing with April, I missed a call from Will. Adrian Winsted's work schedule matched the dates the victims disappeared. They were arresting him and beginning the search of the house when I called for help. He was the only one at home, but there's an APB out for Jamal Greene, the African American man I saw with Patsy. Everyone in three states are looking for her too. They can't get far. At least I hope not. She may have prepared for this contingency and could be halfway to Mexico with her lover by now for all I know. This may have not been the first time she's had to move on quickly. At least now we have her name and photos. Some other werewolf is bound to recognize her. We should probably put their photos out to the press too.

The police and campus security descended on Tim and me within a minute, and I was in no fit state to control the scene.

271

All I could do was keep him unconscious and insist on being in the same ambulance as him to continue that job. It would have been better if I'd have dragged him back to mobile command. Another Alexander screw-up. I'm useless. And exhausted.

She was within my grasp. I had her. She was *right there,* and I lost her. Heck, I had her days ago if I'd only pulled my head from the clouds. If only I'd answered when Will called today. If only…if only. No more. My mess, my job to clean it up. Just after a little nap.

"Babe?"

I jerk awake, wrenching my torso in the process. Fucudge that hurts. Will stands by my side. "Huh?"

"You fell asleep," Will says, helping me slowly sit up. "It's time to go."

"Oh. Good."

Since some co-ed stole my heels after I discarded them, Will slips a donated pair of flip flops onto my feet before aiding me off the gurney into a wheelchair. Even that hurts. Heck, drawing breath hurts. A broken rib will do that. And the hits keep coming. Jason Dahl waits by the front entrance along with two police officers and a drooling Tim Acker in a matching wheelchair. They still have my silver cuffs on him though. I'm gonna need those back. Dahl wheels Tim outside into the frozen night toward the awaiting SUV with us trailing behind.

"Sure you don't want me to come with you?" Dahl asks.

"No," Will replies. "Stay here and guard the son in case they try to spring him."

"Is that wise? If she does come, Patsy could put the sex whammy on him," I point out.

"It's just for an hour or two until Oliver wakes," Will explains. "He'll take over then."

"Shouldn't he go to the other parks Winsted worked to find more bodies?" I suggest.

"That can wait. We're stretched too thin as it is." Will opens the passenger door as Dahl lifts Acker into the back of the car like a bride. "And it's certainly not something for you to worry about right now."

Though it aches like a mother, I somehow stand and climb into the SUV. Damn, even fastening the seatbelt hurts. Yeah, lots of desk work in my future. So not complaining. Will shuts my car door, says something to Dahl, then gets into the driver's seat. If I never see the inside of a hospital again, it will be too soon.

I keep watch on Acker in the rearview mirror as we pull into traffic then the lonesome four-lane road to mobile command. Lying back there, now literally drooling on his seatbelt, he seems so docile. Like a skinny, floppy haired dweeb not a killing machine. Still. One false move and he gets another brain aneurysm. He didn't set off my psychopath radar at all. Maybe because he's only a few years younger than me. Twenty and his life is over just because he fell in with the wrong crowd.

He may have tried to kill me a few hours ago, but I still feel a twinge of sympathy for him.

I can imagine how it all played out. Patsy spots him in her class, this cute weakling with a penchant for domineering females, and has to have him for her harem. She pays him special attention in class, maybe even inviting him over for dinner and "special tutoring." She's an attractive, sensual, experienced woman who probably banged him the first chance she got. What man could resist? Especially when she also offers him preternatural strength, power, acceptance, sex, hell she probably threw in an X-Box as well. She turns him and to prove his loyalty, his fidelity to his new one and only, he kills the girl he loved when she asks. Welcome to the family, Tim.

"What's the matter?" Will asks. "Are you in pain?"

"No, I'm just…I kind of feel for him."

"Why? That little shit shot at you. He was going to kill you. I have half a mind to pull over this car and rip his goddamn heart out for what he did to you."

He could do it too. Literally. Just ask the last man who tried to kill me. "I'm fine. It could have been a lot worse."

Will glances at me, that scowl of his deepening. "Yeah, it could have been. Or it could have been avoided if you had just answered your goddamn phone," he snaps.

"I'm sorry, you're mad at me?"

"Of course I'm mad at you! I'm pissed to fuck! You almost died. Again! Some asshole laid his hands on you, broke your damn rib, shot at you, put you in the hospital and-and-and

274

there wasn't a fucking thing I could do about it! You were out there fighting for your life while I'm miles away on the goddamn phone having to listen to it! When I heard that gunshot…" He shakes his head. "No. Never again. I'm not doing this anymore. This is our last case. The second we get back to Kansas, we're putting in our notice."

My eyes narrow at him. "Wait…what?"

"We're quitting the F.R.E.A.K.S. It's over. We're done."

"Uh…shouldn't we discuss this a bit before we do anything drastic? You don't get to just up and declare I'm quitting my job without *talking* to me first about it."

"What the hell is there to talk about?"

"Um…what we'll do for money? Where we'll live? Or are you going to just make a unilateral decision on those subjects as well?" I snap.

"Why are *you* mad at *me* here?" he snaps back. "We discussed this just this morning."

"Yeah, but talking and doing are two very different things, Will," I point out. "And we barely talked in the first place."

"What, you *want* to stay with the F.R.E.A.K.S? You like getting shot at? Being surrounded by dead bodies? Ending up in the hospital every other day?"

"No. Of course not. But there are practical considerations to work through. Like where would we live?"

"I figured San Diego. We can stay in a hotel or with your grandmother until we find a house."

"Jobs?"

"I could become a P.I. or join a private security firm. Maybe even start my own. I have enough money to last us awhile anyway. And, if you want, you can go back to teaching or tutoring, at least until you get pregnant."

"So you want me to be barefoot and pregnant in the kitchen?"

"I thought that's what we both wanted, Bea. You can work. I don't care. All I do care about is that my wife and kids are happy, healthy, and safe. That can't happen if she's chasing after werewolves and trolls."

"Well, I'm not your wife yet, Will Price," I point out, my blood still boiling.

"That's an easy fix. Hell, there was a sign for a Justice of the Peace on the way to the cabin. We can be in and out in ten minutes."

"How romantic," I say, rolling my eyes. "Can drooly back there be our ring bearer?"

"You want me to stop this car? Get down on one knee? Wait a week so I can organize a flash mob and fireworks for you?"

"You *asking* full stop would be a good start! You just assume I'd blindly go along with all of this!"

"So you *don't* want to marry me?" he shouts back.

"Of course I want to marry you, you moron! I just want to be asked first!" I holler back.

"Fine then! Will you marry me?" he spits out.

"Yes! God! Was that so flipping hard? Ugh! You drive me nuts sometimes!"

"The feeling is more than mutual, babe!"

He stares straight ahead, and I snap my head right to stare out my window. He's so damn infuriating sometimes. Damn it, my heart's racing a mile a minute. He…wait. My gaze whips back his way. "Uh…did we just get engaged?"

Will's scowl softens as his mouth grows slack. "Um…I think so." He catches my eyes, shock morphing into glee and pure happiness just like mine. Even our grins grow together. "Holy shit," he chuckles.

"I know, right?" I chuckle back. "And you meant it?"

"Of course I meant it! I love you so much, Bea, so goddamn much." He grabs my hand and kisses the top. "I was so scared earlier, I damn near lost my mind. If anything happened to you, if I lost you…you're just, you're it for me, you know?"

"Yeah, I know," I say with tears in my eyes.

"Then let's do it. Let's just fucking do it. I love—"
WHACK!

Our car shimmies as something hits us with the force of a boulder falling from the top of the Empire State Building. I barely have time to look back and see another SUV veering towards us before it smashes into us again. There's nothing else to do but scream as Will loses control of the car, sending us spinning and jerking. My head thwacks against the window. Sharp, blinding pain fries my already taxed mind. What...? Another slam. We're sideways. Upside down. Sideways again as we roll, glass raining all around us while metal screeches as it twists and bends. Something big and white explodes in front of me, and a moment later another jolt of searing pain begins in my nose. That anguish is nothing compared to the slice that rockets down my right forearm, and the agony in my side. Then we stop. The car is finally still. What...why...what...something's dripping from my head. Down my throat. Did I eat pennies? Everything's fuzzy. Red. Don't like it. Close eyes. Black. Pain. All over. What...?

"Bea?" Will moans far far away. "Bea, baby, don't—"

More metal and crunching glass. Cold air.

"Hurry," a woman says. "Get him out."

Need to open eyes. Hurts. Everything hurts.

"Now, now, don't do that handsome," the woman purrs. "How's about a kiss instead?"

My left eye opens enough I can make out a woman hovering over a bloody Will while an African American man flings something over his shoulder. I don't have the energy to keep my eye open any longer. A click.

"You want to come with us?" the woman asks.

"Yes," Will whispers.

Bad. Not good. The car shifts. Open...

I force my eye open again to watch as Will, now outside the SUV, kisses the woman again. She pushes him off her with a giggle before taking his hand. They start up the hill littered with bits of our car. Wrong. Bad. Black. Back to black. Bye-bye Will. Bye-bye love.

*

"Trixie. Please. My darling, please. Please, please, please… come back to me. I beg you. Please do not leave me. Please."

Oh, God. Oh God. Pain. Everywhere. Beeping. So loud. I moan but that hurts as well.

"Trixie?"

"Will?" I whisper.

I force open my eyes and glance around. IV. Beeping heart monitor. Concerned vampire sitting at my bedside holding my hand. Same arm wrapped in gauze to the elbow with red stuff seeping through. Blood. My blood. Oh, damn my arm hurts. And my side. And my nose. And head. Okay, everything hurts.

"Trixie?" Oliver asks again, this time rising and saying it inches from my face. Oh, he's so beautiful. No man ever has or ever will be as beautiful as the man before me. He's so worried, with his eyes scrunched and lips trembling. I try to raise my hand to touch his furrowed brow but can only lift a single finger.

"Hi," I whisper.

"Hello, my darling," he whispers back with a sad smile.

279

"Oh, don't be sad," I whisper. "I don't want to make you sad ever again."

"I am not sad, my darling." He kisses my forehead, lips lingering for several seconds. "Not anymore."

"Good," I say, voice sounding distant. Away. Lucky it.

My Oliver returns to his chair, eyes now rimmed red with blood tears. Oh, I've made him cry. I don't want to make him cry. He grabs a tissue to blot them dry. "I…do you know where you are?"

"The hospital. Again. I just left here. What…? Car. Someone hit us. Will. Where's Will? Is he okay? Where—" I attempt to sit up but don't make it an inch before the pain intensifies to eleven along with the nausea.

Oliver leaps up again to stop me. "Trixie, do not move. Please."

"What's the matter with me? What happened?"

"Your SUV rolled down an embankment. You have a severe concussion and inch long gash along your forehead. You almost bled out from it and the cut down your arm. You required a blood transfusion. One centimeter to the right and it would have severed your artery. You may have nerve damage though. You also broke several ribs, your nose, along with a myriad of cuts and bruises. You were…lucky it was not far worse."

"Lucky." I certainly don't feel it. "How long was I out for?"

"Twelve hours. The doctors…" He stares down. "It matters not. I knew you would prove them wrong."

"And where's Will? Is he okay? Tim Acker?"

Oliver stares at me again, all tea and sympathy. "What do you recall about the accident?"

"Uh, Will and I were fighting. Then we…made up, and another SUV hit us. I guess we crashed. Then all I remember is a man and woman at our car. She kissed Will and he…walked away." The nausea rises all on its own this time. "It was Patsy Winsted, wasn't it? It was. I recognize her now."

"The samaritans who aided you after the crash reported seeing a woman fitting Winsted's description, along with Jamal Greene getting into a white SUV with two injured men before driving off. There is an APB out for their car now."

She came back for him. Tim. And she took my fiancée with her as a bonus. Oh God. Oh God, no. This isn't happening. I can't breathe. Panic overtakes even my pain. "She must have enchanted him. Will wouldn't have gone with her otherwise."

"Of course not," Oliver says, taking my hand again. He's so calm. How is he so calm?

"Well, what are you doing to find him?" I all but shriek. "God—" Oliver winces, "knows what she's doing to him! Why aren't you out looking for him? You need to go look for him! Please! Go! Find him!"

"Trixie, you need to calm yourself," Oliver orders. "Dozens are searching for him. Someone had to be here for you, and—"

"I don't matter!" I shout.

"You matter to me!" he roars back. "You stupid bloody woman you matter to *me*! They considered cutting into your brain to quell the swelling! There was a chance you would never wake! And I had to sit here, I *had* to be here in case you…" His face contorts in anguish. It's as if he literally bites his tongue to stop the words. "Hang Will. No matter the reason that man walked away on his own two legs and left you to die. *He* does not matter."

"He matters to *me*," I whimper through the tears which I haven't the strength to even wipe away. "He matters to me."

Oliver stares into my eyes and even through my tears, I see his fury. His fear. His sadness. I cannot bear it. Not one more piece of misery. I'll crack into a trillion pieces. I close my eyes. "If you care about me, truly care about me like I believe you do, if you are really my friend, you'll do this for me, okay? I can't right now, so I need you to. Please. Find him. For me. *Please.*"

I sense him still staring, still fuming, still miserable. He doesn't move or make a sound for several seconds. "I shall inform the doctor you are awake. Rest. For me. Rest."

When I open my eyes a second later, the door is open but my friend has vanished. So I do the only thing I'm capable of right now. I lie in this damn bed in agony. Twenty-four hours. Twenty-four hours ago I was wrapped in Will's arms, making love to the man I adore, and since then I've been cursed, shot at, broken, admitted to the hospital twice, got engaged, and watched helpless as my fiancée left me to die. He left me for an enchantress who is either torturing him or…God help me. God help us both. Please return him to me. Please return him to me.

Please.

FIFTEEN

CIRCLE OF HELL

There is not a doubt in my mind karma exists. What goes around always comes around. It may not happen right away, or how others might like, but in the end we all get what's coming to us. I am twenty-seven years old. I have intentionally murdered two men, been an active participant in the deaths of over a dozen more, almost blew out my brother's brains, and ended the immortality of sixteen vampires. I've lied to my family, I've fornicated out of wedlock, and possibly drove my own mother to suicide. It was all in the name of self-preservation or nobility. I never took a millisecond of joy from my crimes. But the blood isn't just on my hands, it covers me from head to toe, and like Lady Macbeth no amount of scrubbing will ever wash it away. So maybe I deserve this. Maybe I deserve to be consigned to this circle of hell I now find myself in. Stuck in this hospital bed held together by strings and staples. The gash on my arm from thumb to elbow alone required two dozen stitches. Every breath is like inhaling glass, and I can only perform the act through my mouth. But the physical pain I could handle. Your body doesn't go to hell, your mind and soul do. I'm there now. Without question, I am in hell.

I owe Oliver an apology. If he felt half as helpless, as aggravated, as terrified while he waited by this very bed for me to survive as I do now, well I wouldn't wish that on my enemy let alone my best friend. Not that he's come back so I can apologize. Everyone else has stopped by though. Chandler to interrogate me. Wolfe to bring me my book and some chocolate. Carl, Nancy, Dr. Neill, even Jason Dahl and Adam Blue popped by with more questions. Andrew, my self-appointed hospital companion, came at nine AM and hasn't left since. He makes valiant efforts to keep my mind occupied with terrible television, and reading from his Braille version of *The Heart is a Lonely Hunter*. There was even talk of calling my grandmother. I woke just in time to avoid that particular hell, thank God. I've put her through enough already for seven lifetimes.

At least my visitors answer my myriad of questions. If they left me completely in the dark I would probably lose my mind. Authorities found the car that hit us abandoned in a parking lot ten miles from the crash site. It was registered to Jamal Greene. The working theory is Jamal picked Patsy up after our altercation, and they watched the hospital from the parking lot until they saw us load Tim, and followed us from there. One cataclysmic car crash later, they scooped up Tim and Will, stole another car, and are now holed up either in a motel or some secondary location like a cabin purchased under a fake name for just this contingency. It's not the first time Patricia Winsted AKA Patricia Chambeau has pulled a disappearing act with her son Adrian.

Some werewolf in Dahl's rolodex recognized the picture he sent of our hybrid. Finally. Patricia Renee Winsted was born in Edmonton, Canada to a High Priestess mother and normal father sixty-eight years ago. Always the pioneer, she earned her Ph.D. in Cultural Anthropology from the University of Vancouver back when such a thing was unheard of. It was there she met and married her professor Martin Chambeau. Her son Adrian was born five months after the wedding. At some point Dr. Patsy Chambeau began an affair with Daniel Kelley, a member of the Western Canadian Pack. They kept the affair a secret until Daniel turned up missing—how he remains to this day. The affair was uncovered, her hybrid status was not. Prof. Chambeau met with an unfortunate accident as well, dropping dead of an apparent heart attack all of a week before Kelley vanished. No foul play suspected until now. The killing curse mimics a heart attack. The working theory is she wanted to run away with her werewolf lover, he wouldn't leave his wife, so he had to die too. She does not take rejection well.

Unfettered by the chains of domesticity, Dr. Chambeau traveled the world with her then three-year-old son, teaching in St. Petersburg Russia, Norway, even Denmark while publishing multiple articles about the perpetuation of the werewolf and witch "myth" through Eastern and Western cultures. She must have grown bored with said myths or had a feminist awakening became Dr. Winsted who focused on matriarchal tribes and those who worshiped female gods in South America and Africa while working as a fully tenured professor at Vanderbilt

286

University. That is until seven years ago when she was forced out after a scandal involving an affair with a male student and married colleague. Crawford College was the only place that would take her. No waves made since, until now, but I'll bet we'll find more than our fair share of missing persons wherever Dr. Chambeau/Winsted planted roots. The police have already uncovered a body at another park Adrian Winsted worked. In truth we'll probably never know the full extent of her monstrosity. Her son sure isn't talking.

Adrian Winsted hasn't uttered a word except "lawyer" since his arrest yesterday. In light of my attack and Will's abduction, the pneumonic man was stabilized and whisked away to mobile command under the care of Dr. Neill while I was in my mini-coma. To err on the side of caution—really in case Will is forced to spill his guts—both the team and mobile command were moved to new locations. All our passwords had to be changed, and the mansion in Kansas is apparently on lockdown in case Patsy decides to storm the Bastille. No way in hell. She's still around. She took a big damn risk getting Tim back, she's not leaving her own flesh and blood to our mercy.

So in the twenty-four hours since she was ID'd, we have next to nothing helpful to find her. And I'm stuck in this bed, my mind alternating between a snuff and porno film starring my fiancée. He's not dead, that much I know. She took him for a reason. Either she fell madly in lust with him at first sight and just *needed* to have him for her new pack, or she wanted someone she could control to keep as a bargaining chip.

287

Not sure which is worse. I just keep replaying their kiss. Him taking her hand and walking away as I bled to death. Did they even make it off the side of the road before he had his hand up her skirt? Has he even *thought* about me or have they just been screwing like bunnies as I'm lying here helpless in hell?

I know it was an enchantment. I know he wasn't in his right mind. I know he loves me. I know deep down he's fighting through her tricks to come back to me. But as the hours pass with no news, no word, with only those images and my imagination to pass the time, the resentment and anger begin to build until I can't see past them. He should be here. With me. By my side. We should be planning our wedding or looking at houses in San Diego online. *He should be here.* I fought like hell for that man. I took on myself, the entire F.R.E.A.K.S. squad, my friends, a troll worshiping cult, even the man himself, and goddamn it I won. He can't fight through a lust spell and an ancient werewolf? I'm in here hacking up bloody phlegm and consulting with plastic surgeons, and he's in some love shack banging a murderess. Every time I look at him from here on, will I be able to get those images out of my head? I don't know. I really don't. But I do know the alternative, never seeing him again, is a trillion times worse to contemplate. So I'll fight. I will fight and fight and fight until my last breath. Starting now.

"I want to check myself out of the hospital," I tell Dr. Pali.

"That is an extremely bad idea, Agent Alexander," the doctor says. "We don't know the extent of the nerve damage to your arm. You can barely move your thumb. You had very serious head trauma—"

"We have an MD on staff. She can look after me. Just give me the damn form to sign that promises I won't sue you if I keel over and a prescription for pain pills that don't make me loopy."

Dr. Pali turns to Andrew. "Agent DuChamps, perhaps you could—"

"I know this woman, doctor," Andrew says. "I'm surprised she didn't just stroll out on her own yet."

"And I will," I tell the doctor, "leaving you legally responsible for my health. So go get me the damn form before I prove my friend here right."

Pali shakes his head. "Fine. But if you become dizzy or nauseous, you must come back immediately. And someone needs to be with you twenty-four seven for the next three days, and if you sleep, you need to wake every two hours."

"I'm not going to sleep," I snap.

"We won't let her out of our sight," Andrew says without a hint of irony.

The doctor shakes his head again before finally leaving.

"Jesus Christ, I could break out of prison easier," I say, gently removing my covers. Oh hell, even that slow, light movement sends pain rocketing all through my body.

"The doctor is right, you know," Andrew says. "You should stay here. Recover. Will wouldn't want you putting your health in jeopardy for him."

289

"Well, he can yell at me when I get him back."

Okay, here comes the hard part. I take a deep breath, and in one quick movement, I sit all the way up, my fingernails digging into my one good hand to stop the screams. Three cracked ribs. I'm wrapped up like a mummy underneath my gown in Ace bandages which aren't doing a lick of good. "Andrew, three feet to your left on the floor are the clothes Nancy brought. I'm going to need your help getting dressed."

"Beatrice, if you can't even—"

"Just do it, please!"

Even if he weren't blind, I probably couldn't muster any embarrassment as I get naked. It takes all my concentration not to howl in agony with every movement. We don't even bother with a bra and panties. Just purple sweats and an ugly blue sling for my arm. Damn, I just got my other arm out of one of these things a few weeks ago. I'll have matching Frankenstein scars on each limb now. Another fact to care about later. Standing is actually more comfortable than sitting, but I'm exhausted already. This is stupid, so f-ing stupid, me leaving. Like that's ever stopped me before.

Wolfe arrives just before the nurse with my paperwork and pills to escort us to mobile command. Like every other visitor, he visibly recoils at the sight of me. I did too when I first caught sight of myself. Both my eyes are black, and I mean black from the broken nose, which still drains bloody mucous even though it's splinted. They had to shave my hair above my right temple to suture the gash but it is covered with a bandage.

290

Bangs are in my immediate future. I look like the monster that hides under children's beds. But Wolfe doesn't say a word. After my discharge papers are signed, Wolfe wheels me out to the curb, helps both Andrew and me into the car, and off we go. May that be the last hospital I ever see the inside of.

This time I successfully make it to my destination without incident. To err on the side of caution, we double back a few times before reaching mobile command, now safely ensconced on the Ft. Prior National Guard base. No one in or out without showing ID to people with huge guns. I feel safer already.

Adam's the first to see me when I hobble inside the trailer, even greeting me with a smile. "Hey! Do you need hel—"

"I got it," I say, literally waving him off. I may move slower than a sloth on marijuana, but I do make it to the conference room. The white board is covered, not an inch remains, with scribbles and pictures of victims and our perps. Will's picture is off in the corner next to Imelda's. Another victim. Patsy, Jamal, Adrian, Tim, Lars Tinning our Werewolf Doe's DMV photos are dead center. My stomach twists with rage at the sight of Patsy's smiling face. Use it, girl.

It takes effort but I manage to lower myself into a chair. "Really, I can help you," Adam says. "There's no shame in asking for help if—"

"If you really want to help me, then get me everything, and I mean *everything* we have on the case. Every file, every report, every photo past and present. And where are we with Adrian Winsted?"

"He's in real bad shape. A hundred four fever, hacking his lungs out. Your doctor won't let us go at him too hard."

"So he's said nothing?"

"Nothing to help us find Agent Price," Adam says. "Sorry."

"Sorry does me absolutely no good right now. Where is everyone?"

"Most are at the hotel sleeping, but your boss is at the Winsted house, and the Doc is in with the son. There's a staff meeting at seven."

"Let me get this straight. One of our own has been kidnapped and the team is *literally* asleep on the job?"

"We've all been up for over thirty-six hours," Adam points out, "and quite frankly we've exhausted all leads. There's no vacation home or second property in any of their names. Their credit cards are flagged but haven't been used since yesterday. Cell phones and GPS went dead. Their pictures are out to all of law enforcement and even on the news. There is nothing more we can do *but* wait."

"No, there has to be something. Just get me the files. Please," I add as an afterthought.

Adam stares for a second, a pitying smile flashing across his face, before doing as I ask. He plops two boxes on the table and opens the laptop for me as well. "Anything else before I leave?"

"I'm good. Thank you."

I open the first file on the top of the pile about one of the victims at the park. Then the next, and the next with toxicology reports and pictures. Nothing. More files on victims. I give extra consideration to Imelda, re-reading it three times. Besides Tim's current addresses matching the Winsted house, there was precious little that pointed to Patsy. Tim had an alibi corroborated by others and damn video surveillance. And there's sure as hell nothing in here to help me find Will. A damn hour wasted and nothing to show for it.

The second box is filled with the more recent information and evidence collected the past two days. I begin with the file on Lars Tinning, former anthropology Ph.D. student, dead at the age of twenty-four. According to this, he lived with Patsy since he was nineteen. Product of a single parent household. Seems his mother was in and out of rehab. No arrests himself. Excellent grades as both undergrad and graduate. No friends beyond the Winsted house. He took this semester off, no reason given, and just signed a lease for a new apartment in Charlotte one week before his death. Flying the coop and the big bad wolf gobbled him up for it.

Next is the file on Jamal Brian Greene, age thirty but looks eighteen. Parents dead, one ex-wife Rikki and daughter Latishia now eleven, both living in Knoxville, TN. Per an interview neither have seen nor spoken to him since the daughter was four. He met Patsy when she was teaching at Vanderbilt University ten years ago. He was her gardener but in the

293

intervening years he earned his Bachelor's degree in English. He currently works as a bartender. Those at both his and her jobs believed Jamal was her adopted son, or that's what they told people. The son masquerading as the husband, the lover masquerading as the son. I was wrong, the Manson family were The Waltons compared to the Winsted clan. And no one questioned it. Why should they? They kept themselves to themselves, were pleasant when it was called for, and even gave money to charity. Upright citizens one and all. Of course so were Gacy and my ex Steven until they weren't. You never can tell with people.

Adrian's file is just as thin as the other two. Born in Vancouver, Canada but grew up all over the world wherever Mommie Dearest studied and taught. Finally graduated high school in Russia, then earned his undergrad in Botany at the University of St. Petersburg. Right after that Mom got a post at Vanderbilt, and he did his Masters in Environmental Studies there. Applied for US citizenship and worked odd jobs until it was granted and he could join the ranger service. Never married, no children, lived his whole life with Mommy. What a loser.

I comb through their financials next. Two years worth of groceries, Target, Starbucks, the butcher's, all rather pedestrian. No cabin rentals, no local vacations, no payments or mortgages on other properties in any of the werewolves or Adrian's names. They found about $10,000 in cash at the house, so maybe she had more stashed somewhere else. Her son would know.

As I continue climbing paperwork mountain, my anger and determination grow with each boring report. Evidence lists, phone records, photos of the Winsted home each more useless than the last. We have the bastards dead to rites for the murders with the cache of jewelry and other trinkets from their victims, but nothing that guides me to Will. Over two hours and all I have to show for it is a headache. My pain pill's wearing off already. Gritting my teeth, I push myself to my feet but have to take a second to regain my strength. I don't know where Wolfe left my discharge bag before he took Andrew to the hotel. Damn it. I shuffle out of the conference room to medical, but the code doesn't work. Right, they changed them all. I knock. "Dr. Neill? It's Bea. I don't know the code."

The door slides opens a few seconds later. Dang, she looks almost as wretched as I do. Her black circles come from a lack of sleep but are almost as severe. "Um…hi," she says groggily.

"Did I wake you?"

"I, uh, think so. I must have fallen asleep at my desk," she says stepping aside to let me in. "What can I do for you? How are you feeling?"

I expected to see Adrian Winsted lying near death on the exam table, but it's empty. However, when I venture in further, I notice the door to the freezer/holding cell hangs open. There's the bastard, asleep on a cot with fluffy pillows, white sheets, even a comforter to keep him warm. I can hear his raspy breath from here, and he's almost as pale as Oliver, but still he sleeps in a comfy bed. The bastard deserves Guantanamo Bay not the Four Seasons treatment. I stare at him, that rage from before now boiling my blood. He *knows*. He—

"Alexander?" Dr. Neill asks behind me. I snap out of the darkness to look at the good doctor. "Are you okay?"

"Um, my pain medication. I can't find it."

"Oh. I'll get you some from our cache."

"Thank you." Dr. Neill moves over to one of the locked cabinets, and I return my attention to Sleeping Ugly. "How's he doing?"

"The antibiotics are helping. His fever's down, but his lungs are still filled with fluid. He's in and out of consciousness and keeps having fever dreams. He should be in a real hospital but…you know. I'm doing my best."

"I'm sure you've gone above and beyond." She gives me two pills, which I dry swallow. "Thanks." Though my nose protests with intense pain, I manage a smile for the weary woman. "Hey, why don't you take a break, huh? You look like you're about to pass out yourself. Why don't you go get something to eat or take a nap in the conference room? I can keep an eye on him for you."

"No. I don't think—"

"He's not going anywhere, and you're no good to anyone in this state. You'll just be in the next room. If there's any change, any problem, I promise to come get you."

Come on. Come on…

"Okay. I guess," Dr. Neill says. "I'll just need an hour or two. If his fever spikes or if he struggles for breath—"

"I'll come wake you."

The good doctor nods. "Thank you. Really, thank you. I'll just be next door. Oh, and the code's just the old one in reverse."

"Okay. Have a good rest," I say with a smile.

She nods again. I don't drop my smile until that door shuts behind her. That was easier than I thought. I stare at Winsted still snug in his bed. I wonder what he's dreaming about. His mother rescuing him? Evenings with the pack? Burning in the fires of hell for his crimes? Time to wake the bastard and find out.

I manage to wait five minutes to allow Dr. Neill to fall asleep in case there's any noise like screams before I enter the cell. I'd shut the door but I'd be locked in here too. He doesn't wake as I roll the desk chair to his bedside and lower myself into it. I study him for a moment. Up close, I can see the family resemblance. Same chocolate brown hair color, same lips, same almond shaped eyes. Why didn't I notice before? Another damn mistake, and now Will's paying for it. I can't fail him now. I will do whatever is necessary to find him. Even this. God forgive me.

With as much force as I can muster, I slap his clammy face. Adrian jerks awake, wildly staring around the room for the source of this new pain. "What—"

"Wakey wakey, sleepyhead," I say menacingly. His gray eyes settle on my scowling face. "Remember me?"

297

"Who—"

"Don't feel bad. I look a bit different from last time we met. Of course so do you. Looks like the Grim Reaper brushed us both."

"Wa-water," he whispers.

"Oh, you want some water?" I hold up the water bottle I brought in. "We'll call this the carrot." I set the bottle in my lap. "Here's the stick." I backhand his face again, leaving a white mark on his red, feverish cheek. Adrian lets out a raspy gasp before hacking his lungs out. "Now, I'm not a violent person by nature. I'm really not. Sure, I've killed some people. Not to brag but I even slaughtered over a dozen vampires in a single day. But I don't enjoy it. Not even a little. Not like your mother. So personally, I prefer the carrot route. However, it's entirely up to you. Either way, I *will* get what I want from you."

"You-You can't do that," he rasps. "You-You're FBI. There are laws."

"Two more things you should be aware of, Mr. Winsted before you make your choice. First, the man your whore of a mother kidnapped? He's my fiancé, so you're not talking to Agent Alexander right now. You're stuck helpless in a small room with the woman who killed a man at age eight by squeezing his heart," I say, doing that very thing to this man here. Who can't even breathe now and claws at his chest, "Until it burst." I release the organ. Adrian gasps for air as tears stream from his eyes. I feel nothing. "Which brings us to the second point of interest. I can kill you without lifting a finger, without

298

leaving a mark. My colleagues will chalk up your death to the pneumonia." I sit back in the chair. "So. Again. Carrot or stick?"

"I-I-I don't know where they are," he whimpers through the coughs.

"Yeah, don't believe you. You see, according to your mother's phone records, she made a ten second call to Jamal Greene before they both tossed their phones. In spite of this short conversation, they still somehow ended up together to kidnap my fiancée. This leads me to believe there was a pre set-up rendezvous location in case of trouble. Your mother strikes me as a smart woman. Having an exit strategy, especially with us closing in, would be a logical move. But I suppose it is possible she didn't let you in on the escape plan. You are *obviously* the runt of the litter. It is *your* fault we tracked the pack down. If you hadn't gotten sick you would have been in the park to clean up like all the other times. Hell, she didn't even deem you worthy of becoming a werewolf. She brought all those boys into your home, gave *them* the gift, replaced you with them inside her heart, maybe even her bed—"

"Don't be disgusting," Adrian snaps. "I never slept with my mother. And *I* didn't want to become a werewolf. She offered a million times, but I refused. My mother loves me."

"So she *would* have let you in on her exit strategy," I parry. His mouth snaps shut. I roll my eyes. "Carrot or stick?" His lips remain sealed. Gotta admire the loyalty. Slight pressure to the aorta hopefully makes him re-think that particular virtue. As he clutches his chest, face turning as red as blood and sweat pouring from his forehead, his mouth finally opens if only to silently plead for mercy. I pull back, and the hacking coughs begin anew with yellow phlegm this time. Yuck. I pick up the bottle again. "Is it carrot time?"

"Fuck you," he coughs.

"Wrong answer." More pressure this round, for longer as well, until the bastard becomes purple. Nothing. I don't feel a damn thing. Not pity, not guilt. I think I could kill him and sleep well after. At least tonight.

After five seconds, I release him. "Had enough yet? In your weakened state, I truly don't know how much your body can take. Just tell me where she is and this can all stop, Adrian."

"Go-Go-Go," he coughs "to-to hell."

I squeeze. "Tell me where she is."

Release. "Fuck you."

Squeeze. "Where is she?"

Release. "Bitch."

Squeeze. "Tell me where she is!" I shout.

His bloodshot gray eyes stare at me with ire as he struggles for breath. I release again. I really *don't* know how much more he can take. He coughs for ten seconds, and another ten before he catches his rattling breath. "Had enough?" Adrian draws in one big rattling gulp of air, then spits phlegm right onto my cheek. The moment that sticky, viscous fluid hits my flesh, I learn that the phrase "seeing red" is a physical possibility. The world shades fire engine crimson and by the time it clears I realize Adrian's scratching at his chest, rivets of blood welling up, as I squeeze it. I still don't stop. "Tell me where she is!" I shriek. "Where is she?"

"Agent Alexander!"

I lose my concentration, giving that little shit a reprieve. Chandler strides into the cell, hand on his sidearm as if he were approaching a perp. "Step away from the prisoner."

"You don't—"

"*Now,*" Chandler orders voice as hard as titanium.

When I meet his cold eyes any thoughts of protest run and hide. Adrian continues hacking and crying as I rise and walk out with as much grace and dignity as possible. Chandler slams the freezer door shut, muffling Adrian's gasps and coughs. "What the hell are you doing?"

"What no one else has bothered to. Getting him to talk," I say.

"You were using your gift to harm an innocent. We have arrested people for a lot less than what you just did."

"I don't care! His mother has my fiancée. Your best friend. Right now. Right as we stand here arguing. And God knows what she's doing to him. There isn't time for pussyfooting around, Paul. There isn't time for you to apparently grow a pair and do what needs to be done. He knows how to find her, and if I have to drag him to the precipice of death, if I have to flay him alive, I will do it. Nothing else matters but finding Will. *Nothing.* So either help me or get the hell out of my w—!"

The opening door draws both our attentions diverting that way. "What in the hell is happening here?" Oliver asks as he steps in, zeroing in on me. "And why the hell are you not in hospital?"

"Agent Montrose," Chandler says, hand moving to his gun again, "Agent Alexander was assaulting our prisoner. I am relieving her of duty for the foreseeable future, and I require you to escort her back to the hotel. If she resists in any way, you are authorized to use force to restrain her."

"Are you kidding me with this?" I shout.

"Adam Blue is there now and can watch her until I can arrange to have her flown home. You are to return here post haste to glamour the prisoner for his interrogation."

"Is all of this really necessary?" Oliver asks as he steps to my side.

"She is not in any state physically or mentally to help us with this case. She almost killed Adrian Winsted. She's damn lucky I'm not sending her to the Facility." Chandler stares at me. "But I will. Make no mistake about that, *I will*. Go back to the hotel and get some rest before your flight. That is an order, Agent Alexander. Montrose?" Chandler nods toward the door.

"This is—"

"Beatrice," Oliver cuts in, "come."

"I'm not—"

"*Now.*"

"Oh, for…" Pick your battles, Bea. And this isn't one of them. I turn on my own heel and walk out before either can manhandle me. Oliver is by my side almost immediately as I

302

tromp outside without a glance his way. He'll only tolerate being ignored for a moment.

I blink, and he's standing right in front of me. "What the bloody hell are you thinking? Why are you even out of the hospital? You can barely stand."

"I'm fine," I hiss back, "but I'd be better with a solid lead on Will, which wasn't happening."

"So you decided to risk your health, not to mention your freedom, by torturing a sick man?"

"If it got the job done, if it got my fiancée back, then hell yes."

Oliver stares into my eyes, his mouth set as straight as a razor since I uttered the word fiancée. "Well, all it got you was suspended. And Chandler was correct in that action. I know you feel guilty. I know you are frightened and angry and in pain every way possible, but it is clouding your judgment. You are no good to a soul, let alone William, in your current state. Last night you asked me to do what you could not. You asked me to help you. This is me helping you, Trixie. Get in the car or I shall force you. This is what needs to be done. Please trust me on this. *Please.*"

"I would trust you, but the problem is I'm not sure which Oliver I'm looking at right now. The man who sat through my godson's Christmas pageant, who I've spent hours laughing with. Who held me when I cried. One of my best damn friends. Or the man who almost fed me to a werewolf. Who beat my fiancée to a bloody pulp. The one I've heard a dozen nightmare inducing stories about. You know, I hadn't met him until recently. Didn't think he still existed. But he does. And *he* won't lift a finger to find Will. He would just stand in the corner watching with glee as the man I loved came home in a coffin, and the best way to make sure that happens is to take me out of the equation. Send me back to Kansas with platitudes and promises of aid. And I think that's the Oliver before me right now."

He stares at me, shocked and pained into silence for several seconds. "After all we have been through," he all but whispers, "all that I believed we meant to one another, the fact those words just left your mouth, proves my assessment correct. *My* Beatrice would *never* wound me so. She would never think that let alone say it to my face." The vampire lowers his nose to mine, staring straight into my eyes. If I weren't already chilled by the night, those eyes would do the job. "You can curse me. You can hate me until the sun burns out, but I will not let you continue on like this. I will not let *you* ruin *my* Beatrice's life. I will not. So you get in that bloody car or I shall drain you and deposit your body to the hospital where you shall remain for a week."

"You wouldn't dare," I snarl.

"If it saves your life, your soul, then there is nothing I would not do, Beatrice. *Nothing*," he snarls back, exposing his fangs. "So get in the bloody car before you force me to prove myself."

I believe him. Worse, there's nothing I could do to stop him. I could give him an aneurysm, slow him down, but then the others would come after me. I need to stay here, nearby, if I can be any help to Will. So I stare down, hang my head in defeat before getting into the car without another word. I've failed him. Again. Another sin to add to my record.

"You are doing the right thing, Trixie," Oliver says, starting the car.

"Who for?"

SIXTEEN

GOING ROGUE

I don't utter a single word the five minutes it takes to arrive at the Holiday Inn Express. I refuse to even look at Benedict Arnold as he escorts me to my room and deposits me with Nancy after strict instructions not to allow me to leave. As if a ninety pound seventeen-year-old was a match for me, even without my curse. But be it the pills that only take the edge off, the pain still left at a seven, or just general depression and hopelessness, I don't have the energy to even try to escape. Yet. I crawl into bed without even pulling up the covers and shut my heavy eyes.

When I open them again Nancy's gone, the door to the adjoining room is open with the television on in the other room, and an hour and a half was stolen from me. I'm still so groggy when I even attempt to lift my head, it swims. Jesus. The second attempt isn't better, but I power through it, using my not good but less mangled arm to force me into the sitting position.

"Agent Alexander?" Adam asks from the other room. He walks through the door just as I swing my feet to the floor. "You need help?"

"I need to use the bathroom. You gonna offer to wipe my ass too?"

"Not really my kink, but…" he says with a smile.

Jesus, he smiles so damn much. Right now I want to smack it off his face. Not his fault though. Most prisoners feel the same way about their jailers. "Think I can manage."

I hobble to the bathroom and accomplish the task with minimal problems besides the horrific pain in my side when I bend for toilet paper. I muffle my scream by biting into my finger. Maybe Oliver's right. If I literally can't wipe my own butt, what good am I to anyone? At least I accomplish that one task. Adam's waiting at my desk when I return. "Here's, uh, your bag from the hospital. Your pills, necklace, cell, they're all in there. Want me to—"

"I can do it. Thank you. And you don't need to wait in here. I can't exactly make a run for it."

"Just thought you might like to know we got a lead on your boyfriend," Adam says. "The vampire got Winsted to talk. Glamoured him. There *was* a rendezvous point. A Starbucks in Boone. The mother had a safety deposit box in town under an alias with cash and fake IDs inside. He doesn't know the fake names though. Last I heard they were waking up the bank manager to get the surveillance and warrant for the box."

"That's it? That's all he knows?"

"Well, he's making a list of all the victims and marking where he buried them. Thirty plus here and about eighty overall. She is a sick bitch."

"But that's all? All he could give about finding his mother? A place she's come and gone from already?"

"It's something. This is good news."

It's not much. Hell, it's barely anything. A bread crumb that's probably been eaten by a bird already. And I almost killed that man for next to nothing. Christ, as if I couldn't feel any worse.

"You should also know I'm supposed to drive you to the airport in about an hour. You're flying commercial, but Dr. Black will pick you up in Wichita."

"Any more bad news? Did Brad Pitt's face melt off while I was sleeping?"

"I don't think so."

"Then I'm going to rest until it's time for prison transport. If I need anything, I'll scream."

Shaking his head, Adam rises with my hospital bag and steps toward me. "Really. If you need anything…" He sets the bag on my bed. "And we *will* find him. He helped us out when we needed it. We're not leaving until he's safe and sound."

"Then that makes one of us, I guess," I say, I wish with a cruel smile but it'd hurt too much. As does walking to my bed. "Wake me when it's time for my exile."

I lower myself on the bed beside the bag. In case he's needed Adam, gentleman that he is, waits until I'm lying down before returning to his television, no doubt grateful to be away from the rude Gorgon. Nana would tan my hide for being so rude to someone trying to help me. Another karmic point lost. I'll care tomorrow.

Inside my plastic bag I find what's left of my bloody suit after it was cut off me in the ER, the borrowed flip-flops, my pills, my gun, my compass necklace, my purse, car keys for a car probably still parked at the college, my badge, and cell phone. I dry swallow the pills before putting on my necklace. I feel naked without it on. Cell phone next. The first voice mail is from Nana just calling to check in. Yeah, I'm not even close to emotionally ready to speak to her. Delete. I also delete the fateful voice message about Adrian Winsted. Goddamn it, if I hadn't been gabbing with April. If I'd just picked up. If, if, if, if, if. The third message is just silence for several seconds. Delete. Texts next. Text from April: "*Still mad?*" I'll call her later too. The next text is from an unknown caller. "*555-7787. U alone. No tricks or he dies.*"

I almost drop the phone.

Crap. Oh crap. It was sent at noon. Crap. I punch in the number and climb off the bed. I don't want Adam to hear this. Four rings. Five. Oh, come on, you bitch. Answer.

"Hello, Agent Alexander," Patsy says on the other end. "I was beginning to worry you'd never call. Are we alone?"

I shut the bathroom door and turn on the faucet. "Yes."

"I'll keep this short regardless. Not that you can trace this call. This is a pre-paid cell which I will destroy when we're done here. He's alive, by the way. Very much so."

Thank God. Thank you, God. "I want to talk to him."

"Yes, well, perhaps he doesn't want to talk to *you*. He's actually asleep right now. Poor thing, I wore him out."

I am going to kill this bitch, I swear to God. She is fucking dead. "I want to talk to him," I say again with a hard edge.

"First things first," Patsy says. "Your people have my son?"

"We do."

"Then your lover for my son. Simple and elegant, no?"

"I want to talk to Will," I insist again.

"A few conditions, though," Patsy continues, ignoring my request. "This is between us ladies. I deal with you and you alone. If I see or even suspect your little boy band is around or tracking us, I will kill him. You attempt any of your mind tricks or harm me and mine in any way, I kill him. Do you believe me, Agent Alexander?"

"I do," I say without hesitation. "But I need proof of life. I want to talk to my fiancée. *Now.*"

"Fair enough. William! Come here, darling! Someone wishes to speak with you!" Patsy calls as if he were a dog. I'm surprised she doesn't whistle too.

There's thudding and mumbling in the background. "What?" Will asks in the distance.

It's damn good I'm sitting because my knees would surely have given out in relief at the sound of his voice. He's alive. Really alive. Thank you. Thank you, God.

"Say hello to your fiancée, darling," Patsy orders.

310

HOLD SLIP

STEHLIK, MAREN SUE
Unclaim : 07/01/2021

Held date:	06/23/2021
Pickup location:	Joppa Branch
Title:	High moon
Call number:	MYSTERY Harlow
Item barcode:	31526053234891
Assigned branch:	Abingdon Branch

Notes:

"What? Who?" he asks groggily into the phone.

"Will?" I moan.

"There's your proof of life," Patsy says. "I'll contact you again in half an hour with the location of the exchange. One police car, one whiff of the fuzz, I cut off his head and mail it back to you. Do you believe me, girlie girl?"

"I do."

"Smart cookie. Then my son, half an hour. Ta ta."

She hangs up.

Oh crap. Oh crap. What am I going to do? What can I do but what she asks? Because without a doubt that woman will murder Will without a second thought. And the last time we tried an exchange like this was on my first case, and we all almost died. Maybe if I'd been alone that night, just given Walter Wayland his zombie daughter, I wouldn't have been attacked by ghouls, and I wouldn't be missing a chunk of my neck. I can't risk anything going wrong like last time. She gets her son, I get my fiancée, we catch them tomorrow. Of course no one else will agree with my assessment. They'll want to do exactly what we did in Colorado. And what do they say about insanity? If I just do what she says, and let them go on their way, we'll live to fight another day. Of course she could just shoot or hex me on sight, not to mention the problem of getting Adrian out of custody. I don't know what to do. I enlist the others help, Will's life remains in jeopardy. I go alone, mine is. Gut. Go with my gut. And my gut says…crap.

I vomit up the pills with little effort, I need every last one of my wits about me, before stepping out of the bathroom. Preparation first. Gun with silver bullets, silver Mace, my badge, cuffs, cell all present and accounted for. I slip on my flats, turn on the television and increase the volume, hide my purse in the bathroom, take a deep breath, and begin the great escape.

Adam's lying on his bed watching TV when I shuffle into his room. Where are they? I scan the room. Please don't be on him. Where…gotcha. Top of the dresser by his wallet.

"You…okay?" Adam asks, eyebrow raised.

"What? Oh, uh, fine," I say, moving to the dresser. I put my back to it and casually reach behind. "I just, um, wanted to apologize for earlier. I've been acting like a Grade-A b-word when you've been nothing but nice. So I'm sorry. Really."

"It's okay. I don't take it personally. You've been through a lot. You're worried about the man you love…I get it."

Got them! Car keys. Check. "Still. I'm sorry."

"Apology accepted," he says with a smile.

"Anyway, um, I'm gonna take a shower before we leave. Wash the hospital off."

"Okay. If you need help…I promise not to look."

"I got it. Really. But thanks."

With my fingers tightly curled around his car keys, I pad out of the room. Step Two. As if everything were hunky dory, I walk into the bathroom and turn on the shower before shutting the door. I just shut it from the outside. Adam can't see the bathroom from his bed and hopefully with the TV on his werewolf hearing won't pick up there's actually no one in the shower. Step Three. As quietly as I can, I make my way to the door. Turning the handle a fraction of an inch a second, I finally get it open. With the same care, I step into the hall and close it again. Ten minutes. I just need ten minutes before he raises the alarm. I don't waste a second of it. I hustle down the hall to the elevator then to his SUV. Just give me ten minutes.

Hurdle Two presents itself five minutes later at the National Guard gate. I pull up, my stomach churning with nerves, but the teenage guard takes one look at my badge and waves me through. This is proving easier than I thought. Of course Hurdle Three is the size of Mt. Kilimanjaro. There are only two cars in front of mobile command, but that just means anywhere from one to five people with guns inside. If there is a God, there's only one. A forgiving one.

The doors to the three rooms are closed, but I hear voices in the conference room. As quickly and quietly as in the hotel, I creep toward medical. My hand trembles so badly I punch in the wrong code. Twice. I have to take a deep, deep breath before number three. Am I really going through with this? Maybe it's just the head wound taking the wheel here. When the door finally slides open, I'm close to vomiting again. I still step in.

At first glance, it's empty. No Dr. Neill, no Carl, no...I thought too soon.

"What on earth are you doing back here?" Oliver asks as he steps out of the freezer.

At least it's not Jason Dahl. He wouldn't hesitate to physically incapacitate me, and I really wanted to avoid a supernatural international incident. Assaulting werewolf royalty would qualify. On the ride over I tried to work out what I'd do when faced with Adrian's guard. I was going to try and lie my way through, saying that Chandler ordered him back to the hospital or to the hotel. That won't work here. I got nothing.

"I asked, what are you doing here, Agent Alexander?" Oliver asks again, harsher this time.

"I...Patsy called me. She wants to exchange Will for Adrian."

My friend stares at me. "When did she phone?"

"About fifteen minutes ago. She's going to call me back anytime, and I need to have him. She'll want to speak to him."

Oliver strides toward the door. "The others are—"

"No! No, you can't tell them. I have to go alone. She made that very, *very* clear," I say, fear tingeing every word.

"I do not care what she said. There is absolutely no way you are meeting a pack of murderous werewolves alone."

"You don't understand. She—"

"No, *you* do not understand," he says sharp as a knife. "You are terrified, you are grievously injured, and you are not in your right mind. The moment you arrive, they will kill you without a moment's hesitation. All for a man who—" He ceases talking to fume in silence.

"'A man who?' Go on. Finish your thought."

"A man who…may not even wish to be saved. May even fight against the very idea."

I let those words infect the room with their poison. The thought had crossed my mind, but to hear it spoken aloud? My already tender stomach tightens. "So I should just what? Let her keep him? Let her continue to rape him as the best case scenario?"

"No, I am absolutely *not* suggesting that," Oliver spews as if I've accused him of killing Will himself. I think I've truly offended him. "But it is a real possibility you will be facing four hostile werewolves not three, and in your current condition, you could not fend off a pixie let alone a feral pack. And regardless of your physical state…if Will *is* a threat, I do not believe you capable of doing what may be necessary." He pauses. "What even *he* would want you to do." Oliver slowly moves toward me as those words penetrate. "Trixie, I am asking you to trust us. Trust *me*. There is no need, none, for you to be alone in this. For this to be your burden alone. Just please, my darling, please trust me." Oliver takes my good hand in his cold ones and gazes into my eyes. "*Please*," he whispers through gritted teeth.

As I stare into those exquisite gray eyes, so sincere, so pained, I want to burst into tears. I want to lean against him and have him hold me as I sob my terror and misery away. I love Will, I do, but this man has always, *always* made me feel safe. My oasis in the storm. My bedrock. And despite everything, despite his fury in the past few days and my poisoned words from before, deep down I don't doubt his feelings for me. I don't doubt the lengths he'd go for me because they're the exact same lengths I'd go for him. He's proven himself time and time again. I trust him. And if this was just me, just my life, I wouldn't hesitate. But it's not. "I trust you Oliver, with my life," I whisper. "I do." The smile forming on his face quickly hardens along with the rest of him. Every limb locks in place, held still by my will. "I just don't trust you with his. I'm sorry."

"Trixie, let me go," Oliver warns.

I hold onto him, as I back toward the open freezer. "I am sorry."

"Trixie, stop this. Let me go. You are not thinking clearly. Stop!" In my brain, I sense his struggle against my invisible bonds. "Trixie! Help! Hel—"

I squeeze his throat until the noise stops. "I'm sorry."

Needing to keep my eyes on him to concentrate, I lift Oliver an inch off the ground and draw his levitating body inside the cell with me. Adrian lies in bed with a pad, pen, and map on his lap. "What—"

"Your mother sent me. I'm here to free you. Bring you to her."

"No. You—"

"Look, I'm sorry for earlier. I am. And you have no reason to trust me, I get that, but trust your mother. She called and offered me my fiancée for you. Killing and harming you puts him in danger. Trust that. Now, get up. Please don't make me make you."

Adrian glances from me, to the frozen vampire, back to me. He slowly does the math and after several seconds finally pushes aside the papers and blankets to climb out of bed. He winces as he removes the IV. "There should be flip-flops and a coat in the other room. Put them on. Fast."

Adrian pads out of the cell, past the floating vampire whose eyes follow the escaping prisoner before moving back to me, doubling their normal size and brimming with recrimination. With fear, for or of me, I don't know. At this moment I don't care. Oliver floats completely inside the cell, taking Adrian's place as prisoner. As I pivot and back out of the small room, I say, "I'm sorry. Please forgive me. This is the only way. I'm sorry." I shut the door. The moment he's out of sight, I lose the link. I slide in the bolt just as he slams against the door, rattling the eight foot tall barricade. It was built to keep in vampires and werewolves. Time to put its efficacy to the test.

"Trixie, open the door!" Oliver bellows. "You are not in your right mind. Stop and think. This is kidnapping. Open this bloody door now!"

No time to waste. Adrian's slipping on Oliver's leather jacket when I spin around, removing my gun as I do. His gaze moves to the gun trained on him. "I need you alive, but try anything and I'll shoot you in the arm or the leg. It won't kill you, but it hurts like a mother. Walk ahead of me. Let's go."

"Beatrice, this is madness! Open the door!" Oliver shouts as he body slams the door.

Like his mother trained him, Adrian obeys without question, trudging out of medical as fast as a middle-aged pneumatic man can with me a step behind. No one in the hallway yet, but I can still hear Oliver's muffled yells which means the others probably can too. "Hurry." The freezing night air amplifies my trembling when we get outside. I can barely hold the gun. "White SUV," I instruct, teeth chattering from both the temperature and adrenaline. "Get in the back."

Adrian complies, though has a coughing fit from the effort. Just don't die before we get there, douche bag. I hurry around to the driver's side. Just have to clear the gate, and we're home free. I slide the gun into my purse and retrieve the car keys and cuffs. Adrian's fastening his seatbelt when I climb in. I toss him the cuffs. "Handcuff yourself to the handhold. Both hands." I start the car. "And if you try *anything*, if you even look at me wrong, what I did to you before will be a paper cut compared to the agony I'll inflict on you now."

"Just take me to my mother, bitch," he spews back. He does cuff himself though. Ass.

I put the car into gear and drive away. There are no problems at the gate either. Holy crap, I did it. I made it. I probably lost a friend and committed a felony, but I did it. I did…oh, crap. Oh, crap.

What have I done? What am I doing? What the *hell* am I doing?

I've been so focused on getting Adrian I didn't plan past the grab. I'm about to face a damn pack of psychotic

318

werewolves. I have one gun, one arm, and my power. I just assaulted my best friend. He might never forgive me. And Will…he might be…I might have to…oh God. Oh God. Have I made a huge mistake? Judging from the panic that's making it hard to breathe again, I think I have. I—

"Watch out!" Adrian shouts.

Jesus Christ! I realize too late I've run a red light. The pick-up truck careening toward us swerves, barely missing the back of our SUV. I floor it through the intersection, ignoring the honks behind me. Hand trembling, I maneuver the car to the nearest parking lot. "Crap. Crap." I whisper over and over again between my heavy breaths which happen in time to my falling tears. What have I done?

"Maybe I should drive," Adrian says.

Maybe I should let him. My third near-death experience in two days. That's a lot even for me. I rest my head on the steering wheel and force the tears back. I wipe the stragglers as I take deep breaths to calm myself. I can't fall apart now. I fall apart now, all is lost. Oh God, maybe it already is. I can't even drive. How can I save him when I can't even think? Can barely walk? Will needs me. He needs me, and I can't think. I don't think I can do this. I need a plan. I need a *plan*. Think. Think, damn it!

There's blissful silence—save for Adrian's wheezing breath—for five minutes before my cell rings. I was so deep in thought the offending noise jolts me enough I jerk in my seat.

The phone rings again before I locate it in my purse. Okay. I can do this. I *have* to do this. Okay. "Beatrice Alexander."

"I wish to speak to my son," Patsy demands without preamble.

Here we go. I put the phone on speaker and hold it up. "It's her."

"Patsy?" Adrian asks.

"Hello, my darling," she says, actually relieved. "You sound dreadful. How are you feeling?"

"About as well as I sound. You were right, it is pneumonia."

"I told you," she chides. "But they took care of you?"

"More or less," he says, glaring at me.

"You talked to him. I have him. Let's get on with this. There's a mall—"

"*I* make the terms, Agent Alexander," Patsy cuts in. "Remember? Adrian, is she alone? The others, are they with her?"

"No."

"You haven't seen her contact them? There's no one following her?"

"No, not that I've seen or heard. She's on her own."

"Excellent. You've been a good girl so far, Agent Alexander, let's continue the trend. There's a cabin off Route 7. I believe you know it."

Route 7? I don't…oh God. A knife twists inside my heart. Not there. That bitch. Out of all the places… "I do. We're about twenty minutes away."

"Remember: one whiff of anything untoward, I decorate your little love shack with his blood."

"I just assaulted an FBI agent and committed a dozen other felonies. I'm not going to screw this up now. But *you* should know, for every hair you hurt on Will's head, I take one of your son's limbs."

"Noted. See you in twenty. *Ciao.*" She hangs up.

Goddamn you, Will. How could you? How *could* you? He told her about the cabin, *our* cabin. I've been fighting for my life, *our* life, and you took her to our cabin? Our bed? Maybe he's not in there. Maybe Oliver's right. My Will would never be that cruel. If he can do that to me…I stare down at my phone.

"What are you waiting for?" Adrian asks in the back, snapping me out of my pity party. "Let's go."

"You know, you're very rude," I say. "Didn't your mother ever teach you manners?"

"She taught me to show respect when it's earned. You haven't earned a thimbleful." He chuckles. Cruelly. "You don't stand a chance against her, little girl. You know that, right? She's going to eat you alive. Literally. And your boyfriend? He's gonna join in the feast."

I stare down at my phone again. Okay. *Okay.* I slip the phone into my sling. "Well, if your mother tries, she'll be dining

321

in hell with the others who underestimated me." I start the car. "I'm sure she'll save you a seat."

Seventeen

Showdown At
Blood Moon Creek

Forty-eight hours. Forty-eight hours ago I was in this very spot of the wide world driving down this very road beside the man I loved. The first night of a lifetime. Now I'm back here, most likely about to die at the claws of a woman he's been screwing in our cabin for the past day. We should never have left. We should have barricaded ourselves in. Called George. Quit on the spot, and gone back to making love until we couldn't walk for a week. Damn hindsight. Why couldn't I have been born with clairvoyance?

I almost miss the turn. If I had known I'd be coming back here, I would have paid more attention. All I can remember is it was off Route 7 and was the third right after the Shell gas station, the only civilization for miles. We may as well be on Venus. I loved the isolation two days ago. Tonight it's probably gonna get me killed.

"Did that sign say Route 7?" I ask. "It was the third right after the Shell Station?"

"I think so," Adrian replies.

"It's just down that road then on the left. A gravel road."

"Good to know."

Asphalt becomes gravel as we travel down the lonesome road. Beyond my headlights and the moon above, there's no light, nothing but darkness, until a pinpoint in the distance grows larger. His beacon. Will. This is all going to work out. It will. I am going to get him back, we are going to drive away into the moonlight, and once we're safe we'll go after those bastards with the full force of the US government and werewolf community. They will not get away. But Will comes first. Nothing else matters right now but him. *Nothing.* Just please, please God, let me have made the right decision.

My headlights catch sight of Jamal sitting on the porch right in the rocking chair where Will and I made love as the sun rose. Tainted. Every damn memory's tainted now. The werewolf rises from the chair without taking his hard eyes off my face. Werewolves have good night vision. He can probably see every contour, every emotion crossing my face right now. Nerves and fear have top billing.

I stop the car about seventy-five feet from the front door, parking but not shutting off the engine. Ideally I won't leave this car. Adrian will get out, Will in, happy trails. Still, as Jamal moves to the front door, eyes never leaving me, I grip the gun in my lap tighter. Jamal knocks on the front door before stepping aside.

Tim comes out the door first. Unlike what's left of me, there's no physical evidence he was in a car crash yesterday. Not a sandy hair out of place. Patsy follows at his back, long hair flowing around her round face. She's positively luminous for someone on the lam. The afterglow of great sex is great for the skin. Jamal and Patsy approach the car as Tim guards the now shut door.

"I don't see Will," I say.

"I'm sure he's inside the cabin," Adrian replies.

I roll down my window halfway and shout, "That's far enough!"

Patsy and Jamal stop twenty-five feet away. "Adrian?" Patsy shouts back.

I roll down his window too. "Patsy?"

"Did anyone follow you?" she asks her son.

"I didn't see anyone."

"It's just us," I assure her. "They'd be swarming by now if it wasn't. Now, can we please get this over with? You're not the only one now on the run. Where's Will?"

"Let my son out then—"

"You have ten seconds to produce Will Price or I'll reverse this SUV and you will never see your son again," I shout. "One. Tw—"

"No need for theatrics. Tim?" Patsy says.

Her underling opens the cabin door, says something, and finally, *finally* he appears, swathed in the light inside. Oh, thank God. Thank you, God. Like with Tim there's no evidence of trauma either from the accident or his "imprisonment." The only indication something's amiss is the fact his eyes remain slightly closed, as if he's struggling to keep them open. Drugs or exhaustion, perhaps both. He's alive. That's all I care about. "Will!" I shout.

That slow gaze moves my way, shielding his eyes from the headlights. I have the damn well overwhelming urge to leap out of this car and sprint into his arms and shower his face with kisses. To sob against his shoulder until I'm empty. I quash it. Just get him in the damn SUV, Bea. "Your son doesn't leave this car until Will's inside it. Call me crazy, but I find it hard to trust a psychopath."

For some reason, Patsy smirks. "Fine with me. William! Come here, lover! Come!"

Still in his dazed state, he and Tim slowly meander off the porch toward their Alpha. The moment Will's beside her, without preamble, he kisses her. *Really* kisses her like a thirsty man tasting water. My jaw drops, along with my stomach, as his hand moves to grope her butt and pull her into his arms. *He can't help it. He can't help it...*

Patsy extracts herself from his grip, smiling but placing her fingers over his mouth to stop further affection. "Let me go, lover. We have business to attend to."

"But—" Will whines.

"*Now*," Patsy commands. Will's arms immediately drop to his sides. "Good boy. Now, don't be rude. Say hello to your fiancée. She came all this way to rescue you from my evil clutches."

"My who?" Will asks.

Enough of this bull crap. "Will, it's Bea. Beatrice Alexander. Get in the car," I call.

Will glances from me back to the smirking Patsy, almost confused and injured by my words. This simple act terrifies me enough that my heart physically seizes for a moment. No. No…

"You want me to leave with her?" the man I love asks Patsy, each word dripping with anguish and betrayal.

"That's entirely up to you, lover," Patsy replies tenderly.

The hell it is. "Will, get in the car! Please get in the damn car!"

"You have a choice to make, William," she instructs while stroking his cheek. "You are absolutely free to get in that car, drive off, and marry that *girl*. I will not stop you."

"Will, get in the car!" I shout again.

His eyes never leave Patsy for an instant. "Or you can stay here. With me. With your pack. Where nothing will ever be denied you. Where you can fulfill every one of your desires, your instincts. Where you never have to sublimate who and what you are. You are Lycan. You need to run wild, run free, feel the wind in your fur, the blood and flesh in your mouth as you crush your prey."

"Will, get in the car!"

"She will never understand that. She will understand *you*. Not fully. She can't. Because you are better than her, and that girl knows it. There will always be a part of her that fears you because of it. Loathes that inhuman part of you that should be celebrated, not reviled. Not by her, not by you, not by anyone. Your wolf has been shackled for too long because of people like her. She wants to lock you away in a cage of mediocrity. He could be a king, William Price, if you let him."

"Will!" I shriek. Not even a glance. Crap. *Crap.*

I find myself doing the stupidest thing imaginable. I open the door and climb out of the car into the killing fields with nothing more than a gun in my hand. For whatever reason, probably because they're so amused by my misery the others don't attack or even move as I bridge the gap between us. At least they acknowledge my presence unlike Will. His eyes never leave Patsy, not until I shove his shoulder. "William Price, you get in that car right now. Do you hear me? Get in the damn car! We have to go now, okay?" I say voice quaking. "It's time to go."

"I don't think he wishes to go anywhere with you, Agent Alexander," Patsy says.

"Shut up," I snap at her before returning to Will. No matter how hard I try he won't meet my eyes. "Will? Will, baby?" I say, touching his cheek as she did. "It's Bea. It's Bea. Will, please look at me. *Please.*" His green eyes finally turn my way. But there's nothing in them. Not love, not hate, it's as if I'm a stranger. But he's in there. I know deep down he's in there. I just have to tunnel through hell to reach him. "It's Bea, Will," I whisper, voice cracking. "You know me. I-I'm the girl who drives you crazy, remember? The-The one who you taught to pick a lock. Who not two days ago you brought to this very place, who you made love to right inside. Who you asked to be the mother of your children, who you asked to be your *wife.* The woman who loves you. Who wants to build a life with you. Who *you* love almost as much as I love you. It's Bea." His eyes jut to Patsy for a moment for validation, but I grab his jaw and jerk his gaze back my way. "Don't look at her. You look at me, Will Price. Whatever you think you feel for her, it's just an illusion. Magic." I take his hand and place it over my pounding heart. "*This.* This, you and I, what we have is real. I love you. And you love me. I don't hate you, I don't fear you, *I love you.* And I need you. I need you to fight, okay? You've taken on zombies, vampires, my psychotic ex, our friends, hell even yourself, I just need you to fight for me one more time, baby. One more time. Then we can go home. Together. Forever. Goddamn it, fight for me, Will Price. Fight for us. Just…get in the car, Will. That's it. That's all you have to do. Then we can go home. I want to go home, Will. And that's with you, baby. You're my home, and I'm yours. So please get in the car, baby. Get in the car. I beg you. Fight for me. *Please.*"

He stares down at me with those same vacant eyes, the only change are his rapidly blinking eyes as my words penetrate. They *have* to penetrate. This is true love, it's magic can conquer anything. It's toppled countries, saved lives, there is nothing more powerful in this or any universe. He's in there. He has to hear me. Come on, baby. Fight. *Come back to me. Come on, come on, come on...*

No. *No.*

When his confused eyes jut to Patsy, searching for permission, searching for an anchor, I have to actually will my knees not to buckle. Patsy remains impassive, neither encouraging nor discouraging because she doesn't need to be. She's won, and we both know it. I may have the heart of Will Price, but the wolf belongs to her now.

Will removes his hand from my chest, shattering my heart in the process. I literally feel it contort and twist as if it were trying to implode to escape the pain of the moment. I've been shot, burned, bitten, broken bones, but nothing, *nothing* compares to the agony and oppression that swallows me now. Will takes two steps back away from me to join Tim and Jamal. "I'm staying. With my pack."

"You heard the man," Patsy says. "He's made his choice."

When a triumphant smirk forms across her lips, the world blinks to red again. Bright, all consuming red, that fills my every atom with fury, channeled straight from the bowels of hell itself. It isn't until the gun in my hand makes contact with her face that I realize I've pistol whipped the smirk off. Patsy's head jerks sideways from the attack. With the fury cleared, panic takes its place. What the hell have I just done? I wasn't thinking past erasing that smirk. Hell, I wasn't even thinking. Suddenly,

Jamal lurches forward to grab my wrist so hard I drop the gun while Tim and Will move toward Patsy. I'm manhandled, my good arm twisted painfully behind my back and literally brought to my knees, as my fiancée fawns over Patsy, even caressing her cheek. "I'm fine," she assures them before kissing Will. Deeply. I don't even exist in his universe. Jamal could cut off my head at this moment and he'd still continue playing tonsil hockey with her. I think I've busted an emotional fuse because as I watch them, I'm numb. No disgust, no sadness, I can barely sense the real pain in my arm. Small mercies.

Patsy breaks away first, smiling at Will again. "I'm fine. Truly." She pecks his lips again before returning her attention my way. All the mirth dissolves from her face, giving way to steely resolve. "That was very, *very* foolish, Agent Alexander. I was planning to be merciful. One quick snap of the neck. You wouldn't have felt a thing. Now…" She shakes her head. "Our newest pack mate *does* need an initiation."

No matter what she says, this was the plan all along. Have Will hunt and kill me like she had Tim do to Imelda. I just didn't think it would reach this point. I had faith. In myself. In Will. In the power of love. I'm a damn moron. A dead damn moron. I can barely muster the will to care. Judging from the blank expression on his face, my fiancée shares my apathy.

He's gone. It's as if she's erased every part of him. My Will almost killed a man for talking dirty to me. He'd rip these people limb from limb just for suggesting what she just did. I'm on my own here. I could kill her here and now. Squeeze her heart, give her a brain aneurysm, but there's no guarantee she'd die instantly, and the others would attack. Flight before fight. I've learned that the hard way too.

"Jamal, let her up," Patsy orders.

He releases my arm so I can stand. I bite my lip to stop the grimace as pain shoots from my side. Of course flight is a hell of a lot easier without three broken ribs. Patsy's smirk returns at the sight of my agony. "It'll take us three minutes to change. That should give you a sporting chance."

"I'm going to kill you," I say, serious as sin.

Her eyebrow rises. "Are you now?"

"Yes. I am going to kill you. Slowly. Painfully. I am going to kill you. And you are going to suffer like you have never imagined. Whatever you made your victims endure, I will give it back to you threefold. You are going to *beg* me for the sweet relief of death, you fucking bitch, and maybe I'll be merciful. *Maybe*."

Patsy chuckles and all but Will join in. "Of course you will, dear. Just keep telling yourself that." The laughter peters out. "Three minutes. Better start running."

I look at Will, trying to catch his eyes again, but he just stares at Patsy. "Will…?" Nothing. "I love you." Nothing. "Do you hear me? No matter what happens, know that. I love you. I love you, Will Price. I love you."

"How sad for you," Patsy says before dropping her smile. "*Run.*"

My brain doesn't want to leave him. It knows this may be the last time I ever see him again, ever speak to him, but my body has no sentimentality. That word acts like a starter pistol. I turn my back on the man I love and take off the way I came, past the SUV where Adrian's smiling face behind the glass goads me on.

Run.

That isn't exactly what I'd call what I'm doing. All I'm capable of is shuffling at a rapid pace. I clutch onto my side with my good arm. The pressure improves the pain by about 5%. Have to do. There's only one option, make it to the road. There—

The screams begin echoing through the frigid night air.

Run.

I reach the road's bend, finally out of sight of the wailing monsters, and stop a second to catch my breath and remove my cell phone from the sling. "Oliver?" I pant into it.

"Trixie? I am here, my darling," he says, the relief in his voice palpable. I know how he feels. Tears threaten to spill, but I force them down. "I am here."

Common sense finally crept out of its hole a minute after I hung up with Patsy. Five minutes after that, so I could get a head start, I called Oliver. When it would sound natural I mentioned which road I was turning on so he could track us. With the phone hidden from Adrian inside my sling, Oliver could hear me, but I couldn't hear him. Heck, the call could have dropped or not even connected, and I wouldn't have known. But he's there. He's coming for me. Maybe there is a God.

"I-I'm at a cabin off Route 7," I say before beginning my sprint again.

"We know. We have been tracking the GPS on your phone. We are a few minutes out, Trixie."

"They-They're changing. I don't know how much time…I-I'm running toward Route 7. I don't have my gun. I—"

"Darling, just reach the road and hide. We are on our way."

"Will," I choke out. "He—"

"Beatrice Alexander, you reach that road and you hide. Nothing else matters but that, do you hear me? Run, hide, and wait for us. I am coming. You will be fine. I *swear* it to you. What are you going to do?"

"Run, hide, wait," I puff.

"Yes. Run, hide, wait. And do whatever is necessary to stay alive until we reach you. *Whatever* is necessary. Promise me." I don't speak. "Promise me," he orders.

I can't say it. I don't want to lie to him on top of all my other crimes against him. I lower the phone and continue up the driveway to the road. Ow. Ow. Crap. I've had stitches in my side before, but with broken ribs the pain takes triple time to recover. It's all of a quarter mile to the main road, and at this rate it'll take every millisecond of those three minutes to reach it. Ten seconds to gather my strength for every twenty seconds of running. Not a great ratio. *Just make it to the road, Bea.* The

334

cries and screams behind me grow less and less frequent until there's nothing but my heavy breath filling the void. Their silence is worse than the noise. The calm before the storm.

Of course anything is preferable to that first bellowing howl. If I had any breath left, that sound would have knocked it out. Crap. *Crap.* No choice now. I pump my legs as fast as I can, biting my lip hard enough to draw blood, helping to diffuse the pain in my side and head. Not well enough. The white splotches in my vision I get just before I pass out from a concussion trouble me the most. I don't have the luxury of stopping now. What takes me minutes will take a werewolf seconds. I wish I had my gun. Hell, I wish I had a rocket launcher. The second howl spurs me on further. Just keep running.

Oh, thank God. I reach the two-lane road and want to kiss the asphalt. Instead, without breaking stride I cross it, reaching the tree line on the other side hopefully out of sight behind a tall oak. I'd climb a tree if I could find one with low hanging branches. I'm not that lucky. So I just pant and wait as the howls echo. Will's howl. Will…oh God. He just…that wasn't him. It wasn't him, Bea. He *is* still in there. Deep, deep down, my Will remains. And he needs me. I just have to get him away from her. Stick with the plan. It can still work. Everything will be okay. I can save him. Everything will be okay. It has to be.

The sound of crunching gravel across the street ceases my pants. Crap. Crap. Oh God. The crunching grows louder as whatever is about to appear around that bend picks up its pace.

Definitely four legs. Definitely coming for me. Oh God. I can't do this. I can't do this. Please don't make me do this. More crackling. Two more wolves behind the leader. Even with a gun, even at my best, I'm not sure I could fend them all off. And what if Will…? This time I can't stop the tears. A tiny sob escapes before I shove my own hand over my broken nose and mouth to muffle the sound. I sob in silence, my tears obscuring my view of that road. No more. I can't take anymore. *I can't, I can't, I can't…* Even through the torrent of tears and the darkness that only the moonlight assuages, I notice the blur sprint around that bend. Charging toward me. Ten yards. Nine. Eight. Okay.

Okay.

I raise my hand to focus my power. Just as the monster reaches the road, close enough to see the whites of his fangs, lights to the left draw both our attentions. Two SUVs with flashing red lights inside zoom toward us. Beautiful. I let out another sob, this time of relief. The wolf, I'd guess Tim from the light hue of his fur, has a different reaction. Instead of continuing after me, he literally turns tail and begins running the way he came. Once again my subconscious proves far smarter than the rest of me. The werewolf gets three gallops in before he stops mid-stride. I think I did that. My sub-conscious is also smart enough to keep the second part of its plan from me.

Just as the first SUV approaches, a blink later the wolf glides into the middle of the street. Though the driver slams on the brakes, it's too late. Two tons of modern ingenuity careens into the stunned wolf. The yelp and crackling of bones is even more grotesque than the sight of his body contorting as it smashes the front bumper then falls underneath to have the back tires roll over him as well. The second SUV skids to a stop just before running him over too. Jesus Christ.

Jason is first out of the blood splattered SUV, his usual scowl affixed as he stares at the gore and works out what just occurred. Oliver springs out of the passenger door a moment later, not giving the carnage a glance. He scans both sides of the woods wildly, mouth gaping open. "Trixie?" he shrieks in terror. "Trix—"

"Oliver!" I shout. I stumble out of my hiding spot. "Here! I'm her—"

I make it just past the tree line when Oliver suddenly appears right in front of me, pulling me into his arms. Be it the familiar smell, the exhaustion, or those limbs enveloping me, a tsunami of relief washes through me. I all but collapse against his body, hugging him back with what little strength I have left. But the moment I do, his body becomes rigid, and a moment after that, his arms drop as he steps away. I stare up to find nothing but displeasure if not downright ire, at which of us I don't know. The knife Will plunged into my heart twists. "Oliver, I'm so sor—"

The boom of a shotgun charge cuts short my words. Oliver and I both jerk toward the source. Shotgun first, Jason charges across the road toward the cabin's gravel drive shotgun first just as a wolf disappears into the surrounding woods. "No!" I shout.

337

The Alpha ignores my word but can't ignore my mental grasp. I toss him backwards hard enough he rolls like a log toward the SUVs. Nancy reaches the prostrate Jason before Oliver and I do. He brushes off her help in standing. She's all but forgotten when he turns to me, that menacing scowl so intense it'd make Chuck Norris pee his pants. The shotgun in his hands is equally terrifying.

"What the fu—"

"You can't go after them," I pant, once again breathless.

"Wh—"

"Whatever is affecting Will will do the same to you," I instruct. "Remember?" That scowl lowers to Defcon-2, so it would only torture instead of kill.

"Hey, guys?" Carl calls.

We all turn toward the idling SUVs that Carl and Rushmore stand by. Carl kneels between the trucks while Rushmore points a shotgun at something obscured by the gory vehicle. Chandler, who scans the tree line with shotgun for bogies, backs toward the cars. His eyes never leave the forest. "This one's still alive," Carl says.

Oh I'd forgotten about my attempted murder. We join the others between the cars just as Carl rises. Oh Lord. Werewolf Tim lies twitching on the bloody asphalt, his torso flattened in two places, his tail severed and blood pouring from somewhere underneath him. Perhaps death would have been preferable.

Jason must agree, because the moment he reaches the werewolf, he trains the shotgun on Tim and pulls the trigger, splattering his brains on the road. Nancy shrieks in horror, but I'm too shocked to make a sound. But only for a second. "You executed him!"

"*You're* one to talk," Jason snaps.

"I…didn't mean to…he…" I have no defense except I don't *think* I meant to kill him. Still. I turn to Oliver. "Is that the plan? Execute them all on sight? We only kill when we have no other choice. We're law enforcement, not a hit squad. We should at least try to—"

"They murdered another werewolf. Under pack law that is an automatic death sentence in and of itself," Jason says.

"But Will hasn't killed anyone!" I desperately point out.

"He was coming to kill *you*," Oliver says.

"He can't help it!"

"It does not matter!" Oliver parries.

"The hell it doesn't!" I look to Chandler. "Paul…please. There has to be another way. Please."

Chandler meets my eyes, and for the first time ever, I find sympathy. It quickly vanishes as he turns to the group. "How many tranq guns did we bring?"

"One, I think," Carl answers. "And the one cage. We were in a rush."

"Shit. Okay, Nancy you're taking the tranq. Rush, Carl, Nancy you're Team B. Oliver and I are Team A. We'll spread

339

out and search the woods. Chances are *they'll* come to us. When they do, we'll radio in with our coordinates, and Nancy can teleport and tranq the wolf. If possible. But use your best discretion. Take no chances. No matter what." He pauses. "Or who."

Rushmore nods before hustling toward the second SUV with Carl behind. Chandler spins around and opens the trunk where a silver cage fills the majority of space save for the crate of silver shotgun ammo, walkie talkies, four pistols, night vision goggles, and three large knives. Crap, no Bette. My stomach clenches again. "What-What about me?" I ask.

"You and Dahl will wait in the car for Wolfe and Adam." He looks at Jason. The vein in the werewolf's large neck bulges. "She's right. We can't take the chance of you turning on us like Will. Adam either when he and Wolfe get here. You're the last line of defense. You see a wolf, run it down with the car. That worked well enough."

"I should go with you and Oliver. I—"

"You can barely stand right now. You're a liability. You'll just slow us down."

"But—"

"I don't trust you, okay?" Chandler snaps. "We're here to clean up *your* clusterfuck. We were working on a plan before you went rogue. I should arrest your ass. And I still may. So you're going to wait in the goddamn car and if we need you, we'll radio." He grabs the crate before rushing back toward the other SUV with Jason in toe.

I turn my gaze to Oliver as he fastens a knife to his belt. "Don't let him bench me," I beg. "I should be out there with you. I *need* to be out there with you."

"Why? It is as if you do not trust me with Will's life," he says with a hard edge before following Chandler as well.

Those words sting like acid. I even flinch. But the truth is…no. I don't trust a single one of them, not with this. Not even him. Not really. Maybe I shouldn't have called them. Decisions made in fear rarely prove to be the correct one. Crap. Too late now.

I join the others as they affix their earpieces and walkies. Chandler hands a walkie to Jason as well. "Everyone, channel seven." They quickly check their walkies and guns with Nancy sliding in the last tranq dart. "We'll take the left, Team B the right. Zigzag though the woods down along the road until you reach the cabin. We'll rendezvous there. And first group to arrive, secure the son. *Again*," he says glaring my way. "We've done this a dozen times before people, tonight is no excep—" He stops himself. "Just remember your training. Watch each other's backs, and be careful out there. I don't want to lose *anyone*."

"Nor do we," Oliver says.

Chandler nods at the vampire. "Then let's get these bastards. Good hunting, everyone."

"Good hunting," we all say in unison.

Everyone secures their night vision goggles and moves toward the forest, guns already pointed that way. I take a step too, but Oliver blocks me before turning to Jason. "Watch her. Keep her close. *Please*."

Those ice blue orbs narrow at my friend, though for once more intrigued than hostile. He nods at Oliver before the vampire hustles back to the group. I take a few steps until a hand clamps around my arm. "Get in the car," Jason orders. My gaze whips back his way, greeted by another scowl. "Don't make me force you."

Not now, Bea. Not yet...

I snatch my arm away but walk on my own to the first SUV, climbing in the passenger seat. As Tim's blood still trickles down the windshield, I watch my friends dash into the wilderness to hunt the man I love and his lover. Swallowed by the darkness. Chandler is right, we have done this before. In Colorado, in New Jersey, all over. Zombies, vampires, even a giant snake, all hunted and found. All dead. Not a one could be taken alive. Their choice, not ours. Will has to remember that somewhere in his lizard brain. He *has* to.

After moving the second SUV off the road, Jason climbs into the driver's seat. "Surprised you didn't make a run for it," he says putting our car into gear.

"Not without your shotgun."

"So you don't have a death wish." To my surprise he hands me the shotgun. "Good to know." Jason maneuvers the car down the gravel road at a crawl. "Keep your eyes open. Hopefully they'll catch the scent of blood and come right to us. If I smelled my pack member's blood, I would."

342

"We're supposed to wait at the end of the road."

"I don't take orders." He scans the forest for a moment in silence. "Are you sleeping with the vampire?"

"Excuse me?" I snap.

"I've known that vampire since I was a child. He hasn't given one goddamn for anyone but himself in all that time. Will Price is my friend. If you are—"

"I'm not. I never have. He's just a friend."

"And he's okay with that? Because right now the vampire who helped slaughter an entire family of witches to help get his lover back is out there with a shotgun hunting *my* friend."

"He won't kill him. Not unless there's no other option." I pause. "He won't because he knows I'd never forgive him."

"You bet Will's life on that? Because I sure as hell don't." He passes me the walkie and earpiece. "Put it on. Be ready. And there's a flashlight under the seat. Get it."

"Why?"

"Because *I* should be out there. It's my duty to be out there. To kill those fuckers for their crimes. To protect my friend who helped me, helped my wife, many years ago. But I can't. You can. And you will. Besides, I know you're already planning to anyway. I'll save myself the head wound this way. So the moment they come, you be ready." He nods at the shotgun. "Will you be able to use that thing?"

I take the gun in my hand. I may pop some stitches, but, "Yes."

"Good. You'll need it."

"I pray you're wrong, Alpha Dahl."

But when has one of my prayers ever been answered?

After I retrieve the flashlight, we drive in silence save, for the chatter over my earpiece, Carl telling Nancy to stay closer, Chandler checking in with the other team. No sightings yet. Perhaps the pack just ran away. They're halfway to Crawford already. They'll change back, rest and regroup somewhere far from here. It may take a month, a year, but he will be alive and I will find him. I will. He—

The car jerks to a sudden stop. I don't see anything on either side of the road. I have better than average night vision, but I'm not a werewolf. "Where?" I ask.

"Ten o'clock. I saw movement."

"Should I—"

"Wait. It could be nothing."

I don't see a damn thing but branches swaying in the wind. We watch and wait, the air growing thicker with tension each passing millisecond, until I almost can't breathe. Dahl isn't as far as I can tell. His eyes narrow to pinpoints. "It's her."

"I don't—"

The eyes. She must move her head because suddenly two green glowing orbs appear in the darkness. It's her. When she steps closer into the glow of the headlights, I see this wolf is smaller than Will. My hand instinctively squeezes the shotgun. I have a promise to keep.

"She's not coming any closer," Dahl says. "You shou—
"

I've already opened the car door before he grants me permission. Flashlight in one hand, shotgun in the other, pure vengeance and rage racing though my veins, yeah that psycho bitch doesn't stand a chance. She must agree because the moment I set foot off the gravel, she takes off back the way she came. I run as fast as I can after her into the forest. Here I come, you bitch. Game on.

About a hundred feet in, I lose sight of her in the darkness and stop running to scan the horizon with my flashlight. Nothing but dense bare tree trunks inches apart from the others, and branches swaying in the breeze. Crap. Crackling branches behind me, in front of me, I can't tell. Double crap. "In pursuit of Winsted, approximately a hundred feet north of the driveway, in Alpha search quadrant," I pant into the earpiece microphone.

"Trixie?" Oliver asks on the other end. "How did—"

"I have lost Winsted," I cut in, "and—"

Spoke too soon. A howl echoes nearby, perhaps thirty feet away, before the crackling begins anew. I take off after her again, dodging and weaving through the tall trees. "Re-established contact. Heading north-east. Nancy—"

"I need more than that," Nancy says. "Like fire in the air or—"

"Contact left!" Carl cuts in.

"What?" Rushmore asks over the comms. "I don't see…there!"

"He's running!"

"Is it Will?" I ask through my pants.

"I missed him!" Nancy says.

"Don't lose him!" Carl shouts.

They're not listening to me. I can't listen to them either. There's too much shouting. I have to yank the wig from my ear when a shotgun blast rings out over it. Crap. Nothing I can do right now. And I'm tired of running. I cock the shotgun, not easy while running, and push myself harder to bridge the gap between us. I fire. The force and noise cause me more harm than her. As my ears ring and shoulder aches, the wolf continues running, vanishing once more into the black void before I can pick her up with my power. Damn it! After cocking the gun, I give myself seconds to catch my breath and force away the new pain in my arm before following her again. Even with the ringing, I can still hear distant shotgun blasts from Team B. Four, Five. Oh God, please don't let them be after Will. Let him be far, far away from this warzone. Just keep running, Bea. Don't lose her. Don't—

Aagh!

As if I were stabbed by an ice pick the pain in my side from my mending ribs all but brings me to my knees. My lungs beg for me to take deep breaths, but the pain only allows a teaspoon in at a time. My head, front and back from my two concussions, throbs and aches almost as badly as my side in time to my racing heart. The splotches and dizziness don't help either. Too much. I have to stop and the moment I do, my stomach expels its almost non-existent contents out of my mouth onto the dead leaves. Damn it. Goddamn it, I've lost her. There's nothing but silence and my breaths. No footsteps, no crackling, just me. Oww. Damn it, I—

The snapping of a large branch behind me, stops that breath dead. I sense another's presence, and the pain momentarily vanishes as I straighten and twirl around, shotgun and flashlight first, toward the intruder. But it's a damn good thing I'm not trigger happy. I manage to stop my finger from squeezing the moment I realize who I've drawn on. Oliver stands only five feet away, his own shotgun lowered and his mouth open in silent, surprised protest. My jaw drops in time to my gun. "You scared the crap out of me," I pant.

"Are you alright?" he asks, stepping toward me. "I smell your blood."

"I-I think I popped a stitch in my arm." Just as I say it, sure enough all the pain returns to my side, my arm, even my head. "I-I'm fine." About to vomit again but fine. "She—"

I take a step, just one step, and darkness washes over all my senses for a second. One moment I'm upright, and the next I'm leaning against Oliver's chest with his arms holding me, and the vampire himself staring down at me, terrified. My own eyes double in size when a howl echoes through the woods not too far away. I'd recognize that bellow anywhere. I spent the night listening to its mournful, deep bawl less than a week ago. "Will," I whisper. "It's Will!" I push myself away from Oliver, but the moment I'm upright, the world tilts again.

I manage a step, but this time it's not my broken body that stops me. Oliver grabs my wrist, turns me around, and yanks me back against him. *"No,"* he hisses through gritted fangs, eyes as intense as his voice. *"No."*

"But—"

"No. No more. I shall go. You will stay here. I promise, I *promise,* to deliver him back to you. I promise. Trust me. *Trust me."*

And as I stare into those terrified, pained, intense gray eyes, I do. There is not a doubt in a single one of my cells that he'll keep his word. That he'll save Will, a man he loathes, for me. So I'll be happy. He'll do this for me because I can't. He'll take the weight of the world from my shoulders and charge into hell with it. This is the vow we've made to one another. That we'll be there for each other no matter what. And it's been forged in tears and blood and life and death, down to our very souls. How could I have ever, *ever* questioned that? Him? Never again. *Never.*

I blink back my tears and hug my best friend as tight as I can. Without hesitation, he does the same. Why is it I never feel as safe as I do in his arms? "Thank you," I whisper. "Thank you."

He kisses the top on my head, my forehead, and breaks our embrace to gently kiss my lips, sealing his promise, before leaving nothing but the cold night in his wake. Lips still puckered, I open my eyes, and he's gone. Vanished. I'm alone. And dizzy. Finally giving my knees permission to buckle, I slump to the ground, hugging my flashlight and shotgun for comfort. He'll save him. He will. For me. And it'll all be okay.

He promised. He'll always come for me, and I'll always come for him. Until death and beyond. My dark angel. Thank you.

I hug the shotgun tighter. He'll be fine. They both will. It'll all be okay. They—

A howl of anguish echoes through the silence. A human howl.

Oliver.

No, no, no, no, no… Another wail of agony. I struggle to my feet.

A growl. A roar. Another scream. I'm upright.

A shotgun blast. I'm running.

Inhuman yelps and growls mixed with human grunts guide me through the night. A bloodcurdling scream followed by gurgling pushes me to my limit.

What I find at the end of my journey will haunt my nightmares into the next life.

Oliver lies against a tree, his breathtaking face ripped to ribbons, head shaking violently as a massive wolf bites into his neck, blood caking both victim and assailant. Hearing my fast approach, the wolf releases his meal, about to bare its teeth at me. It doesn't get the chance. The moment it loosens its grip on Oliver, the wolf flies as fast as a rocket in the opposite direction, out of sight. Judging from the yelps and thumps, several trees get in her way. It doesn't matter. Nothing matters but him.

I drop to my knees beside my best friend, my already taxed brain unable to comprehend all I observe. Blood. So much blood. His chest is covered in deep slashes inches deep, arms a mess of puncture wounds and claw marks, scalp to jaw slit so the skin on his wan face folds and flaps. I only have a second to take this in before I realize those aren't the real concern. The blood gushing like a river from his neck just below the jaw line from one of the million holes of the wolf's fangs left is. His carotid artery has been severed. He's losing almost a pint a second. Not even a vampire can survive this much blood loss. Heal. He needs time to heal. How...? Okay. I drop the shotgun and flashlight on the ground before sliding my fingers into the hole. Oliver groans in pain and I almost gag, but I quickly feel the worst tear among his warm, squishy flesh. Blood still escapes, but I've plugged the dam. For now.

"It's okay," I whisper, voice trembling as violently as the rest of me. "You're gonna be okay. I promise, I promise, I promise..."

Help. We need help. Help.

My free hand quakes so hard I can barely lift the wire attached to the walkie to speak into the microphone. "A-A-Agent down," I sputter out. "I-I re-repeat, a-a-agent down. C-Code red. We-We are...I don't exactly know where..." I cry. "I..."

The sobs are about to overtake me. I can't let them. I meet Oliver's eyes. He can barely focus on my face, but as the life literally drains from him onto my hands, there's no mistaking the gratitude, the fear, the pain in them. Absolving me. No. *No.* Neither of us gets off that easily. A calm clarity

350

washes through me, erasing all my fear. Forged in blood and tears. Never again.

"I repeat, Agent down, code red. We're in Alpha sector, and haven't reached the road or river." I lift the compass on my necklace. "My compass reads NW. The constellation Orion is to my left, and the Big Dipper is directly over my right shoulder. One, possibly two bogies still in the area. Please hurry."

"I'm on my way," Chandler responds.

I wrap the wire around my neck before pressing my other hand to the other oozing teeth marks on his neck to staunch their bleeding too. Not good enough. This is bad. He knows it too. He stares up at me, blinking slower than usual. He's fading. I'd feed him my blood, every drop, but I need my two remaining wits left to protect him. "Hey. Hey!" I shout right into his ear. He's back for the moment. "You stay with me, alright? No naps now, you hear me? You are not leaving me alone in this. Okay? You-You..." I say, voice quaking. I take a second to compose myself. God, if he felt even an ounce of the helplessness and terror I'm experiencing now while he sat by my bed yesterday, I owe him a lifetime of apologies. "I-I'm sorry," I whisper. "I'm so sorry. For everything. I was cruel and unfair and from the depths of my soul, I'm sorry. You are my best friend. You are the best man I have ever or will ever meet. You are...my angel. And-And I have no right to ask for anything else from you, I know I don't, but I'm going to. I am going to beg this of you. Stay awake. Stay with me. Don't you *dare* leave me, Oliver Smythe. Don't you dare die. Not tonight. Not for me. We promised we'd always be here for one another. To fight for one another. Don't you dare renege on your end of the deal now. I need you. Do you hear me? I *need* you, Oliver. Don't you dare, *dare* leave me now. Not you. You promised. You promised me *always.* I am damn well holding you to it, you bastard. Don't leave me. Not you. Please."

His red tear stained eyes crinkle as I think he attempts to smile as he reaches with his mangled arm to touch my hand, squeezing with the strength of a newborn. I kiss that hand, those graceful fingers, and smile back. He should hate me. I shunned him. Assaulted him. Caused this whole mess. I'd hate me. I do hate me. But not him. Never him. His mouth moves to say what I can't, but I shake my head. "I know," I whisper. I kiss his fingers again. "I *know.* Me too."

He breaks eye contact first as his grin drops, gaze whipping forward into the dark forest. The familiar crackling begins a moment later. She's coming to finish the job. Fast. Not while I'm around, bitch. Plan. Need a plan. We're literally sitting prey. Okay. Okay. I can't remove my hand or he'll bleed to death. Shotgun's out. Which leaves…

All the pain and throbbing in my head doubles to nausea proportions, blood trickling out my nose even, as I yank on one of the skinnier trees with my mind. The trunk cracks in two about five feet from the base, the top crashing with a boom, rattling the ground like a tremor. Timber.

There's just enough time to blink the spots away before the wolf sprints into the dim light, fangs already exposed. Mine

352

are sharper. Just as she begins to bound over the downed tree, with one thought, still airborne, she turns 180 degrees and rockets, neck first, into the jagged remains of the rooted trunk. I watch without a grain of guilt as the wood enters her flesh, impaling her like a roast pig from neck to torso where the bloody end exits once more. Not even her yelps, her whimpers, or as those gray eyes of hers meet mine, touch me. I just smile at her. I warned she'd be begging for mercy. Never underestimate—

The growl to my left wipes my smile away. My brain barely has time to process what I'm seeing as I glance in that direction. A bloody, drooling, enraged two hundred fifty pound werewolf descending upon us mid-air, claws first.

Will.

Before I can react, there's a strong thrust against my chest. I blink and I'm suddenly rolling sideways the opposite direction from the wolf. After the third rotation my heads whacks against a tree, ending my journey. A torrent of misery jolts from that already tender spot on my cranium. I roll onto my back and stare up at the spots dancing with the stars above in time to the grunting and snarling. I could lie here…ow. Something hard collides with my hand. I look left toward the source of the new pain, the shotgun Oliver tossed, but all pain is forgotten in an instant. *No.* Four feet away Will has Oliver's forearm in his powerful jaws, the only thing keeping the feral wolf from going for the jugular. *No.* I try to push Will with my mind but all that happens are more spots and pain induced nausea. *No.* Too much. Too…there's a sickening crack as

Oliver's bones finally break. They didn't…they should have already if…oh God. It wasn't her before. It was…oh, God. No. No, no, no, no…

Will's toying with him. Making it last. Making it hurt. Torturing my best friend. I just lie here for a second hoping the darkness will take me. Damn it. Oliver whimpers again. Why won't it take me? I can't do this. Not this. Anything but this. Will growls. But it was always going to come down to this, wasn't it? Always. Okay. My hand seizes the shotgun. Okay.

"Will, get away from him," I say, drawing the gun to my chest.

He doesn't listen. He never listens.

"I said…get away from him," I demand, somehow finding the strength to sit up. Nothing. The wolf finally acknowledges me when I cock the shotgun. "Get away from him. *Now*."

Those green eyes narrow at me as his lips curl back to bare his bloody fangs, a low warning growl beginning. "Will…please," I whisper. He digs a claw deeper into Oliver's chest as a warning. Oliver contorts in agony. Okay. I point the shotgun at him. "I'm begging you. Don't. Don't make me do this. If you are in there, if you love me, don't make me do this. Don't make me do this. *Please*."

We stare at one another for seconds, eons, not moving or even blinking. He's in there. My Will is in there. He is. He'd never do this to me. *Never*. He loves me. He's coming back to me, and we'll leave this horrible place behind us. We'll live happily ever after just like he promised. He'll keep his promise, or I'll have to keep mine. *"Please."*

Those lips stretch back further, and his cold eyes leave mine as his head jerks back toward Oliver.

Okay.

The shotgun bucks in my arms, practically knocking me backwards as it does Will. As a burst of blood blossoms from the man I love's hip, he rolls off Oliver. I cock the gun again. It's done. It's done. It... Will recovers within a second, turning the full force of his hatred my direction. Without a second thought, he leaps over Oliver, flying toward me claws first. No hesitation, just like I promised him. No hesitation.

I pull the trigger.

At this range, the full force of the concentrated buckshot hits its target. Half his head, from snout to neck, vanishes in an explosion of bone and brain. The force knocks him back the way he came. Away from me. Away from his executioner. He lands on the other side of Oliver. Dead before he touches the dirt.

Okay. Okay. *Okay.*

Good-bye.

There are no tears. There's no pain. No sadness. No relief. No guilt. There is nothing as I crawl over to my best friend to keep him alive, literally opening a vein, and watching as the monster morphs back into the man I loved. Who I swore I would save from himself. The man I planned to spend the rest of my life with. Fall asleep beside every night. Have children with.

The man who brought hope into my lost life. All gone. Never was. There is nothing left inside me but a black hole where my soul should be. He takes that with him as well. He's welcome to it. Only one thing left to do then. I close my eyes and let the void finally swallow me whole.

Fuck it.

EIGHTEEN

REMAINS

We buried William R. Price with honor three days later in the small cemetery behind the mansion where ten other F.R.E.A.K.S. rest in peace. Like them, and all the other agents who've lost their lives in service to others, his picture will adorn every FBI field office across the world. I was worried there would be objections to bestowing these honors to him, but not a person raised a word of protest. One bad deed does not blot out the million good ones. It never should. Chandler and Jason folded an American flag in the traditional triangle and presented it to me, the former, his best friend, with tears in his eyes. Nancy's sobs carried on thought the entire service and even George blotted his eyes when Jason's wife Vivian sang "Amazing Grace." My own remained dry. I haven't cried once.

Dr. Patricia Renee Winsted, Ph.D. the most prolific supernatural serial killer in American history, eventually succumbed to her wounds that night. In all the commotion we all forgot to remove her from that tree for several hours and even then she was impossible to pull off. They burned her where she perished. No grave for her. The only people left to mourn her are her son, who was apprehended with no resistance, and Jamal

Greene. Team Beta captured the lone remaining wolf after the third tranq took effect. Both men will spend the rest of their hopefully short lives alone in an 8X12 cell deep underground, never to see or smell a flower of feel a gentle breeze on their faces again. They deserve a hell of a lot worse, but when does deserve ever factor into life?

I discovered all this after the fact. Oliver took a lot of blood, so I woke in the hospital. Again. Three pints of blood and five new stitches later, I busted out of the hospital and busted into mobile command. Even with five pints of blood and a hundred stitches himself, he was still so fragile. The worst of his wounds were red and oozing, and per Dr. Neill he was in and out of consciousness. I came when he was out. A good thing too because I couldn't give him more than a glance. The moment I set eyes on him my throat seized, my stomach dropped, and my heart went so wild I feared I'd have a heart attack. I was right back in that forest with the gun bucking in my hands as Will...

I just turned and walked back out. I don't think I can ever look at him again. So I haven't. When he woke and asked for me, I never returned Carl's call. I just continued cleaning up my mess. Cataloguing, uncovering more bodies, anything the others didn't want to do until Oliver was stable enough to bring back to Kansas, and we all flew home. His coffin kept Will's company this morning. I brought them both home.

My job is done.

I zip up my suitcase just as there's a knock on my bedroom door. Vivian, a willowy redhead with a great singing voice and backbone of steel if she's married to Jason, stands in the hallway. Like me, she's changed out of her funeral attire into jeans and a sweater. "Hey. Five minute warning. Adam's already loading the car. I thought you might need help with your bags."

"I guess I do. I can get one of the suitcases, but—"

"Oh, I've got them," Vivian says, stepping in. Her eyes scan the rest of the room, especially the boxes scattered around. "So just the suitcases?"

"Um, yeah. They'll, uh, send the rest later."

"Oh. Okay."

It was decided that due to my actions in Crawford I be suspended without pay for three months. I took the reprimand without a word of protest or defense. If I were George, I would have sent me to the Facility with what's left of the Winsted gang. I didn't even want to come back to the mansion. If it weren't for the funeral, I would have caught the first flight from North Carolina to San Diego with just the clothes on my back. Wish I had. When we landed this morning I walked into my bedroom and the bed was still unmade from when Will and I...well, I ripped those damn sheets off and started packing. Still had the boxes from when I came. I haven't called April or Nana but know they'll welcome me back with open arms. Maybe then I'll be able to cry. At least I don't have to spend the night in that bed. Or be here when the sun sets and he...my flight leaves in two hours. I'm ready.

Vivian lifts the handles of my suitcases and smiles at me. "Five minutes, okay? I love my husband but patience is *not* one of his virtues."

"I'll be right down."

With another smile, Vivian nods and rolls my bags out, leaving me alone once more. I take one last pass around this room. My dream room. Powder pink walls, bay windows, pink silk couch, canopy bed, all the latest gadgets. My sanctuary. Where I've spent so many hours watching old movies, reading, just talking and laughing with my friends. Where I first met Will. Where I planned our future. Where he told me he loved me. There's nothing here for me now. I grab my purse and walk out without looking back. Just one more thing to pack before I go.

It smells like him in here. His musk. His aftershave. Clothes are strewn around on the floor and chair. In the hamper. Pictures of his parents, his wife sit on his dresser. Nothing's been touched. It's just waiting for his return. I considered staying longer to pack everything up. Make sure it's not just thrown out like trash. That what remains of a good man's life is treated with respect. But in the end it's just stuff. None of it really matters. Except the reason for my invasion. I find the wedding ring in the desk exactly where I first saw it. He loved her until the end, I have no doubt about that. She died and he was reborn, but the love never changed. That should never be forgotten. *Love* should never be forgotten. It hurts, but I manage to remove my necklace and thread the ring on the chain beside the compass before fastening it again. That's what I'm taking with me. The best of them.

I hate good-byes. All the tears, the fake promises to keep in touch, I don't have the stomach for them anymore. Probably why I didn't tell anyone but George I was leaving. They're as they should be, off in their own worlds. Nancy and Carl at the movies, our three agents getting shitfaced at No Exit, Andrew in his bedroom with a book on tape, George in the parlor reminiscing with some straggler F.R.E.A.K.S. here for the funeral. I managed to get through that event somehow. All the condolences from strangers, the stories of Will's bravery, the praise of his leadership, I said all the right words, smiled sadly, and thanked them. I was the perfect almost widow. So much so everyone understood when I excused myself to "rest" upstairs. No one bothered me since. Or now. I walk down the hallway, the stairs, through the mansion unmolested to my final destination.

This room, this beautiful room, my most favorite place in the world, how I'll miss you. Thousands of books two stories high, thousands of portals to other worlds. Centuries of stories of love and hate and heroics. Some of my happiest memories are of me sitting by the window curled up on that couch with the sun or moon shining through the two-story bay windows. But no memory tops the first. Because this is where I first saw *him*, standing where I am now in the doorway. The most beautiful man I'll ever set eyes on. Not that I knew that then. Then I just thought he was pretty. Shallow. Narcissistic. Cruel. Not much else. How wrong I was. And *God* how I'll miss him. My dark angel. All or nothing. He'll find the note in my bedroom when he rises with those very words inside. I spent the entire flight home from North Carolina staring at a blank sheet of paper trying to find the right words, but none came except those. Because they're all I need. "Good-bye."

I turn away and slowly trod toward the front door. George and Jason step out of the parlor and shake hands as I pass by. I glance at the old man, the same one who sat by my bedside a year ago with promises of control. Of home. Belonging. Another man of his word. He delivered on every one. He's earned the slow, reverent nod I give him. I'm just not sure I deserve the one he bestows upon me. I'll take it though, with pride, as I walk out that door.

One year ago, almost to the day, I saw a little boy about to die. I had a split second to decide: risk my life for his or do nothing. And in that split second, with my decision to act, I changed the course of my whole life in ways I never could have imagined. I've seen and done things I never knew possible. Things that have challenged me, changed me. The same frightened girl who arrived here isn't leaving. The girl who hid from life, who hid from her own voice, from what she was capable of, who was sweet, optimistic, full of hope, is gone. The one who believed in happily ever after. Who thought if she fought hard enough, if she earned it, love could conquer all. But as I climb into that car, as the mansion fades from view, I honestly don't know who she's been replaced with. Because if I had to do it all over again, knowing all I do now, seeing all that I have, I can't safely say I'd run toward that boy again. The cost has been too great. Will wasn't the only one who died in those cold, dark woods. What remained of that girl died the moment I decided to pull that trigger. She wasn't strong enough to look into the abyss. It swallowed her whole and spit back nothing but a husk. I'm what remains.

And nothing good has ever been spawned from that hopeless place where angels dare never tread.

THE

END

ABOUT THE AUTHOR

Jennifer Harlow spent her restless childhood fighting with her three brothers and scaring the heck out of herself with horror movies and books. She grew up to earn a degree at the University of Virginia which she put to use as a radio DJ, crisis hotline volunteer, bookseller, lab assistant, wedding coordinator, and government investigator. Currently she calls Atlanta home but that restless itch is ever present. In her free time, she continues to scare the beejepers out of herself watching scary movies and opening her credit card bills. She is the author of the Amazon best-selling F.R.E.A.K.S. Squad, Midnight Magic Mystery series, The Galilee Falls Trilogy, and the steampunk romance *Verity Hart Vs The Vampyres*. For the soundtrack to her books and other goodies visit her at www.jenniferharlowbooks.com